ACCLAIM FOR MEGAN'S CURE
AND AUTHOR ROBERT B. LOWE

"Another engaging thriller in the Enzo Lee series."
  –Kirkus Reviews

"Lowe's writing style is both engrossing and informative lending to the believability and integrity of the story."
  – Kindle Book Review

"It will grab you from the beginning and not let go."
  – Amazon Reviews

"I loved the good guys. I hissed at the bad guys. And I wondered how I would have acted if I were in the different character's shoes." – B. Reed

"The Enzo Lee mysteries are for me the epitome of what a good mystery should be. Fully developed characters with whom the reader can identify, and settings that are skillfully and accurately drawn." – C. Ray

"It was nearly 3 in the morning when I put it down." - Chakata

"Buy the book; you'll enjoy it. As for me, I'm off to buy the first two." – Lesley G.

MEGAN'S CURE

An Enzo Lee Mystery Thriller

Robert B. Lowe

Enzo Publications
San Francisco, California

Copyright © 2014 by Robert B. Lowe

ISBN 13: 978-0988644823

Dedicated to my daughters Chenery and Halle

Chapter 1

Gulf Coast, Alabama
April 2006

LUCY QUAN FINISHED her peanut butter and honey sandwich, licked the last of the sticky residue from her fingers and giggled across the picnic table at her best friend, Megan Kim.

When she swung her legs over the bench, stood up and gave a little wave to Megan – still eating fried rice out of the wide-mouthed thermos that came inside her battered Dora the Explorer lunchbox – Lucy didn't need to explain where she was going. After two years sharing classes, lunches and walks to school and back home again, both girls knew Lucy was making her usual quick trip to the girl's bathroom. A careful observer would have been able to set his watch by the event – 14 minutes before the bell signaling the end of lunch.

Lucy walked down the pathway between the tall chain-link fence and the 30-year-old, two-story school with beige, brick walls and oversized windows. Just before she reached the corner of the building, Lucy turned back and glanced at her friend. She saw Megan looking away from her in the opposite direction, toward the street that ran along the side of Langford Brice Elementary School. Lucy saw a white-haired man. He stood on the sidewalk with his hands resting on the waist-high fence. Megan seemed to be talking to him across the 20 or 30 yards that separated the two. It was odd enough to cause Lucy to stop, just for a second, before turning the corner with a flip of her ponytail and continuing on her mission.

1

She rushed her trip back, disturbed by the change in routine – the strange man – even as she tried to assure herself with innocent scenarios. Maybe he was just someone asking for the best way into the principal's office. Or wondering about the name of the school. Lucy's heart beat faster than normal when she turned the corner. At the empty table she saw Megan's lunchbox packed and sitting with the handle up. Dora's smiling face on the side seemed to be asking her, "Why did you leave?"

Lucy quickly surveyed the other half dozen tables and the yard of the school that held them. She saw that Megan wasn't among the 50 or so other children sitting with their lunches or playing kickball and four square. Lucy knew she was prone to overreacting. Of the pair, Megan was the cool and confident one who reeled Lucy back to earth when she panicked too soon or jumped to hasty conclusions. She tried to control her breathing as she slowly walked from the picnic table to the place on the sidewalk where she had seen the man.

Lucy stopped at the fence and looked all around her. She scanned the ground, the sidewalk beyond the fence and the thick grassy strip that spilled onto the sidewalk and the asphalt road beyond. Cars sat empty on the street. Nothing. The bell rang. The other kids began moving back to their classrooms. Lucy was in a daze.

"Wait...wait...wait..." She told herself. Maybe Megan had gone back to class early for some reason and just left her lunchbox. The yard was empty when she got back to the picnic table and picked up Megan's lunchbox.

In her heart, Lucy knew before she entered Mrs. White's fifth-grade classroom that Megan's seat would be empty. Her fear of overreacting was replaced now by sheer dread. She sat the lunchbox on Megan's desk, Dora's face down. She took her seat across from Megan's and placed her hands flat on her desk. Then she peeled them off the faux wood grain made sticky by the humidity, wrapped her arms tightly around herself and stared down at her lap.

Mrs. White was writing something on the chalkboard. After a minute she stopped and turned. Her eyes swept the class.

"Lucy," she said. "Where is Megan?"

Lucy felt her chest constrict until she couldn't breathe. Her face crumpled and tears quickly ran down her cheeks to her chin. She continued to hug herself, struggling to get air into her lungs. In a moment, Mrs. White was at her side, kneeling down, enveloping the 10-year-old who wept on her shoulder.

The teacher glanced around her. Sitting near the door, Mrs. White saw the red-headed boy who was two inches taller than anyone else in the class and looked three years older, although he was only 11.

"Jack," she said. "Go get Mr. Rayburn."

Lucy fought to get the words out.

"She left...she's....she's gone," Lucy said between sobs. "There was...there was...there was a man."

Mrs. White looked up again. Like the rest of the class, Jack stared at them. He was frozen in place with his hand on the knob of the half-opened door. The teacher locked her eyes on those of the tall red head.

"Run!" she ordered.

Chapter 2

POLICE CHIEF CLIFF Davidson placed his elbow on the picnic table, scratched his jaw and realized he had forgotten to shave the left side of his face eight hours earlier. He wasn't surprised. It was the least of the balls he had dropped in the past seven months.

Before Katrina, he had felt reasonably in control of the Gulf Coast town of Bayou La Batre, his 18-person police force and his life. Two days in late August had changed all that. When the sea receded and the skies cleared, 20 of the shrimpers that provided the economic lifeblood of the town had been washed up on the scrublands along the Gulf. A few of the boats still were there. Half of the housing in the town of 3,000 had been destroyed or battered until it was no longer fit for human habitation.

Luckily, the early warnings and the long history of hurricane devastation along the Gulf Coast had chased every sane person to higher ground so the death toll in the immediate area was minimal. But, the mess, the dislocation...the sheer havoc wreaked in everybody's lives still reverberated throughout the town and the entire region. Half his force had quit, most abandoning the area to be near helpful relatives or at least somewhere with an unbroken economy and functioning infrastructure.

And now this.

Davidson let the teacher ask the questions for him because the girl, his only real witness at this stage, was so distraught she seemed on the verge of shutting down entirely. He guessed that her family and that of the missing girl had emigrated from

Vietnam, Laos or elsewhere in Southeast Asia over the past two decades. Almost all of the sizable Asian community in his small town, drawn by the familiarity of the local fishing industry, traced their roots to that part of the globe. Maybe the girls' families worked the boats or were employed in the shrimp, crab or oyster plants.

"Now, that's a job," Davidson thought. He recalled the summer a decade earlier when – hard up for cash – he had spent weekends moving mountains of oyster shells from the plants to vacant lots around the area. Even with a damp bandanna tied over his nose and mouth, the stench had nearly killed him. Every movement of his pint-sized bulldozer had unlocked a thousand stinking pockets of decayed raw shellfish. Just thinking about it made him nauseous.

For him, one level of Hell would be spending entire days inside a plant, picking the meat out of an endless progression of oysters or even crabs while bathed in the hot, humid odor of shellfish. Maybe the families had moved up the economic ladder to run the small groceries or restaurants in town. Oh well. He'd know those details before the end of the day.

At 55, Davidson was eligible for retirement in three months and would be entitled to three quarters of his pay. But, he knew he'd delay it for at least a year. He couldn't leave the department short staffed and the community flat on its back. It just wasn't his nature. As it was, he was out here today because all his veterans had left. Davidson had been divorced for five years now, and had lived alone since his only kid left for college two years earlier. He needed to stay busy but the past months had taken him far past his ideal level of activity. Maybe one day he'd kick back, take up fishing and move back to Pensacola where he still had some family. But, not yet.

Across the street from where he sat, he could see two of his officers, banging on the doors of houses that fronted the school, interviewing the residents. Both were sweating through their shirts in the unseasonably warm weather as they moved slowly from bungalow to bungalow. They spoke first through the louvered windows that covered the fronts of most of the homes until the occupants opened their front doors.

Had they noticed anything amiss? Had they seen an older man with white hair splayed out, maybe wearing brown pants and a work shirt? Had any unusual cars parked in the neighborhood earlier in the day, or any other time recently? Had they noticed leaving the school grounds a petite, 10-year-old Asian girl with bangs, short hair, turquoise pants, a purple shirt and a killer smile?

In the pre-Katrina era, Davidson might have gone all out. Haul in off-duty officers. Gather volunteer searchers. Call in the television stations from Mobile and New Orleans. But, he, his department, the town, the entire region and all the press still were reeling like punch-drunk fighters. This was looking bad. But, the nearly 2000 deaths on the Gulf Coast from the hurricane had been bad, too, not to mention the $100 billion in damage. Hundreds of thousands had seen their homes flooded, lost jobs or uprooted themselves to start over. It was all too much. Too much pain. Too much turmoil. And too exhausting.

Davidson closed his notebook and wriggled out from the picnic table. The police chief was six foot two, and 25 lbs. past his ideal weight of 210. He liked to joke that his hair growing ability had shifted to the Deep South, from the top of his head to the bottom of his chin.

He heard more than felt the crunching in the knee joint that he knew would have to be replaced with molded pieces of new-age plastic in the next five years. He grunted involuntarily as he stood up straight, threw his shoulders back, put his palms against his back and stretched out most of the stiffness in his back. This was bad. What in God's earth had happened to Megan Kim and how was he going to find her?

No. A place still numb from the pounding of bad news didn't need this at all.

Chapter 3

San Francisco

AS HE CAME through the door, Enzo Lee heard the click of the automatic switch and then the fluorescent fixtures in the hospital room snapped on flooding the room with light.

"God," he thought. "How does anyone sleep in here?"

Yet, the two small mounds curled up under the pale blankets in each of the two beds in the room were proof that you could, at least if you were sufficiently sick. The curled shape nearest the door was Lee's grandmother. The other was another woman, also in her 80s and Chinese, as were virtually all of the patients at this facility in San Francisco's Chinatown.

Christian missionaries had founded the Chinese Hospital in the early 1900s when the denizens of Chinatown were banned from San Francisco hospitals – even during epidemics of bubonic plague and other serious diseases. Those racial restrictions had lapsed over the decades but the facility survived as a mainstay of the community, particularly for the elderly with limited English and little experience with modern western medicine.

At first, Lee's grandmother's symptoms had been hard to distinguish from the aches and pains of old age. But finally, the weight loss, fragile skin that bled from minor scratches and the recurrent fevers had convinced his grandmother at Lee's urging to seek advice beyond that offered by Chinese pharmacists and acupuncturists. The blood work quickly confirmed what her internist had suspected from the outset. She had leukemia and the cancer was already starting to spread to her lymph nodes, spleen and liver.

Over the past two months, he had witnessed her battle with all of its swings: Feeling energetic and upbeat one day and then exhausted, nauseous and depressed the next. Lee had seen her lose her hair, even more precious weight and, at times, perhaps even her desire to live. He had often questioned why they were struggling so hard to keep her alive when the net result in all probability was giving her just a few more months of painful life.

But then she would wake up one morning with a smile on her face and a twinkle in her eye. She was her old self. Master Chu, Lee's long-time tai chi instructor who had married his grandmother 18 months ago, would join them for a walk outside in the fleeting warmth of the San Francisco afternoon. Lee would push the chair and he could see his grandmother lean her head back as she soaked up the sunlight like a malnourished houseplant. Then he knew he would do everything he could to keep her with him as long as possible.

A lean six-footer with wavy black hair carrying the first traces of gray, Lee was still getting accustomed to listing his age with a "4" at the beginning. He had spent his entire working career as a newspaper reporter, moving from job to job on the East Coast before returning to his hometown four years earlier. His mother was Chinese. His father, Scottish-Italian, had died when Lee was young. His mother, who raised him in Chinatown, had passed away six years ago. Now he considered his grandmother and Master Chu his only close family.

He felt a hand on his shoulder and caught the familiar scent. Mostly floral – maybe jasmine – with a hint of musk. He knew the smell well now and it made him smile as he turned and saw Dr. Ming Wah Choy, trim in her white lab coat and stylish pumps, standing beside him in the doorway. She was in her mid-30s with shoulder-length hair, prominent cheekbones and the most perfect lips he had ever seen on a woman. Lee liked the way Choy's eyes smiled when she grinned at him.

"You're here early," she said in her slight British accent, a holdover from her Hong Kong roots.

"So are you," said Lee. "I'm driving to Napa for an interview this morning. What's your excuse?"

"Softball practice," said Dr. Choy. "The first of the season so I need to leave on time tonight."

"I play softball," said Lee. "What's your position?"

"Pitcher," said Dr. Choy. "Sorry. It's a women's league. You can come and watch us though." She shrugged her shoulders apologetically as she stepped across the room and stood next to his grandmother. She inspected the intravenous line and bent down to get a closer look at the displays on the monitors behind the bed.

As if sensing her presence, Lee's grandmother stirred, stretching out her legs a little. She blinked sleepily a few times and then was able to focus on Dr. Choy as the physician moved closer to her and bent her face down.

"Mrs. Chen," said the doctor. "Good morning. Look who is here. Your grandson."

Lee stepped closer to the bed as Dr. Choy moved back until they were standing side by side in front of Lee's grandmother.

She looked at them for several moments, lifting her head off her pillow. She wore a pink and blue knit hat that looked as if someone had stitched the top of a French beret to the bottom of a ski cap. Lee knew the hat was more to hide her baldness than for warmth. His grandmother returned her head to her pillow and smiled at them dreamily.

"Such a pretty couple," she said, closing her eyes.

Lee and Dr. Choy looked at each other. Lee winked and flashed a quick smile. His grandmother had been trying to set him up with her oncologist for the past two months. He knew that it was a good sign whenever her matchmaking instincts kicked in. It meant she was feeling better – more energetic. She probably was in for a couple of good days.

"You've slept too long, Grandma," said Lee. "Ming Wah and I are married and have three children. The oldest is only five and has already been accepted to Yale."

"He's such a brat," said Dr. Choy, playing along. "But, a very smart one. Jonas will make a very good doctor."

"Writer!" said Lee. "And his middle name is 'Faulkner.'"

Her eyes still closed, Lee's grandmother smiled happily as she slowly shook her head and drifted back to sleep.

Chapter 4

THE TRAILER HAD started out pure white but was covered now in a thick layer of brown-red dust. Two identical trailers stood nearby in a lot that had been cleared of debris just a day or two before FEMA brought in the temporary living quarters.

Chief Davidson walked up the four steps to the landing of the small, movable staircase. It was made of plywood and painted gray. His footsteps sounded like muffled drumbeats. The silver metal door was ajar.

Through the opening, a small child popped into view. The little boy stood a couple yards back from the doorway. Skinny, tanned and clothed only in a disposable diaper in the afternoon's damp warmth, the kid tilted his head curiously at Davidson as he sucked steadily on a pacifier. His mouth was hidden by the white plastic circle with a raised yellow button in the middle. Maybe it was supposed to represent the sun.

The kid looked so focused and serious that Davidson almost directed his first question at him.

"C'mon. Get serious," the police chief said to himself. "He's barely two. Still in diapers." Plus, it looked as if it would take a crowbar to pry the pacifier loose.

Instead, Davidson gave the metal door three sharp raps with his knuckles.

"Hello," he said in a loud voice. "Missus Kim? Police department."

He heard footsteps. Then, the door was pulled open by a slight Asian man wearing a white undershirt and old khaki pants a size too big. He looked in his early 30s. His teeth were a mess. Davidson immediately thought of his son, a junior at Ole

Miss. Six extractions, three years in braces and $8,000 had fixed him. This guy probably needed a lot more than that.

"Chief Davidson," he said, gesturing to the badge on his shirt. "And, you are?"

"Billy Kim," the man said. "Her cousin. I live here, too, with my family." He nodded at the boy in diapers who had retreated two steps but still regarded Davidson with an impressive intensity.

"I get," said Billy Kim. He opened the door further, gestured toward a small dining table just inside the door with four chairs around it and padded down a hallway covered in thin blue carpeting toward the opposite end of the trailer. Davidson had been in a few of them and knew the basic layout. Two bedrooms and a single bath with a shower. Fake wood paneling everywhere. It was designed for four but you could squeeze in six without camping out in the living room if you didn't mind sleeping with your kids.

Davidson heard them at the other end of the trailer. Was it Cantonese? At least it sounded similar to the various Cantonese dialects he occasionally heard. But what did he know? Linguistics weren't his strong point. He liked to say he spoke Southern and non-Southern. It could have been Vietnamese or Laotian for all he knew.

The woman who trailed Billy Kim was thin and looked tired. She wore white polyester pants and a red short-sleeved shirt with a diamond pattern. Her hair was long and hung straight down. The left side of her face was lightly scarred, perhaps from acne when she was young or some other skin disease. Her knuckles were red and her hands worn. Davidson guessed she was someone who had worked hard all of her life. She looked over 40 but could have been closer to 30.

When she sat down with her cousin across from Davidson, Mary Kim positioned herself to face Billy and stared down at her hands. She shrank away from the police chief as if he was a

13

bright flame throwing off too much heat. If he made a sudden move, Mary Kim looked as if she might jump out the window.

Davidson had gotten accustomed to similar reactions over the past few weeks. It had started when the federal immigration agents began periodic sweeps through the bars, restaurants, seafood plants and even selected homes in the area. They were mainly looking for immigrants with criminal records but the sweeps had terrified anyone who had padded the truth – even if just adding a non-existent job skill – on their applications to enter the country. Davidson suspected many if not most of the Asian immigrants in his town fell into this category. The police chief had nothing to do with immigration but he was the face of law enforcement. Lately he'd seen people turn and disappear into the trees when they saw him coming.

"Missus Kim," began Davidson.

"Mary," she said, still looking away from him.

"Mary," repeated the chief. "You know why I'm here. It's about your daughter, Megan."

Billy Kim translated rapidly and Mary Kim nodded toward her cousin as he spoke.

"We've searched the neighborhood and interviewed the people who live in the immediate area," said Davidson. "No one saw her leave or saw anyone suspicious...or a stranger...except for her friend, Lucy."

He waited for the translation and Mary Kim's slight nod.

"Lucy thinks Megan was talking to an older man, a white man maybe in his 50s," he continued. He noticed that Billy Kim used "American" to describe the mystery man.

"He had white hair, sort of sticking out." The police chief put his hands on either side of his nearly hairless head and made a motion as if pulling out tufts.

"Lucy thought maybe he had on a blue work shirt and brown pants," Davidson said. "She wasn't sure." He waited for the translation and another nod.

"Do you know anyone who looks like that?" he asked.

A head shake.

"Do you know why Megan would willingly leave school to go with someone like that?"

Another head shake.

Davidson waited for a few moments. He flipped through his notebook as if looking for something. But, he was really just delaying. He had found that the best information often spills into an awkward silence when people get uncomfortable and search for something to fill it.

Mary said something to Billy. It took several seconds. Billy nodded his head as she spoke. Then, he turned to Davidson.

"She says Megan is very smart," he said. "Very smart for her age. Not just in school but outside, too. She not leave with stranger. Only if reason. Very good reason." Mary nodded as Billy finished.

Davidson got the best phone numbers for Billy and Mary Kim. Hers was at a nail salon in nearby Mobile where she worked during the days. As he stood up to leave, she looked at him directly for the first time. For a moment, at least, parental concern overrode her fear of the lawman.

"Please," she said in English. "Please. You go. Find Megan."

"I'll try, Missus Kim," he said. "I'll try." As he said it, Davidson was counting the hours since Megan Kim had disappeared from her school. At least five. Within the first two hours she could have left Alabama and been in Louisiana or Mississippi to the west, or Florida to the east. By now, she could even be in Georgia or near the Tennessee border. She could be a mile away or 300.

He had already sent out an initial bulletin to all the law enforcement agencies in the area. He would expand the reach now, adding more details about what Megan was wearing. He had a photo from the school he could include. Where had she

15

gone? Why had she gone? If she had fought, some other kid in that school yard would have seen it. He prayed she still was alive.

"Where the hell are you, Megan?" said Davidson softly as he steadied himself on the handrail and clumped down the stairs from the trailer door to the red dirt crisscrossed with hardened tire tracks. He got to his cruiser and then turned back.

The little boy in the diaper was standing on the landing facing him. Suddenly, the pacifier shot out of his mouth and arced in Davidson's direction for a fraction of a second before falling toward the ground. The kid stared at Davidson. He looked mad. The chief half expected the kid to flip him the bird. Instead, both of his hands shot up in the air and he shrieked.

"Eeeee."

Then, he spun around, raced back into the trailer and slammed the door. It hit so hard it made the trailer shake.

Chapter 5

Ann Arbor, Michigan

NANCY JOHANNSEN WAS proud of her 36 years teaching children at Clancy Elementary School in Ann Arbor. When her husband had died eight years earlier, it kept her from spiraling down. It gave her a sense of purpose and plenty to keep her busy. When you spent half of your day negotiating the emotional ups and downs of 28 extremely busy second graders you don't have the time or energy to feel sorry for yourself.

She put off retirement for two years even after she maxed out on the pension scale. She had no children. She wasn't particularly close to any of her relatives. What would she do with herself?

Then the school district undertook a round of layoffs. Johannsen retired so a teacher with a young family could keep her job. Retirement had gone better than she expected. She tutored, gardened, volunteered at the library and managed a discussion blog that focused on the Ann Arbor school district. It was the blog that had invigorated her the most. She often felt that she was back in the classroom. The first thing she did was set a filter to stop all posts that contained the two-word sequence "Go Blue." She had explained to a dozen University of Michigan alums that non-Michigan folks might be offended and, yes, she thought there were even a couple of Ohio State grads who subscribed to the blog.

She had to talk down contributors who thought all whites were racist, assumed male teachers were universally gay and child molesters, and believed every principal and teacher cheated on their students' standardized tests to increase their bonuses. She kept the contact information for the school district's ombudsman and a psychologist who specialized in crisis intervention taped to her monitor.

When the scientist from San Francisco called her, she was excited to hear from him again. It had been more than a year since his first call when he offered her a chance to help a child. It was soon after her retirement and it seemed fitting, being able to help a youngster. She had leapt at the chance.

But now he was warning her about some sort of danger. She might be in jeopardy. Did she have somewhere...maybe relatives some place...where she could spend some time, perhaps a month?

She could stay with her niece for awhile, she said. But after the call, it all seemed too bizarre. It was hard for her to imagine bad things happening on her bucolic street filled with leafy maples, flowering honey locusts and good neighbors. Spring had come early and she had tomato, cucumber and basil plants on the back porch waiting to be planted. She put off calling her niece.

It was noon the next day when the knock on the door came. The man had dark hair with a single streak of white in it. He was reasonably good looking and wore a black jacket over blue jeans. It was after Johannsen identified herself that he pulled the gun out from inside of his jacket and pushed her back into the house.

He told her to sit down on the couch. Then he made her lie on her stomach with her face in a cushion.

"Don't look," he said.

What was he going to do? Molest her? Shoot her in the back of the head like some gangster?

Johannsen obeyed the order not to look. But she listened. She heard him walking around the living room as if searching for something. Then she heard something being moved on the wall above her. Scraping. It was her plaque – the surprising heavy wooden one that fellow teachers gave her when she retired, honoring her 36 years of service.

"What does he want with that?" she thought to herself just before it came crashing down flat against the back of her head, knocking her unconscious.

When Johannsen came to, she was under water. She could see the man above her, pinning her arms to the bottom of the bathtub. His expression was blank, not even a frown or grimace. He might have been a photograph.

She tried to flail but it was as if her limbs were fastened to the bottom of the tub. Something was holding her legs down. Maybe someone else. She inhaled water. Choked. Inhaled more. She finally gave up. She relaxed and looked up at the expressionless man with beseeching eyes that said, "Please don't do this." But she knew it was a plea that would go unanswered.

Chapter 6

ENZO LEE LOOKED down his row of brown metal desks and then turned to the three rows before him that formed a buffer in front of the editors' offices at the San Francisco News. How long ago had it been when every desk was filled at deadline with reporters flailing at their terminals and chattering on telephones in panic as they glanced up at the clocks ticking away on the wall? Now, high-speed Internet was devouring low-tech newsprint and delivery trucks. After three rounds of layoffs in 18 months, the newsroom was decimated. Half the desks were empty.

It reminded him of the way soldiers described it pouring out of the trenches in World War I. Half way across no-man's land, they would look down their row of humanity, see the huge gaps and wonder how much longer Providence would shield them from exploding artillery shells and machine gun fire.

Not that this had been quite that dramatic or lethal. It was more as if a team of accountants lined up at the front of the newsroom every six months. Ready. Aim. Fired. Another eight reporters gone, plus a couple of editors.

Lee considered his long tenure in the reporting business a liability in the age of downsizing. It left him firmly ensconced at the top of the union pay scale – all the more reason to hand him his walking papers. All he could think of was that his steady stream of daily fluff stories – the light features that often graced the front page in a highlighted box – had been deemed valuable enough to keep him on for now. Ironically, he guessed that if he had continued in his original specialty – the tough investigating work of exposing crooked businesses and corrupt politicians – he'd probably be out of a job now. Investigative reporting was a luxury few newspapers could afford these days.

Remembering his professional vulnerability, Lee refocused on his story of the day. He had interviewed Roger and Beth, a married couple, in the wine country that morning. They had known each other when they attended Sonoma High School in the 60s. Roger had asked Beth out back then and she had declined. More than three decades, two spouses and five children later, they met again when his Lincoln smashed into her BMW. Within 90 days, they had married.

"*Roger Barrett obeyed Beth Wilson's stop sign thirty-four years ago*," Lee began. "*He wasn't going to make the same mistake twice.*"

An hour later, the reporter put the finishing touches on the piece.

"*They used the insurance settlement to pay for the honeymoon.*

"*'It's amazing how much car repairs cost,' said Wilson with a mischievous smile. 'It just felt like a love tap.'*"

Lee had just sent the story over to the copy desk when his cell phone rang. The caller ID told him it was the Chinese Hospital.

"Mr. Lee," said the voice on the other end. "Your grandmother has had a cardiac arrest...Mr. Lee? Mr. Lee? Are you there?"

Lee was already running across the newsroom heading for the stairs.

A cab ride and twelve minutes later, he was at the hospital. He was out of breath when he walked through the door into his grandmother's room. He saw Dr. Choy standing next to the bed. She saw him and extended her arm toward him, palm outward, as she finished tucking in a blanket around the sleeping form.

She led him out to the corridor and pushed him into a chair standing against the wall on the pale green linoleum.

"You look worse than she does," she said.

Lee took a deep breath.

"How is she?" he said.

"She's doing well," said Choy. "Her heart stopped but the monitor caught it. The nurse came in and began to give her CPR while everyone else was getting the crash cart. All it took was a couple of pushes on her chest and she was back."

"So, that's it?" said Lee. "No other damage?" Choy sat down in the chair next to Lee, twisting to face him. She had her hand on his arm.

"Hopefully, not," she said. "We'll have her checked out. It was very quick. I'm hopeful any damage was minimal. It's possible it's not really a circulation issue...such as a blocked artery. It could be more the impulses telling her heart when to beat. If that's the case, they may recommend a pacemaker and defibrillator. Cardiology will tell us."

Lee settled back into the chair and closed his eyes for a moment while he exhaled slowly.

"How much more of this can she take?" he asked, directing the question as much to himself as to Choy.

"She is very strong for her age," said Choy. "What is she? 84?"

"Actually, 85," said Lee. "Yes. She is in remarkable shape. But, 85 is 85. This would take a lot out of anyone."

"Unfortunately, what we are doing does not eradicate the cancer," said the doctor. "It only slows it down. And, she seems to be responding less to each treatment. Resistance is building and we started with the most effective drugs.

"I wish...well...it doesn't matter," she continued. "It's not available."

"What?" said Lee.

"Well…it's just…I thought by now there would be a new drug out," said Choy. "A couple of years ago, I met someone at a medical conference. He was working on something that seemed very promising, especially for this kind of cancer. I've checked all the literature. There were a couple of early mentions but nothing recent. Not even trials. I don't know what happened to it."

Lee was quiet for a moment. He just looked at Choy.

"You're saying there could be something else out there that we can try?" he said. "Even if it's experimental?"

Choy shrugged.

"Let's find out," he said. "Let's make sure. Tell me everything you know about it. I'll find out what's going on."

"I haven't been able to find anything useful," said Choy, shaking her head doubtfully. "It just…disappeared. It's not uncommon for drugs to be delayed…or abandoned altogether during late testing."

"Look," said Lee, taking her hands in his. He noticed that her palms were warm but dry. "You've been right about everything the last two months. The progression. The treatment. Side effects. You've answered my many, many questions."

"You can be…well, uh…persistent," she said.

"Thanks for not saying 'stubborn' or 'annoying' but I know I can be both those things as well," he said. "The point is that I trust your instincts, Ming Wah. If it sounded promising to you, let me take another look. I'll find out what happened. Let's get the story. There's always a way."

"Leave no stone unturned?" said Choy, gently disengaging her hands from his and smiling indulgently.

"Well," said Lee. "That's always been one of my mottos. Plus, it will give me something to do."

Choy was silent for a moment. Lee could guess her thoughts: "Let the grandson have this project. Make him feel less helpless…less anxious.   It might make life easier for everyone."

"Okay," she said with a resigned sigh.   "I know better than to try to stop you.   Here is what I remember."

Chapter 7

THEY STOPPED FOR gas and a bathroom break once and then continued on to the outskirts of Fayetteville, Tennessee before stopping again. On the way, the man said little. He told Megan to find anything on the radio. So, she played with the dial a few times in the first hour as different stations came in and out of range. Preachers. Old rock and roll. Country. She would glance at him to see if there was anything he liked, but she got no reaction. He seemed totally focused on something far ahead of them. Finally, she turned toward the passenger window, gazed out and watched the countryside roll past in silence.

The forests flew by in an unending montage. Some were little more than tall scrubland and she could see hills in the distance. Other stretches were so lush with tall trees and thick vines she imagined you could burrow in and disappear within 20 feet of the highway. Places where the hills had been gashed open by the highway builders remained red and raw.

Their second stop was at a Wal-Mart. First, they bought her a toothbrush. Then, they went to the kids clothing area. He let Megan pick out some panties, three T-shirts, socks and pajamas. She stayed away from her usual favorite choices of pinks and pastels, opting for white and primary colors. She wasn't feeling frilly. She picked the pajamas with soccer balls all over them.

It was when they stopped at a Hardee's before getting back on the highway that she decided, finally, that he really was a bit strange. It wasn't just her imagination. While they sat across from each other eating their hamburgers and French fries and sipping their sodas, he just gazed past her into the parking lot.

25

She looked up when she heard his voice and then realized he was murmuring softly to himself.

Megan tried to remember what he had told her at the school.

She was in danger, he had said. She had to come with him right away, at that moment. No delays. How long? Maybe a week or longer. Don't worry. He would take care of everything. Didn't she remember him? Of course she did. Megan assumed he would explain more. Fill in the details. But, they had driven in silence almost the entire time.

She wasn't too worried about him. She'd learned early to talk to adults, the Americans, because her mother relied on her so much to negotiate the English-speaking world. She knew more about renting apartments, bus schedules and getting refunds for broken appliances and ill-fitting clothes than any of her peers. She also had a pretty good idea what people were thinking. Were they angry? Impatient? Friendly just long enough to get what they wanted? She often had to decide on the spot.

The ones that she and her mother could trust she kept engraved in her memory. She went back to them for help when she needed it, and sometimes when she really didn't. They wanted to help. They liked her. For no particular reason, she would visit the assistant librarian, the man who owned the no-name convenience store and the older black woman who sat on her porch all day and told stories. She made sure they knew her name was 'Megan.'

She felt her companion was one of those – a bit odd perhaps but still deserving her trust.

When they finally stopped an hour after nightfall it was at the Magnolia Motel, a small establishment a few blocks off the highway. It had a dozen units with parking in front and an office on the far right side. A gigantic magnolia tree stood on the other side of the office, towering above it and covered with big pink and white blossoms. The fragrance on the evening air reminded Megan of sweet lemonade with a dash of vanilla.

The door to the office had a bell attached and it brought out a young man who left the television on in the other room. It was a game show.

She heard herself described as "my daughter" and knew enough not to look surprised. She saw a $100 bill passed over the counter and some bills and change returned. Megan wandered over to a table set against the wall that was stacked with game boxes, many held together with tape. Monopoly. Clue. Chutes and Ladders. Checkers. Yahtzee. Some she didn't know. There was an old pack of playing cards with a giant ace of spades on the front. She picked them up, studied the pack and looked over at the counter. They both watched her.

"You can borrow those," the young man said.

Megan flashed her biggest smile.

"Thank you," she said in a strong voice. She clasped them in a tight grip and led the way out the door.

Chapter 8

ALL 14 INTERNS were in their second year of graduate business school. Most of the top MBA programs were represented, including Harvard, Stanford, Chicago, Wharton and Sloan. They were half way through a six-week program at Merrick & Merrick, the third largest pharmaceutical company in the world.

It was supposedly a mix of work and education. But everyone in the conference room that looked out from San Francisco's China Basin waterfront toward Oakland across the bay knew that this was a courting ritual. Merrick was strutting its stuff as an exciting employment opportunity – hot products, great management team, wonderful city. The MBAs were mainly trying to avoid disproving anything in the glowing resumes and transcripts that had resulted in their selection to the program.

Vice President Troy Axmann began the session on product development in the darkened conference room with a click of the handheld keypad that controlled the overhead projector. He stood to the side of a screen filling the wall behind him that was immediately transformed into a floor-to-ceiling banana split. A mountain of whipped cream decorated with slivered almonds and Maraschino cherries filled the top half of the screen, sitting atop chocolate and caramel sauce that oozed over pistachio, French vanilla and coffee ice cream.

"This is what awaits us at the end of the presentation," said Axmann. Someone away from the screen said, "Yes!" in a stage whisper that sent a wave of smiles rippling toward the front that splashed onto Axmann himself. He sent a smile back the other way.

"Perfect," he thought to himself. It always amazed him that Ivy Leaguers and Wall Street analysts responded to the promise of a quick sugar high in pretty much the same way as five-year-olds.

Axmann's movie-star good looks were a huge asset to his presentations. But he knew that more than ten minutes of Powerpoint slides in a darkened conference room about his area of expertise – getting drugs from concept to approved medicines – would bore at least some in the audience. He wanted to leave a positive, lasting impression. If they recalled nothing else about this session three months from now, the MBAs should remember the banana splits. He'd had the chocolate sauce flown in from Belgium.

The next slide was an old black-and-white portrait, circa 1900, of an anonymous gentleman with an impressive set of white whiskers who looked to be somewhere between 80 and 100.

"Compared to our brethren here in the Bay Area at the high-tech software and hardware companies, we might seem a little stodgy," said Axmann. "Look at the executive teams at the top 10 drug companies – 'Big Pharma' as we're called – and you'll see many people who have been at their companies a long time.

"People who started out 25 years ago as researchers, chemists, salesmen," he continued. "It's true that there is a premium placed on people who know the science, know the history and – most important – understand how this industry works."

The next slide was of a living room filled with folding tables and a half-dozen young programmers working in front of multiple computer monitors arrayed in front of them. Pizza boxes were scattered around and a huge, overweight ginger cat slept on top of a large piece of computer equipment in the foreground.

"Looks like my frat house," said someone at the table.

"Exactly," said Axmann. "Or any one of 100 software startups around here in Palo Alto, Fremont or San Francisco.

"Don't get me wrong," he continued. "There are plenty of start ups in the drug business. But, they won't look like this, of course. The software crowd might get a workable prototype of whatever they're making – maybe a Windows app – up and running in a year. If they can attract, say, $5 million, they've got a shot. They can run it up the flagpole, wave it around. See if it's useful and if they can get people – businesses, consumers or whatever their market is – to use it."

The next slide showed a room with a dozen people wearing lab coats sitting at laboratory work benches surrounded by microscopes and other equipment.

"Here is how a biotech startup looks," said Axmann. "There is probably more than $5 million worth of equipment just in this room alone. And, getting just one drug out of here and safely on the market will cost more than 100 times that amount and that's on the cheap end. A price tag of $1 billion to get a drug from concept to market is not unusual. And, on average it will take eight years from discovery to FDA approval."

The image on the screen disappeared and another one appeared showing a man wearing a tuxedo at a craps table. He was preparing to throw a pair of dice.

"Billion-dollar bets," said Axmann. "That's what we're about. Billion-dollar bets. It's not for the faint of heart. Sure...we have to execute. We have many thousands of people devoted to making, marketing and selling our products. But make no mistake. Where the rubber meets the road is deciding *where* we place the bets. Bet wrong and you're out hundreds of millions of dollars. Hit it right, and you've got this."

The screen now changed to show bars of black and blue running lengthwise. Each colored bar had a drug name next to it. There were dates running along the top of the slide, starting at 2006 and running out to 2016. A few of the bars ran across the entire slide. Most stopped part way across.

"The six black bars represent Merrick & Merrick drugs earning at least $1 billion a year in revenue," said Axmann. "The blue ones sell less than $1 billion but more than $200 million annually. Where they end is the year that we lose patent protection and the generics enter the market.

"The top two are, of course, our entries for the cholesterol and the anti-depression markets," he continued. "Those two bring in $4 billion a year...each! Next, is Morceptin, our flagship cancer treatment that is now used for four types of cancer. Annual sales are $3 billion but it is the fastest growing of our major drugs and our patents on it run through 2016.

"There have been breakthroughs historically in the drug industry, such as antibiotics and chemotherapy," said Axmann. "But, the application of genetic technology combined with better understanding of the human genome – that's a true revolution just beginning to take off. It will save tens of millions of lives. It will add billions of years of improved quality of life to the world. How many software apps can claim that?"

The executive directed everyone's attention back to the screen behind him.

"Does anyone see any problems ahead for us?" he asked.

Halfway down the table, an attractive woman with auburn hair in her mid 20s raised her hand.

"Stanford," thought Axmann. "Chemical engineering major with two years at McKinsey Consulting."

"Yes," he said.

"In 2012," she said. "A third of your patents go away along with half the revenue stream."

"Correct," said Axmann. "That's our challenge over the next five years. Replenish the pipeline. And, that's also our shareholders' leap of faith – that we have the smarts and the guts to make the right bets. We either discover and develop them ourselves, or buy them probably from the startups we discussed. Either way, they must be on the market before the ones you see here hit the wall.

"And, of course, if any of our cash cows, the drugs currently represented by the black bars, drop out before they're supposed to for some reason – it might be competition, patent problems, FDA issues – the consequences are enormous. To be honest, that's what I lose sleep over at night."

The executive paused while he looked around the room at the MBA candidates watching him. He felt a pain in his gut. Stomach acid washing over his ulcer. He needed to sit down. Axmann clicked the projector controller one more time. The banana split reappeared.

"I'm getting hungry," he said with a thin smile. "Ice cream, anyone?"

Chapter 9

WALTER NOVAK KNEW he had cut himself before the blood appeared on the right side of his jaw and dripped into the sink. Even clamping his left hand on his right wrist for added support after he saw the razor quivering in his hand hadn't been enough.

He rinsed off the blood, tore off a piece of toilet paper, twisted it between his thumb and finger, and put it on the cut to stop the bleeding. He dried the razor on the motel towel, put it back in his toilet kit and zipped it closed. He had shaved earlier that day but it had been before dawn in California, before the flight to New Orleans, before the trip along the Gulf Coast to get Megan and before the long haul to put as many miles behind them as he could.

Panic had consumed him early on. He kept expecting a patrol car to pull up behind him with lights flashing. Or maybe someone else. He kept watch behind him for the first hour, looking for anyone following him. How would hired killers look? What would they drive? Probably something big, dark and powerful.

Finally, he settled down and fixed on a couple of key objectives. He would keep it at a steady 75 miles per hour, fast enough to eat up distance but without the risk of getting pulled over for a speeding ticket or otherwise attracting attention. He would stop only the one time for gas until they were out of Alabama. He really didn't know if that was important or not – getting across the state line. Maybe the police communications broke down between states or were somehow delayed. He had no idea. But it gave him a goal that he could focus on. And when he saw the "Welcome to Tennessee" sign he felt better.

Novak looked at himself in the bathroom mirror and blinked hard. He felt better after the shower and shave. He had on a plain blue T-shirt and jeans. His white hair was slicked down from the shower but already started to spring back to its usual uncontrolled state.

He could still feel the anxiety coursing through him as if it had its own system of veins and arteries. But, he felt in control this time and knew its source. Nine months earlier it had been a much different story. Back then the panic attacks that hadn't plagued him for years returned. They hit him like a set of massive waves.

They left him breathless, then huddled in bed unable to leave the house, and finally in abject terror of things he knew were impossible but wouldn't stop invading his consciousness. Giant spiders cocooning him in sticky silk when he fell asleep. Tiny insects entering his brain through his ears. He thought he could hear the scratching. The air being sucked out of the room, making it nearly impossible to breathe. He thought he felt the faint breeze of oxygen escaping.

Ninety days of psychotropic drugs, therapy and long walks in the mountainous foothills outside a private psychiatric facility in Arizona had eased the paralyzing fears and brought him fully back to reality.

Upon his release and return to California, he took a few more days to adjust. With the help of a local psychiatrist, he continued to push back the old fears until they felt as if he had experienced them in another life. He thought of them as being locked away in a closet that he was starting to forget even existed.

When he got back to work, he expected the stares, the careful slaps on the back as if his co-workers feared he would break or, even worse, somehow infect them with the crushing weakness that had possessed him. But what he didn't expect was the assault on his work. Had he gone from genius to fool in three months? Was he still crazy? Had he been crazy for a long time, misinterpreting everything that had gone on in his life and seeing it through some fractured reality?

He searched for anchors, hard facts he could use to moor himself and the past as he remembered it. There were the degrees. Those were real. They documented a brilliant scientific career that spanned both mathematics and, later, biology. He could find his old papers, published in prestigious journals and representing more than two decades of research.

The money in his investment accounts and financial statements was real, too. They had paid him tens of millions of dollars for what he had developed. It would only have happened if his work had been valued as he recalled. What had changed? What had happened while he was away? He untangled the data, slowly at first and then with urgency. Roxanne, the only person he trusted at work, provided an email that she had been copied on by mistake while he was incapacitated. It hinted at much more.

When he dug deeper he saw that he had been excluded from the questions and doubts – the steady drip of misgivings about his work. It made no sense. The accusations couldn't be right. And, then he saw it. In the reports of damaging side effects and even death, he saw the hints that something else was at work. At first he wondered if it could really be true. Was he seeing the world clearly and accurately now? Could he trust himself? Or was he slipping back into fantasy?

Novak suddenly remembered that he was in a Tennessee motel room, staring at himself in the bathroom mirror. Had he been standing immobile for three minutes or 30? He looked at his jaw. He peeled the paper off. The bleeding had stopped. Novak forced himself to move, turn to the door, open it and walk out.

It was only a step but he felt the change of worlds. Low lights instead of bright fluorescence. Wood paneling, brown upholstery and yellow bedspreads instead of white tile. There she was, sitting at the foot of one of the beds watching for him. She was shuffling a deck of cards. Looking down at them. Then, back at him, tilting her head up just for a moment. But all the questions were there in the glance. What had he been doing? Was he okay? What in God's name were they doing here? Was he capable of handling this situation? Had she made a mistake?

"Don't freak her out," he said to himself. "Act normal. Act normal. Act normal."

"Want to play cards?" she asked, looking up again from her shuffling.

"Okay," said Novak. He moved to the other end of the bed that she was on. He sat with his back against the headboard and his long thin legs running along the side. She swiveled to face him.

"Five-card draw?" Megan asked. He nodded and smiled. It occurred to Megan that it might have been the first time he had smiled at her all day.

They played the first game in silence.

She drew a pair of kings to go with the one she had kept when she discarded three cards. It beat his two pairs. She shuffled again. As she began to deal out the next hand, Novak slumped against the headboard. The long day was sinking in.

"Walter," he said as she finished the dealing and picked up her cards. "It's my name."

Megan nodded as she studied her cards.

"'Walter Novak,'" she said. "I remember. Plus, there's a luggage tag on your suitcase."

She gave him two cards. He added a third jack to the pair already in his hand.

"Are you a doctor?" she asked.

36

"No," he said. "Well, not a medical doctor. You see, when you get a doctorate degree…"

Megan nodded her head twice.

"I know the difference," she said. She turned her cards over. "Straight. Beats three-of-a-kind."

Novak looked at her and then down at his cards which he hadn't shown her yet.

"Where did you learn to play poker?" he asked.

Megan shrugged.

"A boy at school taught me," she said.

"A friend?"

"He is now," said Megan. "He's the biggest kid in fifth grade."

Novak was feeling better. The cards. Having a game to focus on, to talk about. Had she planned that?

He held out his hand for the cards. She picked up the ones on the bedspread, added them to the stack in her hand and handed it to him.

"Do you know how to play gin rummy?" he asked.

Megan shook her head.

"It's a good game for two," said Novak. He shuffled twice and began dealing out the cards.

Megan nodded her agreement, settled down to learn the new game and, almost imperceptibly, breathed out a long sigh born as much from relief as her fatigue.

Chapter 10

"GODDAMN LAZY GOVERNMENT bureaucrats," Salvatore "Murph" Murphy thought to himself as he pulled into the parking lot of the Magnolia Motel a little after 9:30 in the morning.

The FBI clerk in Las Vegas who was on the payroll of his organization had dutifully put an unofficial watch on the handful of numbers they had unearthed that were thought possibly connected to Megan Kim's mother, Mary. The call had come in at 9:45 pm the previous evening to the cell phone of An Dung "Billy" Kim, Mary's cousin.

It was a simple matter to trace the calling number to the motel. Unfortunately, that had only happened after the clerk got to work the next morning and obtained the information from AT&T. That was just a little more than an hour ago.

"Bastard probably had three coffees and four donuts before he got busy," thought Murphy. He used the rear view mirror to check his hair. He ignored the lump on his nose, the product of repeated breakings during a respectable boxing career in his youth. Then he opened the briefcase in the passenger's seat and pulled out his Smith & Wesson 4506. It was a lot of gun but Murphy didn't like to take chances.

As Murphy got out of the car, he slipped the gun into the Galco Summer Comfort holster strapped to his belt and pulled down his black nylon windbreaker until he was sure the gun was invisible. A small, throw-down .22 was already in the pocket of the windbreaker.

"Quaint," he thought when he heard the tinkle of the bell that signaled his entrance into the Magnolia's office. He heard the guy in the back making his way to the front desk. No one else was around. The parking spaces in front of the motel were all empty. Still, he moved down the counter so he could keep his back to the far wall and see the parking area and the front door.

"I'm looking for them," said Murphy, as he put down on the counter a sheet of paper with color photographs of Walter Novak and Megan Kim.

The clerk studied the page and then looked at Murphy.

"Police?" the clerk asked.

Murphy shook his head.

"Private," he said. "Custody matter. He took the kid and her mother wants her back. They called last night from here."

The clerk bit his lip for a moment as he continued to stare at the photos. Then, he shrugged his shoulders.

"Guess it don't matter," he said. "They checked out...oh. I don't know. Call it 40 minutes ago."

"Figures," said Murphy, shaking his head. "Say, you wouldn't have a license number, would you?" He pulled two $20 bills out of his pocket and laid them on the counter.

The clerk barely glanced at the money before turning around to a desk and pulling the top card from a small stack that sat there. He placed it on the counter and gently picked up the twenties and slipped them into his front pocket while Murphy jotted down the car information. Murphy grunted his thanks when he left the office. On his way back to the car, he noticed the thick, cloying stink from the huge flowering tree on the other side of the office.

On the other side of the highway, directly across four lanes of traffic from the Magnolia, Walter Novak sat in the Waffle House and watched the man with the lumbering gait drive away in the blue Navigator that he judged as big, dark and fast enough.

Megan had her back to the window. She was eating a waffle smothered with blueberry syrup. With the height of the booth,

Novak knew she wasn't visible from the street. He said nothing to her.

Five minutes later, they left the Waffle House and walked along the sidewalk in front of the restaurant to the parking lot on the side of the building. Novak saw the clerk in the motel office watching them closely even after Novak returned the stare. He knew then that luck had been on their side. He hoped it stayed there.

* * *

The telephone rang as Enzo Lee was putting the finishing touches on a story about a new dromedary at the San Francisco Zoo whose over-the-top sex drive was terrorizing the female camels. The zoo had posted signs warning families of potentially traumatic X-rated displays.

("When 10,000 voters gave 'Humpy' his name, they couldn't have known exactly how appropriate it would be. Or, maybe he just took it as a challenge.")

"Hi," said Lorraine Carr. "It's me."

"Hey you," said Lee. "I've just spent the afternoon watching a desperately horny camel on the rampage at the zoo. It was breath taking."

"I see," she said. "Give you any ideas?"

"Yes, actually," said Lee. "I've been trying to find costumes for Richard III or the Hunchback of Notre Dame."

"I see," she said. "For you or for me?"

"Umm. Both?"

"You know," she said. "That would be pretty funny, if politically incorrect."

"Yeah, I know. We'd have to wear masks for the video."

Carr laughed.

"You're just trying to put these images in my head so nothing erotic can get in, right?" she said.

40

"You got it," said Lee. "At least until you hop off the plane. Speaking of which…when are you flying in?"

In her half-second delay, Lee knew he would be spending the weekend alone again. Carr had been his boss as city editor at the San Francisco News as well as his lover for almost a year when the last round of layoffs hit the newspaper. She hadn't been dumped unceremoniously as had so many others, but Carr received a clear signal from her superiors that her best move was jumping off the sinking ship while she still had a choice.

So, she had taken a long-standing job offer from the Wall Street Journal. The problem was that her position was covering East Coast high tech companies from New York. She and Lee had been trading monthly trips back and forth. But his grandmother's illness holding him in San Francisco and Carr's incessant travel up and down the East Coast had taken its toll. They hadn't been together in six weeks.

"I'm sorry, babe," she said. "I've got to be in Munich on Monday. A big Siemens announcement. Fiber optics breakthrough or some such nonsense."

"Aarrgh," said Lee loud enough to get a few stares in the newsroom. He put his face in his hand and took a couple of deep breaths as his emotional state cycled quickly from anger to desperation before settling into self pity.

The weekends they had together now – usually stretched to three days – were incredibly intense. But just when they were getting back to their old rhythms – past satisfying the pent up passion and the celebration of reuniting – Carr was gone again. The emotional rollercoaster was getting old. Each time Carr slipped away, Lee could feel the gulf between them widen a bit more.

"Are you still there?" said Carr.

"Yes," said Lee with a heavy sigh. "This is getting a little ridiculous."

"I know," she said. "Look. I will try, try, try to be there next week, okay? Meanwhile...I don't know. Maybe we should resort to phone sex."

"*Phone sex*," said Lee, drawing a few more glances. "Then I'll have *no* idea if you're faking it."

Carr laughed and then switched to her seduction voice – low and purring.

"I *never* fake it," she said.

"Okay," he said. "You can convince me of that the next time we're in bed."

"The pleasure will be mine," she said. "And hopefully yours, too."

They both laughed.

"Listen," said Lee. "Before you go I need to ask you something...non-sex related. It's about my grandmother. Her doctor was telling me about some new drug...some big breakthrough that seems to have vanished mysteriously."

"Okay."

"I'm trying to track it down and see what I can find out," he added. "There are a few mentions of something that looked pretty exciting a couple of years ago. I don't know if it's the same thing or not. Maybe there are some trials going on somewhere.

"I came up with a guy's name, but I'm not finding much when I Google him," Lee added. "You have access to the scientific journals, right? There must be a huge database of that kind of stuff."

"You have no idea," she said. "You're right. There are services that have all that. We have access."

"Okay," said Lee. "Maybe you can run this guy through them and see what turns up."

"I'll do it tomorrow," said Carr. "What's his name?"

"It's Novak," said Lee. "Walter J. Novak."

Chapter 11

Las Vegas

THE MERCEDES CONVERTIBLE pulled into the cool shade of the Palladian Hotel and Casino parking garage and Gray Axmann pressed the button to raise its roof. He watched the rear view mirror with quiet satisfaction as the panel behind the back seat lifted open and the black hard top slowly emerged, reached upward and then pivoted down over his head before finally clicking gently into place.

Smooth. It still tickled him six weeks after buying the car, his latest toy.

"Those Germans," he thought. "They know how to make a car."

Axmann shifted his gaze in the mirror to himself, running his fingers through his hair to tame it from windblown to merely tousled. He still was getting accustomed to seeing chestnut brown hair in the mirror rather than the natural yellow bleached nearly white by the desert sun.

Growing up in Las Vegas with his twin brother Troy, the pair had attracted confused glances wherever they went. They might have been identical twins with the kind of good looks that garnered attention, twins or not, except that he was blonde while Troy had dark brown hair.

The other differences were less obvious.

Gray was a born athlete and a natural leader, giving off lead-dog pheromones as if he applied them each morning along with his cologne. He had never had to look far to find the next

43

opportunity – or beautiful woman – waiting in line to be plucked, drawn to his looks and charisma.

Troy, on the other hand, had been an average athlete and both a brilliant and slavishly dedicated student. He rode his nearly perfect college entrance test scores and straight-A transcript to Princeton and a PhD from UCLA in microbiology. Eight years later, Troy started Axology, a biotech startup focused on applying cutting-edge gene technology to the development of cancer treatments.

Meanwhile, Gray remained in Las Vegas, earned a business degree at the local university and then took over their father's business, "negotiating" with the employee unions on behalf of the casinos. The business had evolved from one mainly relying on broken kneecaps and blackmail to the more genteel technique of bribery. Along the way, Gray had diversified the business to handle all the security needs of several of the largest Las Vegas casinos, including the Palladian.

The parking garage elevator came to a stop four floors beneath the one where Gray Axmann had parked and the doors slid open on the far side of the Palladian hotel lobby. He strode across the marble flooring toward the casino floor beyond. Along the way, he checked himself in the mirrored surfaces he passed, adjusting his dark blue blazer over khaki pants and a teal polo shirt. He would be on a golf course in two hours, dispensing tips and giving up strokes to visiting casino bigwigs from Singapore. And, damn – he did look just like his brother Troy with the new hair color.

He glanced around the casino floor with a practiced eye. Lunch time. Still quiet. He saw his floor chief in the middle of a conversation in the black jack pit. They were going to talk about the ongoing problem of drug use in the hotel restrooms. It was mostly meth but cocaine still retained a loyal fan base. He was convinced a couple of arrests with just the right amount of publicity would nip it in the bud without distressing the customers.

While he waited for his chief to finish his conversation, Axmann checked his watch. Then, he felt a hand caress his neck and slide up into his hair.

"Hello, Gray," said Eileen.

She was the new supervisor of dealers at the Palladian. She was 30ish, tall and wonderfully built with long black hair that reached far down her back. Her father was the general manager at another casino on the strip.

"What did you do to your hair?" Eileen asked. She moved her hand deeper into the hair at the back of his head and gripped it so hard it almost hurt. It also triggered images of the night two weeks ago when Eileen had gripped his hair the same way while she wrapped her long naked legs around him and they went at each other like a pair of wrestlers – biting encouraged. It had been their first time together.

From her smile when he caught her eyes, Axmann knew Eileen was thinking of that night as well. He thought he felt a tingling pass through her fingers and race through his body. He actually gasped. Then he regrouped.

"Just trying it to see how it hides the gray," said Axmann. "It's enough to have it in my name...Gray."

"I get it and I like it," she said, releasing her grip and letting her fingers caress his ear quickly and run off his shoulder. Her smile hadn't changed. He smiled back at her as his eyes quickly ran down her front and back up again, taking in everything.

"Dinner?" he said.

"Perfect."

Chapter 12

FROM HIS VANTAGE point 12,500 feet above the Richmond Bridge, Troy Axmann could see the other three main bridges connecting the west and east sides of the San Francisco Bay lying in the distance in front of him, the farthest – the Dumbarton – almost all the way to Palo Alto. The Golden Gate Bridge was off to his right. Its orange-red towers looked like lonely fortresses guarding the comparatively quiet waters of the Bay from the tumult of the open ocean beyond.

It was only when he was up here in his Cessna Skyhawk that Axmann felt truly relaxed. He was new enough to piloting, having received his license a year ago, that most of his attention was consumed by flying itself. He watched every gauge, parsed each radio transmission and scanned the skies for any unexpected aircraft. He continually recited in his mind the checklists he'd been taught.

He treasured this required vigilance, the need to fill his mind with the details of his flight. Elevation. Air speed. Heading. Wind direction. Fuel. Weather.

It pushed all his other worries away for a couple of hours. Maybe not as distant as the ferries, tugs and freighters felt, inching across the Bay far below him. But far enough that he felt the worries lose their constant grip on his insides. He felt he could inhale again.

"Remember. Breathe," he said to himself, adding it to the checklist. "Remember. Breathe."

The purchase of the Cessna had been Axmann's big indulgence when he sold his startup company to Merrick & Merrick along with the rights to its flagship cancer drug,

Morceptin. He actually thought the transaction would make his life easier, reducing the pressure a notch or two. He'd known that sooner or later he would need one of the Big Pharma conglomerates to continue the heavy investment required to get the drug to market, not to mention the marketing and distribution network to get the drug known and available to every oncologist and hospital in the developed world.

It was an easy sell.

Morceptin was one of the wave of cancer drugs designed to turn off specific genetic switches in patients' cells that enabled cancers to flourish. Early results showed it was more effective and had fewer side effects than the scorched-earth chemotherapy regimens it replaced. Axmann knew it would be a valuable piece of any major pharmaceutical company's drug portfolio.

Troy convinced the backers of Axology, his startup, to accept a small initial sum from Merrick & Merrick in exchange for a potentially huge back-end payment that was based on Morceptin's success. Merrick liked the arrangement because it reduced its risk in case Morceptin failed, and gave Troy Axmann's team a huge incentive to make Morceptin successful.

Initially, it appeared to be a brilliant strategy for everyone. And it gave Axmann the resources of a giant pharmaceutical company even though he still had the promise of immense personal wealth.

Morceptin was approved for treatment of liver and colon cancer as well as some types of leukemia and lymphoma. Applications for kidney and prostate cancer were pending. The average Morceptin patient stayed on the drug for 17 months at a cost of $78,000, Merrick's studies showed. If revenue growth stayed on track, Morceptin sales could easily exceed $5 billion annually in another four years. That was the key number in the formula for the back-end payout. It would bring Axology's original shareholders $800 million, one-third going directly to Troy.

But in recent months, that smooth upward flight to success and riches had encountered stormy, uncertain weather.

The new threat was Merrick's purchase of Walter Novak's company, Medvak.

Medvak was bought on the cheap – only $80 million – and mostly due to the whim of Edwin Merrick, grandson of one of the pharmaceutical company's founders and current CEO. Someone – an ex-professor or another Big Pharma executive – had put the bug in Merrick's ear about Walter Novak. "Brilliant but erratic" had been the catch phrase. A man with great ideas but no execution.

Edwin Merrick had judged Novak incapable of managing a pizza parlor much less a team that could successfully move a new drug down the complicated path toward FDA approval. But he thought Walter Novak's raw research was promising and might eventually lead to marketable drugs. The chairman assumed it would take at least several years and, perhaps, a couple of billion dollars to bring anything to fruition.

Within a week of the acquisition, Axmann realized that Edwin Merrick's assessment was totally wrong.

Novak's drug looked good and earlier trials had gone well. It might race through FDA approval and reach patients within two years. If so, it could cut Morceptin sales dramatically, perhaps even blow it out of the market completely. And there were additional longer-term implications in Novak's work.

All this would be disastrous for Troy Axmann and the original investors in Axology. When he realized the possible consequences, Troy called his brother Gray.

In part it was habit. Gray was the one who knew how to fix things. As kids, it had been deterring a bully or convincing a girl to go out. Now it was getting the better end of a tough negotiation or backing down an angry employee threatening lawsuits. But there was another important reason, too.

Gray had brought in all the major investors during Axology's early days. Indeed, once he realized Troy was working on something truly promising, Gray had managed the fund-raising side of the startup while Troy dealt with the science and regulators. Gray Axmann had convinced his bosses, the wealthy owners of casinos from Reno to Bangkok, to buy into Axology.

Climb on the Morceptin rocket, the Axmann twins had told them. It can't miss.

As Troy Axmann brought his plane down to the runway at the Charles M. Schulz Airport in Sonoma he resisted the temptation to touch his wheels and take off again. He had afternoon meetings. He was out of time.

He taxied to his parking spot and went through the final check list.

Turn off the master power and ignition. Lock the doors and windows. Install the gust lock on the tail. Turn off the emergency beacon. Tighten the tie-down straps.

And remember. Breathe.

Chapter 13

"SHE OKAY. SHE say she okay," said Billy Kim. This time, Mary Kim was looking Chief Davidson in the eye, nodding in agreement to what her cousin was saying.

Davidson was back at the square dining table in their trailer. It was two days after his initial visit. He had come to update Mary on the ongoing attempt to find her daughter. He was embarrassed because he had little to tell her. Megan and her abductor had simply vanished.

Now, they were telling him they had talked to Megan. And they seemed almost unconcerned about her, as if she had gone to sleep over at a friend's house instead of disappearing from a schoolyard after talking to a strange man no one could identify.

"She okay. She okay," said Mary Kim, nodding again and mimicking her cousin.

"Let me get this straight," said Davidson. "She called you, Billy, on your cell phone?"

Billy nodded.

"Where was she calling from?" said Davidson. "What state?"

Billy looked at Mary. He hesitated. Finally, he said, "Tennessee."

"Okay," said Davidson. "Now, tell me again exactly what she said. Did she talk to you or Mary? "

"Mostly Mary," said Billy. "I hand her the phone." He mimicked handing a telephone to Mary. Billy said something in Chinese to Mary. Mary answered back.

"She say…Megan say not to worry," said Billy. "She say she with good person. He take care her."

"*Who* is this guy?" said Davidson, getting irritated now. "*Why* did she go with him? Do *you* know him? What the *hell* is all this about?"

The pair had another exchange. Back and forth. Again. "We...we not know," said Billy. "She...Megan not tell us. Just...just everything okay. We not worry. You not worry. She be back...maybe in few days."

Both Billy and Mary were looking away from him as Billy talked, unable to look Davidson in the eye. He knew they weren't telling him everything. And, they were embarrassed at having to lie to him. But whatever was going on, they didn't seem truly worried about Megan anymore. It was as if the matter was settled. But why were they keeping something from him? It didn't make sense.

"Listen Billy...Mary," said Davidson. "You know I'm not the INS, right? I don't care about immigration status...how either of you got into this country. I'm only worried about Megan."

Bingo. He saw Mary shift uncomfortably when he mentioned the INS. The pair exchanged glances. But if he thought he was being reassuring, Davidson now saw that just bringing up the topic of immigration had had the opposite effect. They now sat in complete silence. Interview over.

"Christ," he thought to himself. "Now, what do I do now? What is this? Kidnapping? Child abduction? False alarm?"

Davidson had been in touch with the FBI since the day of Megan's disappearance. That was new for him. Coming from such a small department, he'd had little cause to talk to the feds in the past. He knew they were supposed to get involved in kidnappings, but their reaction had been to ask him more and more questions. It was as if they didn't trust someone from a Podunk town to get anything right.

He wondered if their reaction would have been different if Megan came from a family of wealthy suburbanites. They kept asking him if he was certain it was a kidnapping. How did he know for sure? Was there a note? It was as if they were too busy and didn't have time for this. He got the impression if he found Megan dead in a ditch they'd be relieved.

"Murder?" the feds probably would say. "Not our jurisdiction."

Well, now he knew Megan had crossed over the Alabama state line. She had been taken away in the middle of the school day by an unauthorized person who wasn't a family member. Davidson didn't know much else. Megan might have had the whole phone conversation with her mother while a gun was at her head. He would try again to get the feds to take charge. It was interstate now, not just a local matter anymore. He couldn't very well try to track her down in Tennessee.

Maybe someone else could let it drop. Davidson knew he couldn't. The little girl was from his town. Her school was a half mile from the station. If he did nothing and Megan turned up hurt – or even dead – he wouldn't be able to forgive himself. He wouldn't feel right until he saw Megan Kim back at home – safe.

When he got up to leave the trailer, Davidson gave Billy Kim a withering glare. They were messing with him and he didn't like it. He puffed himself up to full size, which felt huge next to Billy who was the size of a scrawny teenager. He wanted Billy to know this wasn't over and Davidson wasn't happy.

He snatched his notebook off the table and stomped out of the trailer and down the stairs without saying 'goodbye'. When he got to the cruiser, he turned around with his hand on the door handle for a last look.

The little kid was at the rail of the landing watching Davidson. They stared at each other for a moment. Then, the kid pulled down his diaper – it was one of those with elastic on the sides – until it slid down to his ankles. He stood with his hands straight down, his face a still portrait of concentration.

Then, a pale yellow stream of urine shot out of his tiny penis and arced down, splashing on the red dirt four feet below him.

Both the kid and the police chief watched in fascination as the flow continued. Davidson felt a pang of envy, realizing it now took him at least a full minute to empty his bladder and often an extremely slow 15 seconds just to get things started. He often felt compelled to apologize to those waiting behind him in crowded restrooms.

The kid finished and pulled his diaper back into position. He resumed his frantic work on the pacifier as he caught Davidson's eye. Then he turned and ran back into the trailer, slamming the door behind him.

Chapter 14

WHEN HE WAS a boy, Walter Novak visited his grandmother every summer. With his mother and baby sister, they would make the long drive down I-95 from Philadelphia through Washington D.C. and Virginia until they reached North Carolina.

From there, they would head west, passing through Raleigh and then taking the smaller state highways through towns like Carthage and Troy. Novak always wondered who had plucked the names from ancient Roman and Greek history and given them to these North Carolina towns. Had this explorer left a Pompeii or a Babylonia somewhere behind him?

Finally, they arrived at Badin Lake, a reservoir an hour outside Charlotte. He would know they were getting close just by the smell. After leaving the main highway, they rolled down the windows and let in the scent of the pine forest mixed with the earthy aroma of leaves and debris rotting slowly into topsoil.

His grandmother's lake house was an "A" frame with a steeply pitched roof and a wood balcony that sliced the façade in half. Sliding glass doors on top offered a commanding view of the lake from the upper great room, an expansive wood-paneled space where he and his cousins had played games for hours.

A short walkway led from the house to the lake and a pier that ran out more than 200 feet. In the summers, a waterskiing boat had been tied up at the end, usually next to a canoe or two. Novak had learned to sail on the small Sunfish that was overloaded with more than two in it. A red line painted across the pier near the end signaled where it was deep enough to safely dive into the lake. Novak had launched thousands of human cannon ball jumps from that pier during his summer visits.

He wasn't sure who technically owned the lake house now. But, he knew the cousin who lived outside Charlotte and took care of it. When Novak called him the night before he left California for New Orleans, his cousin was happy to let him borrow it for a week. He gave Novak the combination for the lockbox that held the key.

The sun was setting when they arrived. It only took a few minutes to move all their gear in as well as the groceries he'd purchased on the way in. Novak could feel himself unwind as soon as he walked inside the house. It felt like the first time in three days. He knew it was the familiarity of the place where he had spent so many endless summer days when he was young. He thought they would be safe here for a day or two. They needed to rest. He had to relax. He needed time to think.

He unlocked the glass door and stepped out on the balcony overlooking the water. The sun was a blazing red ball hovering over the horizon. The glare from the water was blinding and they both used their hands to shade their eyes as they looked out.

"There should be canoes on the property somewhere," he said, nodding toward the pier below them that was bare. "Do you swim?"

"Yes," said Megan disdain clear in her voice. Novak wondered if the bit of attitude had anything to do with the fact that she was routinely trouncing him in their gin rummy games after two days. He didn't know. Maybe it just came with all girls her age. He knew little about kids.

He left her on the deck and went back inside to get working on their hamburgers.

His cousin had provided the information he needed to turn on the wireless Internet connection in the house. When he had gone for Megan, his only plan had been to take her away from her home where he was certain she was in serious danger. But now what? He wasn't even sure who was coming for her. What were his next steps? He needed more information.

Who was hunting them and what resources did they have? Did he need to fear the police who wouldn't understand the danger and protect Megan? He had watched for any news about Megan on the radio and in the newspapers he glanced at when they stopped for gas and meals. Nothing.

He had to contact Roxanne at work and find out what had happened there. Had they asked about him? Maybe something in the databases at work could help him put more of the pieces together. They might be watching for him to log into the computer system. And they could be monitoring anyone who might help him.

No matter. He had to chance it. He couldn't fly blind. They couldn't stay on the run forever.

Megan came back into the room. She sniffed at the meat sizzling in the frying pan. She was carrying a fishing pole. It was a short one. Maybe five feet long.

"Do you fish?" asked Novak suddenly remembering lazy summer afternoons drifting in a canoe a few yards from shore and waiting for the red and white floats to be pulled below the surface by a hungry catfish or small-mouthed bass.

Megan pointed the pole toward the far corner of the room, closed one eye and peered down it as if looking down the barrel of a rifle.

"My family," she said. "We are fishing experts."

Chapter 15

GRAY AXMANN LEFT Eileen snoring softly in his bedroom and took a bowl of Muesli, fresh bananas and raisins along with a mug of black coffee to the back deck that overlooked the 16th fairway of the Arroyo Verde Golf Course. Thankfully, he was on the left side of the fairway greatly reducing the number of errant balls heading his way. Many evenings he'd sat out with a bottle of Bordeaux watching hacker after hacker slice their tee shots into the side of the house across from him.

He picked up the cell phone on the table next to the Financial Times and dialed.

"Hello," said the man on the other end. Axmann knew that he wouldn't recognize the incoming number. It was his third phone of the month.

"Jerry," said Axmann. "It's Gray."

"Christ," said Jerry in a low whisper. "I can't believe you're calling me here. Let me call you back. Five minutes."

Axmann had figured out most of the daily adjustments he would make to his stock portfolio – mostly reducing exposure to the possible devaluing of currencies in Latin America – by the time his phone rang.

"We really shouldn't be doing this," said Jerry. "Can't you call me at home?"

Axmann pictured Jerry, a middle-aged clerk in the FBI's office in Las Vegas, standing out on the back balcony of his office next to a waist-high ashtray filled with sand and scores of cigarette butts.

"No time, Jerry," said Axmann. "We need this...pronto, buddy."

"It's like I told you," said Jerry. "It's a two-step process. First we identify the ISP which in this case is a cable television company – Cox to be specific. Then, the ISP breaks down the IP information from the database session. It should identify the gateway – probably someone's wireless router – and Cox can match that to an address."

"Timing?" asked Axmann.

"It's a 24-hour turnaround," said Jerry. "Tomorrow morning at the latest. Any higher priority and it needs supervisor approval. And we're fucked."

Gray Axmann said nothing. He knew the silence would unnerve Jerry. He preferred applying pressure without threats if he could. He found that the imagination came up with more frightening scenarios than any he could concoct. He wanted his informant to be totally on top of this one. Every minute was crucial.

"Look," said Jerry, finally. "I'm doing everything I can. I'll get the information to you as soon as I can."

"Okay," said Axmann. "Jerry, you know what I'm going to say about your performance the past six months."

"I know. I know," said Jerry quickly. "I haven't done jack shit. I've had a lot of...uh...distractions. You know what I mean? I'm back on it. Just let me know what you need and I'll do my best."

Gray Axmann knew Jerry and his wife had a swimming pool, summer trips to Italy and two expensive foreign sports cars they could only afford because of the monthly, tax-free payments Jerry received from an offshore company that Axmann controlled. He had been careful to describe half of the payments as "loans" knowing Jerry could never repay them. If he ever needed to, he could squeeze the informant like a juicy lemon by demanding repayment to an organization which, in the not-so-distant past, had been famous for arranging one-way trips to the Nevada desert.

When he finished the call, he dialed another number.

"Yes," answered Murph Murphy, his voice always nasal due to the pounding other boxers had given his nose.

"Hey," said Axmann. "Where are you?"

"Knoxville," said Murphy. "They seemed to be heading in this direction."

"Okay," said Axmann. "And what's your plan?"

"Disappear them both," said Murphy. "If there's a problem, the fallback is the girl asked for help, Novak pulled a gun and they both got nailed in the...uh...mayhem. I've got a throw down."

"Good," said Axmann. "We should have an address by tomorrow morning. I'll let you know."

The sun was just winning its battle over the morning chill when Gray Axmann felt Eileen's hands running through his hair.

She shifted to his right side and he saw she was wearing his Runnin' Rebels T-shirt as she guided his face into her chest. He rubbed his face against her and nipped her left breast through the fabric, making her giggle. He hungrily inhaled the scent of sex, sweat and last night's perfume. Then he ran his hand up the back of her thigh to see what she had on underneath. Nothing.

Chapter 16

IT WAS A little before 6:30 a.m. when Enzo Lee ran past Washington Square in North Beach. As he passed the twin spires of Saints Peter and Paul Church, he paid silent homage to Joe DiMaggio, a fellow San Francisco boy who was married in the church and had had his funeral there just a few years earlier.

Lee was aware, of course, of DiMaggio's 56-game hitting streak for the Yankees – a still unbeaten record. But, it was his Marilyn Monroe streaks that seemed even more impressive to him.

The marriage between the movie star and sports legend lasted barely a year. Seven years later, DiMaggio had reportedly proposed to Monroe a second time mere days before she died of a drug overdose. He sent roses to her grave steadily for the next two decades. Six flowers arrived three times a week. Then DiMaggio went to his grave at the age of 84 steadfastly refusing to ever talk about Monroe. He even got his close friends to keep their lips sealed after he was gone. *Those* were the streaks and what they represented that impressed Lee – the Yankee Clipper's iron will standing guard over a broken heart.

As usual on this route, Lee started trying to calculate in his head exactly how many roses DiMaggio had sent during those 20 years. He knew that before he would finish the math in his head a changing traffic light, a bad driver, a pretty girl or some other distraction would derail his train of thought.

He continued down Columbus and then turned down Mason to the waterfront. He ran west on Jefferson past the crab stands that would be jammed with food and tourists in a couple of hours. He continued by Ghirardelli Square to Fort Mason, the old army base before its transformation to civilian uses. He traversed the upper part of the Fort and took one of the dirt trails to the lower level. He continued to the Marina Green, did a shortened loop, and began to retrace his route.

He cut the return short with a half mile jaunt to the end of the Municipal Pier, a decaying concrete structure that juts out from the shore toward the middle of San Francisco Bay with amazing views of Alcatraz and the Golden Gate Bridge. He stopped at the end of the pier, walked in slow circles and let the strong winds blowing off the Bay dry his sweat. He inhaled the ocean smell and listened to the sound of surf washing up on the shore behind him.

Then Lee headed back and slowly jogged the few blocks to the Hyde Street cable car stop. It was one of his luxuries – a four-mile run with the uphill return trip courtesy of the city's old cable car line.

When he got back to his second-floor flat in North Beach near the border with Chinatown, Lee started the coffee maker working on a pot of Peet's Sumatra and popped open his laptop. Attached to a series of emails that Lorraine Carr had sent to him, were eight articles from an assortment of technical journals, all authored or co-authored by Walter Novak.

The earliest were published in the late 1970s and had all appeared in math journals. Lee had no idea what they meant: Triangulations In Hyperbolic Geometry; Random Flows For Incompressible Fluids; Arithmeticity of Holonomy Groups.

Then there was a gap of several years, and the next papers appeared in journals devoted to molecular biology: Evolution of DNA Restriction; Antigenic Structure and Immune Response; Transcriptional-Related Factors in Selected Human Proteins. These made slightly more sense to him. Carr had also found a short summary of a conference held three years ago that mentioned a presentation Novak had given about his research. It had excited the attendees.

Lee could trace Novak's geographical movement at least through academia. First Harvard and then Duke University for mathematics. Then, MIT and Johns Hopkins for the molecular biology work. But he found no articles or other references to Novak since the conference three years earlier. However, Lee noticed that Novak had coauthored the last two articles with the same person – someone named Roxanne Rosewell.

He ran a search on his laptop for Rosewell, adding the term "biology," and found a listing that showed her as a senior researcher at the Merrick & Merrick pharmaceutical company based in San Francisco.

When he called the company, Lee was quickly patched through to Rosewell.

"Hello?" she said. Rosewell sounded older. Lee placed her as middle-aged.

"Uh…hello," he said. "My name is Enzo Lee. I'm looking for Walter Novak and I'm wondering if you know how I can reach him."

"You're who?" she said. "Why do you want him?"

"My name is Enzo Lee. I'm a reporter for the San Francisco News. But, I'm actually calling on a private matter. My grandmother is ill. She has leukemia. And I just wanted some information about the drug that…uh…Mr. Novak was working on. Her doctor…my grandmother's…remembered hearing about it. I guess she heard Mr. Novak speak about it and…"

"I can't talk about that," she said. "I can't talk about that. And you're with who? The media?"

Lee could hear the rising stress in Rosewell's voice.

"Look," he said. "I'm just trying to get a phone number or email address. My grandmother's sick. I just want to know what's out there."

There was silence on the other end. But Lee could hear her breath. It was coming fast. Her heart was pumping. He could feel her indecision. Then, he heard the phone bang against something as if she missed the cradle the first time before she hung up with a loud click.

Chapter 17

THE CLIPBOARD WAS everything.

John Average hadn't been sure when he first heard the suggestion. But, now he knew it was absolutely true.

The scrubs were, of course, essential as well. Thankfully, he had found that the four sets he'd bought – two shades of blue and two of green – covered almost everything. He could drive around a hospital at almost any hour and spot somebody in the parking lot or just inside the emergency room lobby wearing whichever color was standard for the facility.

Then, he simply pulled those on over his jogging pants and T-shirt. Add running shoes and the clipboard and he was good to go.

It all worked together as a package but it was the clipboard that sealed the deal. It was better than a name tag or any badge or credential he might have conjured for the occasion. Something like that was just an invitation for someone to read his name and title, and start asking questions. Who was he there to see? What was a physical therapist doing at 2 a.m. in an oncology wing? If he was a radiology technician, where was the gurney to wheel away the patient?

The clipboard gave him purpose without details – authority without any fine print. He had placed graph paper on the clipboard and filled it with words he was pretty sure would be meaningless to anyone who looked closely. They were random Latin words written hurriedly in his own handwriting which was atrocious. Finally, his Catholic education was proving useful.

If questioned by some particularly territorial nurse, he had two replies ready.

"Inventory," he had answered twice when asked his purpose on a ward. Then, he had gone back to looking closely at all the medical equipment in the room he was in, from beds and chairs to heart monitors and oxygen tanks.

Once, when he was questioned by a particularly prickly woman, he had replied, "Surprise hygiene check."

Then, he had stepped back and closely scrutinized the overzealous, middle-aged registered nurse from her white orthopedic shoes to her dyed red hair tied back in a bun. He made a few marks on his clipboard, gave her a polite smile and continued down the hallway.

Tonight, though, no one had done more than glance quickly at him as he walked through the hospital. He was late-30s, a normal weight, medium height and wore glasses. He had light brown hair and was not particularly attractive. When he left his house, he tried to forget his real identity. Blend in, he told himself. Be average. John Average. That's how he thought of himself. Weight, height, hair, accent, shoes, type of ballpoint pen. Average, average, average.

He found the room using the number he had memorized. He checked the name of the lone patient written on a whiteboard near the bed against the one he had also committed to memory. From his pocket, he pulled out a syringe filled with a bluish fluid. He had no idea what was in it. Each time, he was given an unlabeled vial, the name of a hospital, room number and patient name. He kept a bag of new syringes. He filled one and replaced the plastic cap over the needle. He was careful to dispose of the vial in a convenience store trash can, as instructed.

He suspected the drugs were different because the amounts and colors varied. All he knew was that after he injected it into the intravenous line, he had at least ten minutes before anything would happen. Whether that was a heart monitor alarm going off, a careful nurse noticing a change in breathing patterns or the patient turning over and releasing a polite fart before going back to sleep, he had no idea. He didn't know if what he was doing would leave the patient dead, blind or feeling like a million dollars the next day. And, he didn't want to know.

John Average still was holding the clipboard when he replaced the plastic cap over the needle of the now-empty hypodermic and put it back in his pocket. He would dispose of it later that morning in another convenience store trash receptacle.

Then he left the room and walked back down the hallway toward the bank of elevators. They led down to the lobby with an exit that opened onto the parking area. He walked at four steps per each relaxed breath. He counted off the steps as if he were a soldier on parade but more slowly. Half speed. One...Two...Three...Four. One...Two...Three...Four. It was a carefully calibrated pace. It was exactly average.

Chapter 18

"I HAD A dream last night," said Megan. "There was this girl in it. I think she was a little bit older than me. She was blonde, with pigtails."

Her fishing pole was high in the air. She examined the worm on the end, still curled into a tight brown knot. Satisfied, Megan pressed the thumb button on the reel, pulled the rod behind her on the right side and then cast next to a half submerged log.

Walter Novak had been watching his own line inattentively, keeping the float in sight while his mind wandered. His thoughts had shifted from working through math problems – mental games really – to tracing the main points of the medical research that had consumed the past 15 years. His conclusions. He recalled yet again the trail of evidence he had uncovered that had convinced him of sabotage and of the threat to Megan.

The scientist's greatest breakthroughs had come when he set a task for himself – such as finding the single gene in a cluster of thousands that had suddenly gone bad – and allowed his subconscious to grind out the answer. After weeks or months, he would suddenly awaken with the solution or it would come to him while he was planting tulips or watching the sun set.

Novak had given himself the task of figuring a way out of the mess that had ensnared Megan and him but he was getting nowhere after two days. A math or science problem was one thing. He wasn't equipped to handle real danger. He couldn't see a path. Everything felt too dangerous – more risky than just staying here where it at least *seemed* safe.

Megan's account of her dream, though, had grabbed his full attention.

"She seemed familiar," she said, slumping in her seat at the front of the canoe after her cast. "It was like I knew her. But I didn't."

"Did she...did she say anything?" asked Novak.

"No," said Megan. "She was high up in the room. Filling it. I was below. And she was just, you know, watching me. I usually don't remember my dreams."

They were silent for a minute.

"How is your mother?" asked Novak. Megan had called her mother on the cell phone Novak had bought at a convenience store on the way to the lake just before they climbed into the canoe.

"She wants me to come home," said Megan. Her voice jumped half an octave as she mimicked her mother: "Come home. Come home."

Novak nodded sympathetically.

"But I said I can't," she continued. "You said it isn't safe. Not yet. I told her soon. Everything is okay. You are taking care of me."

"She remembers me, right?" said Novak.

"Of course," said Megan. "How can she forget?"

"And I told her, 'Don't tell anyone,'" she continued. "Like you said. 'Don't trust anyone.'"

Novak nodded his agreement to the messages conveyed. They were quiet again, watching the water that was disturbed only by the occasional touch of a flying insect .

"Look!" said Megan as the red and white float ducked below the water and then popped to the surface. It dipped again. The third time, it stayed down. She flipped her wrist to set the hook and began reeling it in. After a few seconds, the fish broke the surface in a splash of brown and white. In another 20 seconds, she had the 11-inch bass in the boat.

It was Megan's third fish, equaling her catch of the previous day. She had caught their dinner again. Novak had caught his one and only fish an hour earlier. Megan had hooked her fingers securely into the gills of that one and held it up admiringly as it flipped in desperation.

"It's BIG," she had announced, although it looked to Novak no larger than ones she had caught.

It was a hard 20-minute paddle back to the house. The sun was already down when they tied up and unloaded the gear on the dock, Megan looked at him questioningly. He knew she wanted to jump in. She was wearing denim shorts, a white T-shirt and flip flops. They hadn't bought a swim suit for her.

He nodded. Two shakes of her feet to remove the flip flops and one leap later she was under water. She came up eight feet away, spitting out water and tossing her head to shake the water out of her bangs. Her grin was infectious.

She swam 30 feet away and then floated on her back, staring at the darkening sky for awhile as she slowly moved her arms back and forth as if she were making a snow angel. Then she turned on her stomach and swam back.

Novak reached his hands down toward Megan. He grabbed her wrists and pulled her up, holding her high for a second as if *she* was the trophy catch. Then he set her down on her feet. They gathered up their fish, poles, oars and other equipment and ambled up the dock, across the small yard to the house.

An hour later, Megan was cleaning the fish when Novak turned on his laptop and checked his private email account. In his in-box was a message from a sender identified by a string of seemingly random numbers and letters. He knew who had sent it. He clicked it open.

The message was short and to the point.

"The British are coming," it read.

Chapter 19

CHIEF CLIFF DAVIDSON walked up the front steps of the small, well-kept house surrounded by a lawn watered to a lush thickness by the fickle but heavy Gulf Coast rains. It sat on supports that held it two feet off the ground. The gap underneath was hidden by lattice panels. He knocked on the door.

The barrel-chested man who opened the door had long gray hair tied in a ponytail in the back. He wore glasses and a thin-lipped smile on his cherubic face.

"Mr. Whitten?" Davidson asked.

"Yessir," said Whitten. "Yessir. That's me. Indeed. Indeed. Come in!" He wore a short-sleeved shirt that was white with a purple floral design sprinkled over it. He opened the door wider and gestured inside.

Just inside on the left was a deep sofa facing a big flat-screen television. On the right was a black-leather recliner surrounded by adjustable table surfaces so that computer displays surrounded the chair on three sides. It was a makeshift cockpit for a computer jock.

"Coffee or iced tea?" Whitten offered.

"Thank you, sir," said Davidson. "Coffee would be fine. Black."

Whitten walked quickly through a door into the kitchen. A few seconds later he came out with a tan-colored mug he handed to the police chief.

Davidson blew on the hot brew a couple times and then took a sip. He nodded appreciatively at Whitten.

"Why don't you show me what ya'll got, Mr.Whitten," he said before his second sip.

Whitten nodded and moved over to the recliner. He slipped through a gap along the side, seated himself and then pulled a keyboard strapped to an adjustable tray down to his lap. His fingers started tapping the keys as he talked.

"After one of your people came by asking me about...what's her name?" said Whitten as he continued to work the keyboard.

"Megan Kim?" said Davidson.

"Right. The little girl," said Whitten. "Well, as you can see, I'm totally hooked on gadgets, computers, video games...you name it. And I have these cameras all around the outside of the house.

"It took me a while to get around to it," he continued. "Had a lot of work to get out. But when I looked at that day, I found this."

Whitten swiveled the monitor on his left side so Davidson, standing to his left, could see it clearly. It was a photo of the street looking from Whitten's house toward the end of the block. Just past the intersection, Davidson could see the elementary school where Megan Kim had vanished five days earlier.

"I run the cameras on video at night," said Whitten. "During the day, they're all set to take a picture every five minutes. This one was taken five days ago, five minutes past noon. This is the car that I thought was interesting."

The image vanished and was immediately replaced by another. It was a close up of the back of a car. It was a Ford Escape. The license plate was from Missouri. The numbers were clear.

"It wasn't there five minutes earlier," said Whitten. "Ten minutes later, it was gone. I've never noticed a car with Missouri plates on it in this neighborhood."

"Okay," said Davidson. "Let's start with any pictures with the car in it. I may come back for more. But, can you give me copies of those?"

"Sure thing," said Whitten. "USB drive okay?"

"Yep," said Davidson. "That's perfect. And, you know what?"

"No. What?"

"Y'all just made my day."

Chapter 20

MURPH MURPHY SPOTTED the Escape as it passed him going the other direction just after he made the turn down the small road that led to the lake house. He had driven more than seven hours from Knoxville to get there. It was a long haul but beat the hell out of waiting a day and a half to finally get a physical street address. Damned bureaucrats. It had taken them forever to finally establish the chain of connections and figure out where Novak had been when he logged into the computerized database at Merrick & Merrick.

He waited for the Escape to drive past the next curve before he turned around. No matter how easy the target, Murphy knew the element of surprise was an advantage worth preserving. This was particularly true when the goal was a quiet disappearance without witnesses, evidence or drama. He knew Novak would be worried about being pursued. Why else would he have left his cell phone in California other than to eliminate tracking him through the device? But there was no reason for the scientist to suspect that danger was only a few seconds behind him. Novak and the kid probably were just running an errand – heading into the nearest town for supplies.

As long as they kept to country roads with little traffic, Murphy was content to hold back more than a quarter mile. He didn't want to stampede his quarry. He could afford to be patient. Maybe an empty parking lot at a supermarket would be the place. He could force Novak to drive the Navigator until they found somewhere isolated. It looked as if they could take almost any of these side roads and be totally alone within a few minutes. Or, he could wait and follow them all the way back to the lake. That was probably the best choice. Take his time in the lake house. Disposing of the bodies would be the hardest part. He could work out that step at his leisure. He knew mountain reservoirs were deep. Hundreds of feet. Good places to drown secrets.

That was it then – the lake house if they led him back there. Now that he had them in sight, Murphy was in hunting mode. On high alert but patient. He was confident he would recognize when to strike and be ready. Some people thought this was easy, particularly when the targets were amateurs. But, he knew better. The one thing you had to expect was the unexpected. An extra person at the scene. Someone who fights instead of runs. Or runs instead of fights. Making the right decision in those frantic seconds, managing the situation, doing the right thing to stay in control and bring the job home. That's what made him a pro.

* * *

They had packed and were loaded within 20 minutes after Novak opened the email warning. They left the fish in the freezer. Before they loaded the car, he went out the front toward the lake and slowly circled around the back to the car. He stopped and listened. All he heard was the gentle lapping of the water. He saw no cars, no lights. He had to assume no one was there, that they had gotten the word in time.

Once on the road, he was immensely relieved. He invited Megan to find a station on the radio. He tapped his fingers to the music and rested his arm on the rest between them. He had only told her that they needed to pack and be on the road in 15 minutes. Novak hadn't said why. He didn't want to freak her out. He was trying to put her at ease now.

Then he saw the blue Navigator drive past. It was too coincidental. It had to be the same one he had seen at the motel through the window of the Waffle House. Novak used the mirrors to watch behind them and saw the SUV follow them onto the larger road from the small street that led to the lake. It stayed pretty far behind. He assumed they were taking their time, waiting for a good opportunity. He was thankful for that. He could imagine the big SUV running them off the road and then being stuck in the car while they finished the job. They were being patient. Novak tried to think of something, some kind of plan.

He knew the area, Novak thought. That was his advantage. He knew it from his many summer trips here. Where was he heading? What could he reach in 15 minutes? Not much. Unless...maybe.

Novak knew there was a turnoff coming shortly. It was a road that ran off on the right. It eventually hooked up with another highway after a few miles. But, halfway there, it crossed a railroad line. There was a railroad yard near that intersection. It wasn't large. It was a strip of land maybe 400 yards long with two extra sets of tracks that ran parallel to the main tracks. A dead-end asphalt roadway ran next to it until it ended in a pile of gravel. The yard was used to store extra equipment and freight cars which sat empty until needed.

As a kid, Novak had tagged along with his cousins who rode their bikes there, drawn irresistibly to the huge empty train cars like moths to a flame. He watched while they played on the empty cars, climbed up the ladders to the top and jumped around trying without success to make them boom like giant drums. As far as he knew, the grownups had never guessed what they were doing.

Novak also recalled that past the end of the storage tracks was an open field that led to a big farmhouse a half mile away. When he was a boy, the farmhouse had always had cars and a pickup or two parked there.

It was all he could think of other than driving on until the people pursuing them got tired of it and decided to stop them.

This way, he thought, perhaps he could at least keep Megan alive if he got lucky.

Novak made the right turn. In another three miles, he saw the railroad crossing sign reflected by his headlights. Instead of crossing the tracks, he turned left along the dead-end service road that paralleled the extra tracks in the yard. His headlights enabled him to see the line of empty cars sitting at the far end of the yard.

He drove down the road until it ended at the gravel. The line of empty cars was further down the tracks. He quickly turned the Escape around to face the way they had come. He turned to Megan.

"You need to get out here," he said, urgency in his voice. "Run down next to these railroad cars. When you get to the end of them, you'll see a farmhouse in the distance across a field. Go there. Knock on the door. Tell them anything. Say you were kidnapped and need the police. Just do anything to get them to call the police."

"What about you?" asked Megan. The fingers in her right hand were wrapped around the door handle.

"I'm going to slow them down," said Novak. "Get out. *Now.*"

Megan stepped out of the car and hesitantly turned and headed toward the empty train cars. She looked over her shoulder at Novak.

Even if Megan got home safely, Novak knew the people hunting her would try again. They couldn't afford to let her live, not with the story she was carrying. But he couldn't worry about that now. He was only worried about her survival tonight. It was the best he could do.

Novak saw the blue Navigator turn off on to the dead-end road, following him. The big SUV stopped after the turn, its headlights shining in his face. He couldn't see the face behind the dark windshield.   But he knew the driver was waiting patiently to see what Novak would do next.

Chapter 21

MURPH MURPHY WAS puzzled when the Escape turned off just before the railroad tracks. It hardly seemed like a road. It certainly didn't look as if it went anywhere. He slowed the Navigator. Then he saw the headlights of the vehicle turning around. Maybe they knew he was there. He started worrying that they were going to leave the car and run for it. He made the left turn down the dead end road so he could use his headlights and see what was happening.

The Escape started moving. It was heading toward him. He flipped his headlights on bright. He thought he saw something moving behind the Escape. The girl. It must be. Novak had let her out and was driving back out to the main road.

Well, Murphy wasn't going to let that happen. He wasn't going to chase Novak while the girl ran off. He would block the Escape and keep everything in front of him in one place where he could use the headlights to see. This was as good a place as any. There was no one around.

He moved the Navigator slowly toward the Escape which still was heading his way. Murphy scanned the area in front of him to see how Novak might try to evade him. There wasn't much room unless the Escape left the asphalt and went into the field to the left. The main railroad tracks to the right were on a bed of gravel. That would be hard to negotiate but it might be possible. Either way, the Navigator ought to have as much traction as the smaller vehicle. Murphy would cut him off.

What was it now? Damn. The son of a bitch was speeding up and heading straight toward him. Christ. Was he really doing this? Was he trying to get Murphy to take evasive action so he could dodge the larger car and get back to the main road? No way, thought Murphy. I'm not getting out of the way until you make a move. Try and get through me, mother fucker. See who wins.

"Okay," Murphy said aloud. "Let's do this!" He pressed down on the accelerator.

* * *

Walter Novak took a last look in his rear view mirror and saw Megan moving down the track away from him and brought his focus to the pair of headlights that faced him. He hit the accelerator and started rolling forward. He squinted sharply when the Navigator's bright headlights switched on but he knew exactly where he wanted to go. There was nothing in his way.

He let his speed increase steadily. The Navigator seemed stuck in place, just waiting for him. When he got close, he saw the headlights of the opposing vehicle dip down and bounce back up into his eyes again. It was moving straight toward him, not trying to get out of his way. Novak jammed the gas pedal to the floor. He was breathing heavily now as if he was sprinting instead of sitting. He gripped the steering wheel so tight his arms shook. He felt ready to explode.

"Give me the strength...give me the strength...give me the strength," Novak murmured as he gained speed and closed on the other car.

When the headlights were so bright and close he thought they would pass through his eyes and smack the back of his skull, Novak let go of the steering wheel, put his arms at his sides and closed his eyes.

* * *

Megan walked quickly in the darkness down the line of train cars. She could see the lights from the farmhouse far in the distance. She could hear the car accelerating behind her, moving away.

Suddenly, she heard the horrible sound of the collision. First, the noise of metal crashing together and glass breaking followed a split second later by a thud as the Escape nosed up at the moment of the collision and then came back to earth. She turned and saw the wreckage. The Escape rolled back a few feet before coming to a stop.

Megan didn't know what to do. She started walking toward the cars and then stopped. He had told her to go to the farmhouse. But what if Walter was hurt? What if he needed help? She stood transfixed, staring at the two smashed cars…waiting.

* * *

The airbag stunned Murphy. It felt like getting hit flush in the face by someone chucking a basketball at point blank range. He hadn't seen it at all. When his vision cleared, the bag already was deflated, hanging in his lap from the center of the steering wheel. The smell of rubber surrounded him.

Murphy rubbed his face. It felt numb. He could feel some blood on his upper lip draining out of his nose. He knew without touching it that his nose was broken again. As he opened the door of the Navigator and twisted to get out, he felt a pain in his chest as if someone had taken a bat and whacked him there a couple of times. He was shaky on his feet at first and still a little groggy. He left the driver's door opened as he moved forward to the Escape. The windshield was broken and the front was crumpled. Novak was still in the front seat, his head hanging limply to the side. He looked unconscious or dead, certainly not going anywhere soon.

Murphy stumbled forward past the Escape heading toward the empty train cars in the distance. The girl had to be down there. He needed to stop her before she got away. He felt steadier with each step. He soon broke into a lumbering jog down the road even though every step made his head ache. Where the hell was she?

Chapter 22

MEGAN FINALLY BROKE out of her trance and resumed her quick walk to the end of the railroad yard and the farmhouse. When she heard the crunch of footsteps far behind her, she knew they were coming for her and she picked up her pace.

She reached the last train car and stopped. The farmhouse was in the distance. She saw lights shining through the windows. But it seemed so far away. She could hear the footsteps behind her running now, closing fast. He would see or hear her in the open field and catch her before she could make it even half way across.

Megan imagined being run down out there. In her imagination, she saw a baby deer being pulled down and torn to shreds by a wolf. Instead of going into the field, she circled around the end of the last train car to the other side of the tracks and started doubling back.

She tried to be quiet. She could hear him in the gravel on the other side of the car as the man ran to the end of the train cars. Then he stopped. Silence. He was looking and listening for her.

Megan froze. She was at the end of one of the cars. She moved as quietly as she could, taking the four or five steps until she was deep in the shadowy space between the huge cars. She moved backward until she felt the metal of the undercarriage touch her shoulders. It was cold and solid, like part of a building or a huge rock. Then, she squatted and scrabbled backward slowly until she was underneath the car. She got down on her knees in the dark, stifled her wince as the sharp gravel dug through her pants and into her skin. She waited.

She heard him walking toward the end of the cars and then crossing over to the other side as she had done. He moved slowly up along the side of the cars in her direction, retracing her route. He was patient and unhurried now. Megan heard his steady breathing. He stopped every few paces. Maybe he paused to see if he could hear her. Perhaps he was dropping down to peer under the cars. It was pitch black underneath in the shadows away from the light of the stars. Megan held her hand directly in front of her face. She couldn't see a thing.

She suddenly was shivering uncontrollably. She clamped her jaws together so her teeth wouldn't clatter. She was so scared she could hardly breathe. She fought to control herself. Surely, he could hear her gasps.

Megan tried to relax. She closed her eyes and thought of something else. She pictured herself wading in the bay at home. The sun reflecting bright and hot off the water. Her feet sinking into the fine mud, raising underwater puffs of silt with each step in the warm ocean.

She heard him walk past her hiding place and then continue on several paces until he stopped again. Silence.

* * *

The hand that suddenly grabbed Megan's arm felt to her as if it was made of metal, it was so strong. There was no resisting as it jerked her from underneath the train. It was all she could do to keep from slamming her head against the undercarriage and limit the damage to a glancing blow.

He pulled her roughly away from the car as if she was a bag of potatoes dragging on the ground.

"Got you, you squirt," he said as she pulled away from him. He held her in that iron grip as he used his other hand to feel around his own waist.

"Dammit, dammit, dammit," he swore under his breath as he reached the holster strapped on the left side of his belt. His Smith & Wesson was gone. It must have fallen out in the collision. In the confusion, with the airbag smashing him in the face, he hadn't checked to make sure he had it.

He held the girl by the upper arm. She was fighting him. He squeezed her arm until she winced in pain. Then he gave her a hard shake. She was his. It was over now.

Murphy grabbed her at the throat with his free hand. The girl stopped moving completely now and stared at him, eyes bulging. He could strangle her like this. It would be over in five minutes. But Christ. She was just a kid. He had nieces about the same age. Hell. Thank God there was no one else around to witness his squeamishness. He was alone. He could do what he wanted. He'd get the gun. Finish her that way. Fast. He didn't need to feel her death throes. Hauling her back to the car would be easy enough.

Murphy hoisted Megan above his right shoulder and carried her with his arm pinning her around her middle. She wasn't heavy. He'd carried bags of fertilizer around his yard that were heavier.

He slapped her hard on the side of her face with his free hand. He held it poised for another blow.

"Stop moving," he said. "Or I will *make* you stop moving. I'm not kidding."

Megan was still and let herself hang from his shoulder as Murphy walked back to the two damaged cars. Murphy could feel her silent sobs.

His arm ached a little by the time he reached the cars. He was ready to set the girl down. When he drew even with the front bumper of the Navigator he glanced back at the wrecked Escape. It was empty. Novak was gone.

"Oh shit," he said. It was his last thought before Novak stepped out behind him from the opened door of the Navigator and swung the SUV's tire iron with both hands as hard as he could. It smacked into the side of Murphy's head.

If Megan hadn't hit the asphalt and lain alongside Murphy, Novak might have immediately swung the tire iron a second time probably permanently rearranging Murphy's face. But the girl was too close. It gave Novak a moment to see that Murphy was completely still. His first blow had caught him perfectly. In fact, Murphy would see double for the next two weeks and would never regain his sense of smell.

Novak threw the tire iron as far as he could into the darkness. Then he picked up a stunned Megan. He held her as he set out toward the distant farmhouse. Novak started to concoct the story he would tell in order to borrow a phone to call his cousin. And as the adrenaline left he began to hyperventilate. He had to stop, catch his breath and force himself to relax. Still he was trembling. He held Megan a little tighter to his chest and hoped she didn't notice.

Chapter 23

ENZO LEE GUESSED that the woman was in her late 40s. Long silver hair held in back by a barrette framed an attractive composed face. She looked elegant even in loose sweats and gardening gloves as she dug with a trowel in the raised planter box in front of her house in San Francisco's Sunset District. The sun was just breaking through the morning cloudiness.

He had parked a block away and worked his way up checking the street numbers along the way. She glanced up at him when he still was a couple of houses away and then returned to her work. She looked up again when he stopped in front of her, holding his notebook and looking both at her and the house number up the stairs next to the front door.

"Roxanne Rosewell?" said Lee. She stared at him silently.

"I'm Enzo Lee of the San Francisco News," he continued. "We talked briefly a couple of days ago."

He watched it register with her, the recollection of the call. In her expression annoyance battled with resignation. She plunged her trowel aggressively into the dirt in front of her a couple of times, breaking apart large clods of dirt.

"*You're* persistent," she said finally, her attention still focused on her gardening. Lee watched her work for a moment.

"Look," he said finally. "This is personal for me. My grandmother is very sick. This is probably it for her unless they come up with something different than what they've been giving her. I just want to find out what happened to Walter Novak – the drug he was working on."

He waited while she packed black earth around a small, fragile-looking plant.

"And you're right," Lee added. "I am persistent."

Rosewell stuck the trowel into the box, removed her gloves, stood up and brushed dirt from her clothes. She turned and started up the stairs to her front door.

"C'mon then," she said, gesturing for Lee to follow her.

She made them tea and they sat on opposite sides of a natural wood coffee table on an Oriental rug that occupied half of the hardwood floor in the living room. While Lee and the pot of tea sat, Rosewell changed. When she reemerged, she wore a long dress with a floral pattern and ruffles around the neck and arms. She had unfastened her hair in the back and wore a silver chain with a pendant in the shape of a dragonfly.

They both sat back with their tea and studied each other.

"You and Novak worked together for a long time," Lee began.

"Yes," said Rosewell, nodding. "I guess 15 years qualifies."

"I've looked up some of his articles. And yours," said the reporter. "He started out in math?"

Rosewell sat down her tea and moved forward in her chair.

"He was a very talented mathematician," she said, smiling wistfully. "And just switched careers. He had, uh, personal reasons. And he got frustrated with academia. It seemed like ego for ego's sake."

"And so what specifically did he...and you...work on?"

"Walter started the company, Medvak, and I was his first hire," she said. "I was a year behind him in the PhD program at Johns Hopkins. He had some wonderful insights into the genetics of cancer...how to find and repair mutations in cells that let the disease flourish. It was very exciting."

"And there was a drug? What was the name?" said Lee.

"We called it 'Roxaten,'" she said.

"Hmm...any connection to..."

"He named it after me," interrupted Rosewell, blushing. "It was silly. But, he insisted."

"I see," said Lee. "And what's happened to it?"

She chewed her lip, looking down at the coffee table. Lee could sense her grappling with a tough decision. He assumed it mainly had to do with whether she could trust him and how much she could tell him.

"Listen," he said. "Let's just make this all confidential...off the record. Nothing gets published unless I get it from somewhere else. It's public record or something. Anything else I run by you first. I'm just trying to find out what happened."

"Okay. Good," she said, relief in her voice. "I hate to use the term 'miracle drug' but it may actually apply to Roxaten. I mean it was just phenomenal...in the lab, animals, the beginning of the human trials. Amazing results. It ate cancer for breakfast and touched nothing else. And that was just the beginning.

"Then we sold to Merrick & Merrick. Things were great at first. Then, overnight, they went bad. And they buried it. They buried Roxaten. And they tried to bury Walter, too. I don't know why. I mean I have my guesses but I'm not really sure."

"Well, where is Walter...Novak?" asked Lee. "Is he still at Merrick?"

"Walter became ill," she said. "He had a breakdown. He went away for three months to a psychiatric facility in Arizona.

"That's when everything changed...while he was gone," Rosewell continued. "They cut me off. Patients started getting sick. They stopped the trial. I wanted to dig into it and they wouldn't let me. They even started to question the rights to Roxaten, the patent rights. It was night and day – a miracle drug one minute and a disaster the next.

"It was insane," she said. "Just completely insane."

Rosewell shook her head sadly and took a sip of her tea. Lee waited for her to continue with her story.

"Walter left almost a week ago," Rosewell said. "I don't know where he went. He said something about 'Patient Zero'.

There's something he was hiding from me. He said he had to save his Patient Zero. It didn't make any sense. I'm worried that he was having another breakdown."

"What is that?" asked Lee. "Patient Zero."

"In epidemiology it is the initial case. It usually is in the context of a disease but it can be anything you are investigating," said Rosewell. "Another way to look at it is that if you're trying to understand something – or prove a theory – it's where you start."

Chapter 24

IF THE FEDS weren't good for anything else, at least they had the clout to get information quickly from car rental companies and law enforcement agencies across the country.

They had taken only a few hours to trace the Missouri plates from the car parked near Megan Kim's school on the day of her disappearance to Avis after Chief Davidson made the phone call. The car rental company had quickly furnished a copy of the rental agreement that bore Walter Novak's name and driver's license number.

By the next afternoon, Davidson had in his hand a colored printout reproducing Novak's California driver's license. It showed a man in his 50s with wispy white hair, glasses, a befuddled expression and an address in San Francisco's Lower Pacific Heights. The next morning he would ask Lucy Quan if it was the man she had seen on the other side of the schoolyard. Even without that identification, he knew he had his man.

Aside from lending their clout to his records research, the FBI had continued their hands-off posture. Could the police chief definitively call it a kidnapping? Mary Kim's assurance that Megan was okay gave the feds an out. It was enough of an excuse for them to avoid responsibility. But it wasn't enough for Davidson.

San Francisco.

It reminded him of a long weekend in New Orleans at one of the few real training opportunities he had had during his time at the tiny police department. This one had been about crime scenes: Securing the site and collecting evidence. So much had

90

changed with new technologies to identify genetic material, fiber evidence, even the precise composition of dirt or tobacco.

Davidson had only been able to attend the sessions designed as a crash course for small police departments because he could drive the two hours from his home to the New Orleans Hyatt where it was held. There was no budget for hotel rooms.

He recalled nostalgically a bourbon and beer fueled evening when he had introduced a fellow cop to the joys of eating a huge platter of boiled crayfish seasoned with cayenne pepper and garlic dipped in melted butter and lemon. The dish was the one exception to his general aversion to shellfish. Keeping him company that night was a hilarious, brassy African-American woman, he recalled, who had been the best of the instructors that weekend. And she was from San Francisco.

"Connors," she had said. "Like the tennis player."

* * *

"Let me get this right," said Det. Bobbie Connors. "This guy from San Francisco flies to New Orleans, drives two hours to your town, snatches this little darlin' and takes her to Tennessee. Then she calls her mother who tells you everything is hunky dory. And that's it? No other explanation."

She laughed.

"In a nutshell," said Davidson.

"Okay," said Connors. "So you've got a 10-year-old *somewhere* out there and you want to know who this guy is. I get it."

"I figured you would," said Davidson. "Think y'all can help me with this one?"

"I'm on it," said Connors. "But I got to say that just hearing your voice makes me very hungry."

"Crayfish," said Davidson. "Any time you're back 'round these parts, you stop on in and I'll boil up a pot for you myself."

"There's that," said Connors. "But I was remembering the key lime pie in particular. I am an expert and that was the best…yes, I would say it was *the* best I've ever had."

"Tell you what," said Davidson. "You get a line on this guy and I will personally send you one of those pies next time I'm in New Orleans. Pack it in dry ice myself."

"Ooh…you got me weak in the knees now," said Connors, laughing. "You got yourself a deal, Chief."

* * *

Troy Axmann was working on the third-quarter revenue projections he would present to the Merrick board two days later when he got a call from the company's vice president for public relations.

An SFPD detective had called the main switchboard and asked for Walter Novak. Novak's office said the scientist had been gone for several days and no one seemed to know when he would return. Since Novak worked in product development – Axmann's department – the PR executive wanted guidance on what to tell the police. Was there any reason to issue a press release?

Axmann hung up the telephone promising a return call in 20 minutes.

In a panic, he picked up the phone again and called his brother, in Las Vegas.

"Gray," he said when his brother answered his cell phone. "We've got big problems. The police have called us about Novak. They're asking if we know where he is."

Gray Axmann listened while his twin brother filled in the details. The top people at Merrick had no idea Walter Novak was missing, explained Troy. How should he play it?

"Play dumb," Gray Axmann instructed his brother. "Novak works in your department. He's been ill. He's home sick as far you know. If anything, you've been too generous, trying not to put pressure on him.

"Tell the police Merrick doesn't know where he is," Gray continued. "He's been out sick. And that's absolutely all that you know."

Chapter 25

MING WAH CHOY had abandoned her stethoscope for a black Mizuno glove and a blue baseball cap. Instead of a stylish Italian dress underneath an opened lab coat and low heels, she wore a shiny yellow jersey, stretchy pinstriped pants and black Adidas cleats.

With her hair tied into a medium-length ponytail, she toed the rubber with her right foot and rocked back with her left, swinging her right arm behind her. Then, she stepped forward as she whipped her arm in a full underhand circle, finishing with a snap of her wrist and a finger flick that sent the yellow softball spinning toward home plate like a cannon shot.

On his knees, Enzo Lee barely adjusted in time to make a backhand catch when the ball dipped to his right as it neared the plate. It hit the palm of his glove with a loud smack. He gave Choy a long look before he pulled out the ball and tossed it back.

"I didn't know they played softball in Hong Kong," he said loud enough for her to hear as she set up for her next pitch. "Fast pitch no less."

"They play some," said Choy. "But they play a lot more in Australia where I went for boarding school.

"'At's a bloody good catch, mate," she added in an Aussie brogue. "The next one rises at the end. Watch 'er face."

Lee was thankful for the warning. It avoided a possible concussion and the embarrassment of having a softball seam engraved on his forehead for the rest of the evening. After another 15 pitches under the lights of the ball field, Choy walked off the mound and joined her teammates and Lee on the small bleachers off the first base line. A handful of family and friends were scattered around, sprawled in the stands and on the surrounding grass, working their cell phones and minding dogs and small kids.

The field was in a remote park in the hills of San Francisco's Bayview, a district in the southeast corner of the city. The neighborhood held rundown homes just a few blocks from the freeway that was bordered by lumberyards and warehouses. The evening winds were picking up, swirling and cold after sweeping over the frigid ocean waters off the coast.

By the time Choy took the mound, her team had a four-run lead. The high point of the game for Lee was in the fourth inning when Choy faced her opponent's best player for the second time. The other team's center fielder had taken her deep for a two-run homer the first time around.

He guessed that a speed gun would have shown Choy adding an extra 4 or 5 mph to her pitches. Her focus was absolute as the first three pitches broke down and away from the batter. Two were strikes. As the slugger leaned in on the fourth pitch to protect the outside of the plate, Choy delivered a waist-high fastball on the inside corner that forced her to pull back. Strike three and a satisfied grin that was erased as soon as it appeared.

After five innings and 90 minutes, the umpire invoked the mercy rule and ended the game. Choy's team was ahead by 13 runs. She had given up four runs. Everyone was relieved. Even the dogs looked cold. Lee and Choy threw their gear in the back of his Toyota Spyder.

He took her to Francisco's in the nearby Noe Valley district, a neighborhood café where you could wear your worst jeans but still have a great dish of pasta, a choice of fine veal entrees and a good Italian Barbera.

Lee ordered them an initial antipasto of sliced heirloom tomatoes layered with slices of fresh mozzarella marinated in herbs and olive oil, and topped with fresh basil leaves.

For himself, he ordered veal marsala with three types of mushrooms and a Perrone beer. Choy opted for vegetarian lasagna and a glass of Umbrian Barbera.

After their first sips and bites of bread, Lee leaned back and studied Choy.

"I always thought our children would be basketball pros," he said. "You know, part of the new wave of Asian backcourt players."

"Hmmm," said Choy. "I was thinking, perhaps, tennis."

"Why is that?"

"You can play it late in life," she said. "It's social. Girls can play boys."

"Uh oh," said Lee. "Do I sense a challenge coming?"

"I do a play...a little," said Choy, shrugging. "If you want, I can get a time at my club."

The reporter laughed.

"Why do I think I'm being set up?" he said. "Okay. Your serves can't be that much faster than your pitching and I know the balls are softer. I'm game."

He held up his beer and Choy tipped her wineglass in return.

"So," she said after returning the glass to the table. "You saw your grandmother today?"

"Yes," he said. "We talked a little bit. But she seemed exhausted. She fell asleep again after a few minutes."

"She's very tired," said Choy, nodding in agreement. "I don't mean just lack of sleep. This type of treatment. The chemo. The ups and downs. It's very draining even for the young healthy patients. And psychologically, when things aren't going as well, it becomes very difficult."

"I know," said Lee. "God do I know." He suddenly felt completely drained as he remembered the past few weeks and the many hours at the hospital by his grandmother's side.

He stared up at the ceiling and exhaled long and slow. Watching her steadily losing strength and seeing her in pain had taken its toll. He remembered how he had felt when his mother died and knew he was already grieving for his grandmother.

Choy reached over and put her hand on his forearm and gave him a squeeze. He smiled wistfully at her and put his hand on top of hers.

"Thanks," he said.

"She's had a long, full life," said Choy. "Sometimes the best we can do is help them at the end. Help them find the most peaceful path."

Lee shook his head.

"She's still fighting," he said. "She hasn't given me any indication she wants to stop. Until she does, I'm going to help her. Do anything I can."

Choy nodded her understanding. She pulled her hand back from underneath his and rearranged her silverware.

"And how is your...your investigation going?" she asked. "Have you found out anything about the 'mystery' medicine?"

Lee shook his head.

"I don't think that's going anywhere," he said. "Merrick & Merrick bought it, or at least the rights to it. But the trials have been put on hold. There might be a story there eventually. At least there's some controversy. But I don't think it translates into anything that will help my grandmother."

"I'm sorry," said Choy. "But I can't say I'm surprised. And...uh...how are you holding up otherwise? Has your girlfriend been out to see you? Your grandmother told me about her. Has she been to visit you?"

Lee shook his head.

"Not for a while," he said. "Her paper has her running around like crazy. She's been trying to get away but things keep coming up."

Lee looked up and saw Choy's eyes fastened on his. Behind her pretty politeness were a hundred questions.

"It's one of those times in a career when you have to pull out all the stops," he said, shrugging his shoulders. "I understand it. I've been there. Believe me."

Choy looked down, picked up her glass of wine and took a sip. Lee wondered how she was able to drink wine and bite her tongue at the same time.

Chapter 26

MEGAN'S NECK WAS still sore where the man had gripped her so tightly she thought he was going to strangle the life out of her right then. Every time she turned her head to the side, she felt it and a little of the terror resurfaced. But she beat it back down quickly.

The first day at Walter's cousin's house outside of Charlotte had been awkward. His cousin had shown them around the three-bedroom suburban house where he lived alone, fed them and made them comfortable. But it was clear he found it unsettling that Walter was roaming alone with a young girl and that they were clearly on the run from something.

He didn't want to know any details. When he suddenly remembered an out-of-state client he needed to visit, he left it unclear exactly when he was going to return. Megan wondered if he had made it up.

They were alone now in the house, finishing scrambled eggs and bacon with a small stack of buttered toast on a plate between them.

"I saw the girl again last night when I was asleep," she said. "The one with yellow hair and the pigtails. She was above me, looking down again.

"She said something this time," Megan continued. "She said, 'Don't worry. Don't worry.' Twice. That was all she said."

Walter Novak studied the 10-year-old girl as she went back to nibbling on a piece of toast.

"Megan," he said. "What do you remember about being in the hospital?"

She paused for a moment in mid-chew as her mind went back to that time. How long ago had it been? More than a year ago. It seemed like another life. She resumed eating her toast.

"Everyone was really nice to me," she said. "I had so many cards and balloons. And the wigs. They kept bringing in more and they looked so funny. Red and blonde. I think they just did it because it made me laugh." She smiled at the recollection.

"But you remembered me," said Novak. "Even though you were so sick."

Megan nodded.

"I threw up a lot," she said. "My mom was there almost all the time. She wouldn't go home. She almost lived in the room with me.

"I remember you said you would save me," she continued. "And you did. How could I forget that? And the whale. You said it was a 'Get Well' whale. I still have it."

Novak smiled. He had bought the stuffed black and white whale in the hospital gift store before seeing Megan for the first time. He had thought of the "Get Well" nickname on his second visit, when she was starting to recover.

"And is that why you came with me?" asked Novak.

Megan looked up at the ceiling as she thought about it. Then she smiled and nodded her head emphatically.

Novak looked down at his half mug of instant coffee that was now at room temperature. He swirled it around, watched it stop moving and then took a taste. He looked back at Megan. He was remembering how tiny she looked when he first saw her lying inanimate, not moving at all. If they had told him she was already dead, he would have believed it. Most of her life seemed to have already bled out of her by then.

"You were the first one, Megan," he said. "The first one to have that medicine. It was so new. I wasn't supposed to give it to anyone."

Megan nodded her head, becoming more solemn. She knew this was a serious moment.

"I know," she said. "I'm glad you did. I know I'm lucky."

"You're a story now, Megan," Novak said. "You are you – Megan. But inside you...in your body...you also have the story of that medicine. What it did for you. How it cured you. How it changed some things in you."

She nodded.

"It's very complicated," Novak continued. "But there are people who don't want that story to get out. That's why they are looking for us. That's why that man wanted to hurt you."

Megan was silent as she thought for a moment.

"Can't we just tell someone the story?" she said. "Write it down. And give them some blood. Is the story in the blood like the cancer was? Whenever I see the doctor they take more blood. Isn't that enough?"

Novak shook his head sadly.

"A test tube of blood isn't a Megan," he said. "And a success story that isn't walking, talking and breathing isn't much of a success story. People can ignore and explain away a piece of paper with test results. They can't ignore someone who is living who wasn't supposed to be, especially if that person is still healthy two, five or ten years later.

"I understand a lot of what happened to you, Megan, but not everything. There is still more that I can learn...that many people can learn...by studying you and then giving the medicine to more people. You and your body are telling the story."

Megan nodded in agreement. She took a deep breath and exhaled slowly as her eyes scanned the room. They stopped at a basket by the back door that was full of sports equipment. A basketball. Baseball glove and bat. Croquet mallets. Rackets of various types.

She looked back at Novak.

"Do you know how to play tennis?" she asked.

Chapter 27

SHORT AND STOCKY with closely cropped white hair, CEO Edwin Merrick sat in a low-back chair with a spectacular view of the San Francisco Bay when Troy Axmann was ushered into his office. Merrick's Italian loafers rested on an oak coffee table. His tie was loose and he had a stack of business plans on his lap.

"Sit down, Troy," instructed Merrick. He gestured at the sofa on the other side of the coffee table. Axmann had taken the company shuttle from his office at Merrick & Merrick's research center at China Basin to the drug company's top corporate offices in its downtown high rise two miles away.

Merrick picked up the stack of business plans and let them drop with a thud on the carpet next to his chair.

"Did you know we're celebrating the company's centennial in four more years?" he asked. "Four years and we're already starting to plan for it. Lining up the goddamned U.S. Surgeon General. Who knows if he'll still be in office...or alive for that matter...in four years?"

Merrick shook his head.

"Well," said Axmann. "One hundred years. That's quite an achievement."

"Yes," said Merrick. "Great Grandad Eddie and Great Grand Uncle Joe knew a thing or two about business. Sons of bitches, too. Had half the army quartermaster's corps on the payroll. That's how they sold tons of bandages in World War I and even more sulfa drugs in World War II."

At 63, Merrick held both the CEO and Board Chairman positions at Merrick & Merrick and was the latest in a long line of Merrick descendants and in-laws who had dominated the company's decision-making since its founding. In the last two decades, he had personally spearheaded Merrick's aggressive acquisition of startups developing promising new medicines. This had led to a parade of successful Merrick drugs targeting everything from heart disease and liver cancer to acne and flatulence, keeping the company well positioned among its Big Pharma competitors.

A shrewd evaluator of both human talent and promising science, Edwin Merrick had devoted much of his attention over the past decade to developing a beachhead in medical biotechnology. He kept a close watch on technologies exploiting the explosion of knowledge of the location and function of the 30,000 human genes. He had understood very early the potential for treatments that were both more powerful and more subtle – better cures with fewer side effects. Within the company, probably only Troy Axmann had a better handle on the biotech startup scene and they met regularly to compare notes on possible acquisitions.

Merrick picked up a four-page memo sitting on a side table. It was folded in half lengthwise. He held it at the bottom and tapped the other end against his forehead as if transferring all of its content directly into his cerebral cortex. He said nothing for a few seconds.

"Amazing," he finally said in a tone much softer than his usual booming voice. "When I read this, I couldn't escape the feeling that I was witnessing an historical moment. It was as if I was watching the signing of the Declaration of Independence or Edison and the first light bulb."

Axmann nodded his agreement. Even as he had written the memorandum, he had felt a little stunned by the enormity of what he described.

In the search for genes that caused cancer – a hunt that the pharmaceutical industry was pursuing with a gold-rush fervor – Walter Novak had apparently discovered the mother lode.

Other researchers had discovered individual genes linked to cancers of the breast, colon, prostrate, ovaries and pancreas, among others. But Novak had found one – a mutation – that seemed present in many if not most cancers. Moreover, it seemed to operate as a master switch, enabling the genes tied to more specific types of tumors and organs to cause their damage.

Novak called this master, cancer-causing mutation the "C Factor." He had used this discovery to develop the Roxaten drug, which early testing had shown strongly effective against multiple cancer types.

Moreover, Novak had taken the C Factor a step further, taking drugs typically used in vaccines to stimulate the immune response against diseases ranging from hepatitis to common influenza and combining them with a C Factor component to build resistance to cells carrying the mutation. The C Factor's apparently powerful and widespread role gave this immunology research – conducted in laboratory and animal research so far – important implications.

"Just finding the common genetic flaw, the 'C Factor,' is a potential game changer," said Merrick. "Hell! It's like finding the goddamn Holy Grail! Researchers have spent 30 years searching for this."

"Right," said Axmann, nodding his head in agreement. "It's a powerful concept."

"The hell it is!" said Merrick, now returning to his normal full volume. "And then coming up with the drug...Roxaten. It's a single-purpose cancer drug. For most cases, the single medicine could do it. It's almost penicillin for cancer.

"And the immunology work," continued Merrick. "It's halfway to a goddamn vaccine! And it actually makes sense if it gives you real protection against the majority of cancers you might get."

Troy Axmann had tried to prepare himself for the CEO's response to his memo. But it was hard not to feel diminished by it. It was true, though, that compared to Novak's Roxaten solution, his own work – and the Morceptin drug he had developed – seemed almost trivial. It certainly held no potential to revolutionize the treatment of cancer as was the case for Roxaten.

"But what's this about the problems with Novak's work?" said Merrick. "Why didn't you spell it out?"

Axmann shrugged.

"I just thought it was better to keep it verbal," he said, lowering his voice a bit as if they were telling secrets in a crowded room. "Keep it off the record for now anyway."

"Okay then," said Merrick, quieting his voice just a bit. "Let's hear it."

"We're having some problems with the first patient trials," said Axmann. "Some evidence of liver and heart damage in some participants after the first treatment. One fatal heart attack. We had to stop the trial. "

Merrick shook his head and grimaced as if in pain.

What Axmann didn't say is that all the problems had only occurred in the most seriously ill patients. They were the ones confined to a hospital and with an IV bag dripping into their veins. They were also the ones whose names and locations he could provide to his brother Gray along with instructions about which drugs that would produce the symptoms that would force a halt to the study.

"And then there's the patent situation," Axmann continued.

Merrick raised his eyebrows in alarm.

"Three years ago, Novak taught a seminar at the UCSF medical school," said Axmann. "He devoted a couple of sessions to his research. He went into some detail about how it worked. These were molecular biology grad students. He got into the science pretty deeply."

"My god!" exclaimed Merrick. "Non-disclosures?"

Axmann shrugged helplessly.

"It was a class, not a business meeting," he said. "And it gets worse. The students combined their notes and shared them."

Merrick nodded his head.

"Sure, we used to do that," the CEO said. "For the large classes, we'd compile a complete set, give it to a Kinko's and anyone could order one."

"Today, it's all electronic, of course," said Axmann. "Now, there are sites where you can just upload them. You can probably find notes for half the classes at Harvard if you searched for it. Novak's class notes have been available – freely available – on this one site for three years."

Merrick went pale and speechless, the latter a rarity for him. Axmann knew he was contemplating the legal rights to one of the greatest breakthroughs in modern medicine slipping through his fingers. What Axmann had described probably was enough to demolish any Roxaten patent on prior art grounds. It had been publicly disclosed years earlier.

Axmann reached into his soft briefcase and pulled out the *coup de grace*.

"Here they are," said Axmann. "The notes on Roxaten. The site where I got them is noted at the top. It's called 'classnotes dot com.' Pretty unoriginal."

Merrick did not reach for them. Axmann set them down on the coffee table in front of the CEO who seemed to make a conscious effort to avoid looking at them, as if he could deny the existence of the pages and what was contained in them.

When he left Merrick's office, Axmann was sure the CEO would quickly overcome his denial and soon send the five pages of notes to Merrick & Merrick's highly paid patent counsel. He also was sure they would find the description of Roxaten disastrously complete. After all, he had written it himself, inserted it into the original set of notes and replaced the old file on the 'classnotes' website.

Chapter 28

ENZO LEE WAS in the newsroom working on his story about the decline in attendance at the annual San Francisco Flower Show. Organizers believed gardeners were shifting from tulips and roses to cucumbers and tomatoes.

"Old gardeners never die," the story began. *"They just vegetate."*

As he labored over the second paragraph of the story, Lee's phone rang.

"Mr. Lee," said the caller. "This is Roxanne Rosewell. I've been thinking a lot about our conversation on the weekend. I'm...I'm very worried about Walter. And...I..uh. I'm wondering if...well, if I put you in touch with him...could you talk to him? I mean. Would it have to be public or could you just listen and...and maybe give him some advice?"

"Call me Enzo, Roxanne," said Lee. "I'll be happy to talk to him off the record, just as I did with you."

"Oh. Good," said Rosewell.

"You understand, though, that my main interest is whether there is anything that can help my grandmother, right?" said Lee.

"Of course," said Rosewell. "It's just. Well, I don't know. I mean Walter is...is a good man. His intentions...they are always good. But there is a lot more going on. A lot that I don't understand. And I think Walter is confused. I just felt...well...you seem to have good intentions. Maybe you can help steer him a bit. He needs someone he can talk to."

Lee wondered exactly what mess Novak could be in. Well, why not? Often when he interviewed someone, he had no idea if it would be a complete waste or the beginning of a great story. It was just a little of his time. And maybe something would come out of it that could help his grandmother after all. It wasn't impossible.

"I'll be happy to talk to him," said Lee. "Do you have a phone number?"

"I'll try to get him to call you," said Rosewell. "He's quite...well, I suppose 'paranoid' isn't too strong a word. It's a very tortuous process. But I can get word to him."

"Okay," said Lee.

"Oh. And one more thing," said Rosewell. "The police called here asking about Walter."

"The police?" said Lee, his reporting side now kicked into high alert. "What did they want?"

"I have no idea," said Rosewell. "All I have is a note someone left on my desk. Do you know a detective named Bobbie Connors?"

* * *

The Tadich Grill in San Francisco's business district boasts that it is the oldest restaurant in California, tracing its roots to a makeshift coffee-and-grilled-fish stand erected on one of the city's main shipping piers in the midst of the 1849 Gold Rush.

It's a throwback with rich wood paneling, white table cloths, dry martinis and waiters wearing starched linen jackets. The extensive menu was too rich and fried to ever be mistaken for health-conscious cuisine – but delicious nonetheless.

Lee had two dry martinis and a half dozen Oysters Rockefeller at the ready – steam still rising from the cream spinach and cheese topping baked to a crisp gold – when Detective Bobbie Connors arrived at his table.

"Enzo!" she exclaimed, barely giving the reporter time to stand before enveloping him in a bear hug that only ended when she had a chance to peer over his shoulder and see the chilled drinks next to the plate of oysters.

"You devil," she said, dropping a huge purse on the floor and taking off a purple velvet jacket which she draped over her chair. She sat down, swept her long braids back out of her way and took a long sip of her martini.

"Okay?" said Lee.

Connors was silent for a moment, feeling the drink descend and the beginning of a warm glow start its ascent.

"Yah," she said. "Hell, yah."

"So," Connors continued, picking up a stuffed oyster and attacking it with her fork. "You're plying me with food and drink so I'll spill my secrets, huh?"

"Well, you can pay half if it will make you feel better," said Lee.

"Let's not be rash," said Connors laughing.

Lee and Connors had become good friends after having helped each other on various stories and investigations over the past few years. They were close in age – 40 and counting. Connors was a veteran in the San Francisco Police Department. She was also active in gay and lesbian rights. She had jolted her superiors early in her career when she openly marched in the city's annual Gay Pride parade in full uniform.

Lee thought the fact that they both had grown up outside the white mainstream of America enhanced their friendship. Connors was African-American and Lee had weathered his fair share of taunts and slights that came to a boy raised in Chinatown. They both fit comfortably into the current mélange of cultures, lifestyles and ethnicity in the San Francisco area. But both had grown up feeling like outsiders, not really eligible for the first-class cabin of power and privilege.

The waiter returned and Lee ordered his usual sautéed sand dabs, lightly breaded and cooked with butter and wine. It came with braised asparagus. Connors opted for the cioppino, a light tomato-based stew crammed with shrimp, scallops, clams, mussels, crab, fish and garlic toast thrown in for good measure. They asked for a Loire white to accompany the dinner.

"So," said Connors after the waiter left and she was able to attack her second oyster. "The elusive Mr. Novak."

"Hmmm. 'Elusive,'" said Lee. "That sounds right. Where is he and what is he eluding?"

"Okay," said Connors. "Let's just cut to the chase. Here's what I got. The guy snatches a 10-year-old girl in nowhere Alabama. Looks like a kidnapping. Molestation. The whole damn thing. Then the guy – or the girl – calls the mother and somehow convinces her everything is okay. No problemo. But no other explanation."

"Are you sure we're talking about the same guy?" said Lee. "I've got a 50-something cancer researcher – maybe a brilliant one – who possibly develops something important, a better drug or some such thing. Then weird stuff turns up in his drug trials. Unexplained results. Things that don't make sense. Then he disappears saying he's got to save someone."

"Well, my guy works at Merrick & Merrick," said Connors. "So that sounds like a match. I don't know anything about his professional life."

"And why are you interested in Novak?" asked Lee.

"Just between us, it's unofficial," said Connors. "It's more of a favor. I know the guy – the police chief – where this happened. Where the girl was snatched...or whatever. Nice guy. Salt of the earth. Small town. Wants to make sure this kid is okay. You'd think it was his own daughter. And why are you onto this? A story? Outside your normal features beat, isn't it?"

"I don't know what it is," said Lee. "I mean I got into this because of my grandmother. She's very sick – leukemia."

"Oh, God," said Connors. "I'm sorry, Enzo. I know you're close to her."

"Yeah," he said with a long sigh while he rubbed his forehead with his left hand. "Thanks. It's been a rough time. She's about my only family."

"Anyway," Lee continued. "I heard Novak had developed a drug just for this...what my grandmother has. So, I was trying to find out about it. And one thing led to another..."

Connors was silent for a moment. She finished her second oyster and stared at the third before picking it up.

"Why don't I put you in touch with my guy?" she said. "Cliff. 'Ol Cliffy in Alabama. You two put your heads together and see what you can figure out. Just let me know what you find out. Sounds as if whatever is happening is a long way from here. But you never know."

Connors held the third helping of Oysters Rockefeller up to her lips and used her fork to push the spinach, cheese and bivalve into her mouth. She chewed for 15 seconds and then washed it down with the last of the martini.

"Man, that was good," she said grinning. "You can pump me for information any 'ol time...please!"

Chapter 29

THE MAN WITH the single white streak in his hair was called "Whitey" by everyone who knew him. It was a nickname he had hated since childhood in no small part because it reminded everyone – including him – of the birthmark in his scalp that robbed the strip of hair of its natural brown pigment.

In high school, the class clown had tried to stick him with the alternative handle of "Skunk." The result had been a mouthful of broken teeth for the clown and the realization that there were worse nicknames. He grudgingly accepted that he was stuck with 'Whitey.'

Late in the afternoon, Whitey would have preferred to be inside the house of Walter Novak's cousin near Charlotte before its owner came home. But when he went up to the front steps to see if anyone was there – ready to adopt the pose of a salesman offering deals on new roofs should anyone answer – the loud barking that greeted him changed his plan.

Instead, Whitey parked his rental car in the shade down the block and settled in with his paperback, a history of World War II. He had learned the cousin was an accountant. Hopefully, he kept normal work hours. Whitey had made it through the German invasion of France when a Jeep Cherokee pulled in front of the house. The garage door slowly opened and the Cherokee parked inside before the door began to wind its way closed.

Whitey waited five minutes before leaving his car. Before he got out, he took the newspaper he had bought at the airport and folded it until it sat neatly tented over his Glock 19 with the silencer screwed onto the barrel.

Novak's cousin was pudgy, wore wire-rimmed glasses and had on his slippers when he answered the door. He opened it six inches.

"Hello," said Whitey, smiling and pointed the newspaper with the concealed gun downward at the man's legs. He held the newsprint pinched closed with his free hand.

"I found this in the gutter and thought it must be yours," he added.

When Novak's cousin opened the door another foot, Whitey let the newspaper fall away and thrust the gun into the accountant's midriff. He used his other hand to guide the smaller man backward into the house. He shut the door behind him with a kick.

"Whaaa. What are you doing?" said Novak's cousin.

Whitey put the end of the silencer under the man's jaw carefully, pressing it up hard enough to get the guy's undivided attention without accidentally blow his head off. Then he spun him around. The dog, a knee-high mutt, was five feet away, growling menacingly.

"Lock him up," said Whitey, through gritted teeth. His voice was quiet but insistent. He grabbed Novak's cousin by the back of his shirt under the collar and pushed him in the direction of the dog.

He stayed behind the accountant holding the fistful of shirt as the dog was corralled and locked into a guest bathroom off the entry hall. Then Whitey walked him into the middle of the living room and made him sit flat on the floor with his legs in front of him.

"What's your name?" asked Whitey.

"It's...uh...it's 'Andrew.'"

"Do you want to live, Andrew?" asked Whitey.

"Yes...yes," said Novak's cousin, looking up hopefully at his assailant. He was terrified.

"You won't unless you tell me right now where Walter Novak is."

"He uh…he uh…left," said Andrew. "I don't know where he went. He didn't tell me. You've got to believe me. Please."

Whitey was still for a moment, his eyes boring into the man on the floor.

"That's not the deal, Andrew," said Whitey. "I don't mind killing you. I've killed a lot of people. One more? It's nothing to me." He sat down on the sofa four feet away from the accountant on the floor and pointed the gun at his face.

"Listen…listen," said Andrew. "I don't know him really. He was here but I hadn't seen him in 20 years. I don't even *like* Walter. I never did. He was always…just strange. I wanted him out of here. I didn't care where he was going. I didn't want to know."

Whitey exhaled slowly.

"This is not going well," he said. "You are not holding up your end of the bargain. You need to come up with something better than this. Can you call him? How do you get in touch with him?"

Andrew shrugged and held his hands out plaintively. He was sweating. His eyes raced around the room, looking for a way out…an answer…anything. Then he closed his eyes.

"He said…he said…I think he said he knew someone," said the accountant. "It was a professor at Duke with a place in Georgia. A professor at Duke with a place in Georgia. That was it! It was a Middle Eastern name. Like Rasheed or something like that. Rasheed or..or..maybe something that sounded like that. Foreign."

"Roll over! Face down!" Whitey ordered. Andrew immediately flopped onto his stomach. Whitey stood up, bent over the prone man and pressed the gun into the back of his head.

"You've failed, Andrew. I'm sorry," he said.

115

"Oh no! Oh no! Oh no!" wailed the accountant. He clenched handfuls of carpet in a death grip and made wet slobbering noises. Whitey could see a wet stain starting to grow in the crotch of his pants. It was then that Whitey was sure he had gotten everything he was going to get from the poor slob. He stood and listened to the crying for a moment.

"If you try to contact Novak, I'll know," said Whitey. "Every phone call. Every email. I'll know. And I'll come back and finish this."

On his way out, Whitey stopped at the guest bathroom, threw open the door and shot the snarling mutt twice.

"God, I hate dogs," he muttered to himself as he left the house.

Chapter 30

ENZO LEE HAD left his grandmother sleeping peacefully at the Chinese Hospital and settled into his desk at the News. He was working on the lead sentence of his daily story and trying to find the creative tightrope of fun and flippant without falling into either the juvenile or the heartless. It was a daily balancing act.

The piece was the tale of a young socialite, Penny Hamilton, who had attempted the previous night to become the $1,224^{th}$ person to commit suicide by jumping off the Golden Gate Bridge. The young woman had been jilted by her fiancé. She fell 20 feet into a safety net set up for a painting crew which pulled her out and then escorted her to an all-night counseling center in the Haight. It was a little more serious than his usual fluff.

Lee's first try: *"A Penny saved is a Penny spurned."*

"Hmmm," he thought, hitting the 'delete' key. Perhaps a bit much given the circumstances. He was gearing up for another try when his phone rang.

"Hello," said Lee.

The man on the other end cleared his throat.

"Mister..uh...Lee?" he said.

"Speaking."

"I...um...I'm Walter Novak."

"Mr. Novak," said Lee. "Well, I'm glad to talk to you. I guess Roxanne gave my number to you."

"She did," said Novak. "She did some research. Roxanne is impressed with your background. And she thought maybe you can help."

117

Lee waited for more. But Novak was silent on the other end.

"Okay," said Lee finally. "Look. I guess I'm in the dark here. I don't really know what is going on with you. What situation you're in exactly."

"Fair enough," said Novak. He sighed heavily. Lee could hear the weariness in his voice.

"It's such a long story," the scientist continued. "And it's an unbelievable one. I can hardly believe it myself. People are trying to kill us. Megan and me."

So, he is with the girl then, thought Lee. That part of the story was true.

"Is Megan okay?" asked Lee.

"Yes," said Novak. "We've had a close call. But she is well. She is alive at least. Listen. I think I need to see you. I need to know I can trust you. And I can show you what I have – evidence. Otherwise...I don't know..."

"Well. You know the reason why I was trying to contact you to begin with, right?" said Lee. "My grandmother."

"Your grandmother" said Novak. "Yes. Roxanne told me. I think we can help her. But really it will be up to you. It will be a decision for you to make."

Lee held the phone to his head and looked out the windows that ran across the front of the newsroom. It was turning sunny outside. He was thinking of his grandmother, a 10-year-old girl he didn't know yet and a scientist who...well, he had no idea if he was a genius or what. And he had to admit that he was curious. His reporter's sixth sense was kicking in big time as well, saying there was something here worth examining. And even a remote chance that something could help his grandmother was better than nothing.

"Okay," he finally said. "Tell me how to find you."

After he hung up, Lee placed a call to Alabama.

"Chief Davidson?" Lee said.

"Yessuh," said Davidson.

"I'm a reporter in San Francisco," said Lee. "My name is Enzo Lee."

"Yes. All right then. Bobbie Connors...Detective Connors said you would call," said the police chief. "And she filled me in a little about this Novak."

"Right," said Lee. "I just got off the phone with him. And...uh...I'm going to meet him. I'm flying out tonight. He's in...uh...Georgia. And he says he's with the girl...Megan...and he says she's fine."

"Megan? Megan Kim? You know where she is?"

"Maybe," said Lee. "I'm supposed to see him. See them. Tomorrow."

"Where are they?" said Davidson.

Lee didn't answer. He was debating what to tell Davidson.

"Listen," said the police chief. "Megan Kim is mine. I mean she's one of mine. She lives here. I need to know she is okay. I *need* to know that!"

"I understand," said Lee. "But you need to understand that Novak is spooked. I mean seriously spooked. He's convinced someone is trying to kill him and Megan, too. I don't know if he's crazy or what.

"But I think he'll show up," he added. "He sounds like he will. But if he gets scared off, that's it. He's gone again and that's not what you want. So, I'll keep you in the loop. I'll check on Megan the best I can. And...and I'll try...I will try to get her home."

Davidson was silent.

"Don't have much choice, do I?" said Davidson at last.

"No," said Lee. "Don't worry. I'll be in touch."

119

Chapter 31

THE 12 MEN who rode the elevators to the basement of the Florentine Hotel and Casino in Macau and then made their way to a windowless conference room were the CEOs, board chairmen and other top executives of the largest pharmaceutical companies in the world. Most of them had close ties to other drug behemoths and would informally represent their absent brethren here as well.

Each of the men had his own preoccupation as they greeted each other and traded small talk before the clandestine meeting began.

The lone Italian was thinking about the 28-year-old Korean woman he had left in his hotel room upstairs clad only in Victoria Secret's panties that she had donned in a nod toward modesty after their post lunch tryst. She was his company's top salesperson in Seoul and their travel schedules regularly intersected whenever he was in Asia, which was four times more often than his predecessor had thought necessary.

The senior member of the Swiss contingent was thinking of the 21-year-old Spaniard whom he expected would knock on his door in two hours. They had met at the roulette table. The tight undershirt the young man wore beneath his open work shirt sheathed his Michelangelo-quality abs like a latex glove. The drug executive drooled at the thought of running his hands up and down – and above and below – those chiseled muscles.

Meanwhile, Takeo Hayashi, the 45-year-old vice chairman of Kimura Pharmaceutical, was planning how to win back the $300,000 he had lost at the craps table the previous night. The gambling relapse, added to his previous losses over the past two years, had him once again pondering how he could kill himself without losing a $5 million life insurance payout. He was running out of other options to ensure his three children the elite educations they deserved and his wife her comfortable retirement.

The meeting location, identities of the attendees and the substance of their discussions this afternoon was secret to avoid inevitable allegations of price fixing and colluding. This was also the reason why Macau had been chosen as the meeting place. It was far from both the attention and the jurisdiction of the United States and Europe where the regulators of Big Pharma were the most vigilant. And, this center of gambling and conventions was a place any of the attendees might visit anyway, even if just to blow $50,000 on an evening of baccarat.

Edwin Merrick surveyed the other men sitting around the long, rectangular table. All were long-term players in the pharmaceutical industry. Most had started as scientists or salesmen and then used their intelligence, savvy, loyalty and dogged persistence over three decades to achieve their places in the corporate suites.

Merrick glanced down at the bright yellow page sitting in front of him. Identical copies sat in front of each of the other attendees. It was a list of the topics they were to discuss, appropriately vague to avoid any embarrassment if any of the pages should leave the room.

"Pricing" referred to the setting of floors for the amounts charged for drugs so the companies could keep their cash cows fat and lucrative and immune from price pressure.

"Regulation" contemplated coordinated efforts to influence key government officials to avoid laws and rules that would stop the drug companies from rewarding doctors who prescribed their drugs – with expensive vacations or outright cash. Since the largest drug companies distributed worldwide, it made sense to combine forces and funnel payments to the regulators – whether legal or not – through a single source.

"Third World" alluded to the pressures to drastically cut prices on drugs for AIDS, malaria and other widespread diseases in the poorest countries. Since one company's concession in this area would be used to browbeat the others, it was important to agree on a formula that would serve as the industry bottom line.

Merrick had invoked his status as the only top pharmaceutical executive who could trace both his lineage and name to his company's original founders and had his own item inserted at the top of the agenda.

It simply read: "New Business – E. Merrick"

Most of the Europeans sat on his left. The Japanese contingent was on the right. His fellow Americans sat across from him along with the Brits.

"We have a…a situation," said Merrick. "One of our scientists has found what looks to be a workable vaccine for cancer. Our people think it could eventually be widely useful for most cancers, certainly the big ones. The immunity could last a lifetime."

Murmurs rippled around the table.

"Finally, a cure," said one of the Swiss.

"Close," said Merrick. "As we continue to get better at finding genetic factors, those at high risk certainly will want the protection. It's not hard to imagine a day in the near future when everyone – at least in developed countries – receives this vaccine just as they do for mumps and measles today.

"You can imagine how aggressively the health agencies, foundations, cancer societies…everyone will push this," he continued. "One by one, they will attempt to eradicate their favorite cancers. Rates will plummet. Cancer cases could be cut by half…maybe more."

Merrick paused while he let his words settle in. He could see each of the executives working out the computations in his head. How much revenue was generated by cancer medicines? What were the implications of losing that? Could they escape the disruption that could ravage stock prices, force consolidations and end careers? How many years would they have to drift away into a quiet retirement?

"And tell us why this isn't great news for you," asked one of the British executives.

"Well...how do I put this?" said Merrick. "Even if we were completely secure in our rights to this, we would have a few years of nice profit but at a long term sacrifice of a pillar of our business. It would be as if we were burning down our house for a night of celebration.

"As it is," he continued. "We...ah...are less than completely confident that our patent rights are what they could be for this. You know how complicated issues of prior art and publication can be."

Everyone in the room realized that Merrick, while admitting nothing that could be used to undermine his company's patent, was signaling that the rights to this cancer vaccine were compromised. The implication was obvious. The rights to the breakthrough could well be in the public domain already. If so, the generic houses would manufacture and sell it at bargain-basement prices once it was approved by regulators. A powerful, cheap cancer vaccine. It would be disastrous for all of them.

"Edwin," said the younger Japanese executive, momentarily abandoning thoughts of gambling losses and suicide. "Please tell us why you don't simply bury this if it is not...convenient? We all have done this for drugs that won't be profitable or that...what is the term...'cannibalizes' one that already is popular."

Merrick slowly surveyed the room. This was the embarrassing moment.

"We have lost some control of the situation," he finally said. "Our scientist has disappeared. He has evidence of this drug...its potential. When he...if he...contacts one of your scientists, approaches a university or health agency in your country, or goes to your media, you must tell us.

"We must deprive him of help and support, certainly from any fellow scientists," said Merrick. "We all must discredit this man. Now you all know what he has. If the world believes an effective cancer vaccine is in the offing...imagine the clamor. We could not control it. And it will cost us – all of us – untold billions."

Chapter 32

IT WAS A humid 70 degrees at 10 am when Enzo Lee's red-eye flight from California to Savannah landed at the airport. By the time he rented a car and drove the 25 minutes into the city, it still was well before noon and he had more than two hours before he was to meet Novak.

As he left the freeway and headed through the old part of the city and toward the historic district that runs along the Savannah River, he remembered why he had found the place so charming during his only visit more than a decade earlier.

Central Savannah was like a movie set conjured up to depict the Antebellum South. Every three or four blocks there was a small park with giant oaks dripping with Spanish moss surrounded by mansions, stately churches and three-story row houses – many of them more than two centuries old.

Lee parked and walked two blocks and down a set of stairs to the riverfront area which was 15 feet below the rest of the downtown. It was now a parkway filled with broad walkways, planters and benches. Shops catering to tourists filled the row of old buildings away from the river. But it wasn't hard to imagine the day when English sailing ships were tied up along the same stretch of river. The buildings that now held antiques and ice cream shops stored cotton bales then until the visiting ships could take them back to the English textile mills.

After a 20-minute stroll, Lee made his way back to the street level and walked down Bull Street away from the river. Every few blocks he passed through another square surrounded by the gigantic oaks and with a statue in the middle honoring a Revolutionary War hero or a Georgia founding father.

Lee finally reached Chippewa Square. The bronze statue here depicted James Oglethorpe, the founder of Georgia. He wore the waistcoat, high boots and tricorn hat of a Revolutionary Era general and held an unsheathed sword. Lee sat in the shade on a bench in front of Oglethorpe and two snarling lions perched at the base of the monument. After five minutes, a thin, lanky man with white, swirling hair sat next to him. Lee recognized him from a photograph he had seen online, even though Novak had been at least a decade younger when it was taken.

"Mr. Lee?" said Novak.

"The same," said Lee, nodding at Novak and giving him a smile. "Roxanne sends her regards."

"Ah," said Novak. "Roxanne. My contact with reality."

"Hmm," said Lee. "Well, she certainly seems well grounded. And she's very worried about you."

"I know...I know," said Novak, wistfully. "It's delicate. Very delicate. She wants to help me...as is her habit. I don't think she fully appreciates the danger.

"This may be hard to believe," he continued. "Although any doubts I had vanished long ago. There are people willing to kill over this..."

"Over Roxaten?" asked Lee.

"Yes. Roxaten," said Novak. "And what Roxaten could lead to. The potential. It's enormous. Much more than I could have guessed...even as recently as two years ago."

"Okay," said Lee. "Doctor...shall I call you Doctor Novak?"

"Walter is fine," said Novak.

"Okay," said Lee. "Enzo works for me. As I said, I'm willing to listen and be convinced. I'm not a scientist. But if you can break it down for me, I'll do the best I can. I don't imagine we can get through it all sitting here in the park. Is there somewhere else we can go? Do you mind my asking where you and Megan are staying?"

Novak nodded across the square at a building that faced it. It was a brown row house. On each of its three floors were large windows with dark wooden shutters that stood open, framing each opening.

"We have the top flat," said Novak. "It belongs to an old friend. He's on sabbatical. There's room enough for you to stay while you're here. In fact, I'd prefer it."

Lee studied Novak for a moment. Then he nodded in understanding.

"Fewer loose ends," said the reporter.

"Yes," said Novak. "These people are relentless. I don't know how they are doing it. But they seem to know where we're going before we do."

Chapter 33

THE FIRST THING that Lee noticed when he walked into the third floor flat off Chippewa Square behind Walter Novak were the bruises on Megan's face and neck. They were starting to fade but they must have been painful. He didn't say anything. He would ask her about them when they were alone. And he made a silent promise that he wouldn't leave her alone with Novak until he was absolutely sure she would be safe.

"Hi," Megan said brightly when she saw him. She put down the paperback book she had been reading and sat up perkily with a ready smile. She wore blue jeans with a yellow T-shirt that read: "Girls Rule."

After introductions were made, Lee could tell that Megan was eager to say something, barely able to hold it back.

"Are you Chinese?" she finally blurted out.

"Half," replied Lee. "My mother is...was Chinese. My father wasn't. He was Scottish and Italian." Lee was accustomed to being mistaken for a variety of nationalities and ethnic groups. Filipinos, Mexicans, Native Americans...even Turks and Iranians had mistakenly claimed him as their own.

Megan nodded her head, arching her eyebrows knowingly. Lee winked at her and she smiled back.

Lee wasn't sure how freely he and Novak could talk with Megan there. So, he decided to ask her about everything that had happened since the day she saw Novak outside her school yard.

It tumbled out of her in a torrent.

The first hotel. The table full of games. Waffles with blueberry syrup...her first time. Learning how to paddle a canoe. Catching the fish. Swimming in the cold clear water of the lake, so different than the ocean off her Gulf Coast home. Teaching Walter the best way to cook fresh fish. The forays to buy clothes. Her rationale behind her style choices.

It sounded like someone describing summer camp. As she talked and exhibited her obvious affection for Novak, Lee's worries about any mistreatment by the scientist began to dissipate. But he also noticed that she made no mention of being pursued, fears in that vein or anything else that would account for her bruises. He decided to wait. He knew he had a lot of ground to cover with Novak and Megan. He wanted to hear it all, parts of it more than once so he could absorb it all and detect inconsistencies. Lee needed to be able to weigh what was true and what it meant. He wanted to get to know them, even if it took a couple of days. He needed to know how reliable and trustworthy they were.

They seemed to trust him. Indeed, they seemed relieved to have someone else share in what was happening. He hadn't dealt a lot with children, but instinct told him to give Megan the time he could to let her reach the difficult parts of her journey on her own.

It was evening when Novak left to buy some groceries and then pick up a pizza and a salad for their dinner at an Italian restaurant on his way back. Lee agreed to a game of chess with Megan using an elaborate board and set that occupied a place of honor on a game table in the flat. Novak had taught her the rudiments and she wanted to test her knowledge.

They were in the middle of an initial skirmish of pawns when Lee asked her about the bruising on the side of her face and neck.

Megan's hand froze over the pawn she was getting ready to move. She stared at Lee. Then her hand moved to her neck, pressing against it as she moved her head back and forth, feeling the last of the soreness that lingered there. The sensation unlocked all the memories of that night as well as the terror. Her eyes filled and she looked down in her lap.

"They came after us when we were at the lake," she said, looking up at Lee. "Walter tried to stop them. He crashed the car but it...it wasn't enough. I tried to hide...in the railroad yard...but the man found me. He...I thought he was going to choke me."

Megan's hand went back to her throat.

"He was carrying me when Walter hit him," she continued. "I think that's what happened. Then we got away. We went to the farmhouse. But we're afraid. They'll come again."

"Do you know why, Megan?" asked Lee. "Do you know why they are after you and Walter?"

She shrugged.

"It has to do with the cancer," she said. "Beating the cancer. It did something to me...to my body."

Megan shook her head.

"Walter says I carry a story now," she said. "They don't want the story to get out. I don't think I really understand it."

Lee nodded in sympathy.

"Must be pretty scary for you," he said.

Megan shrugged again. She was quiet for a moment.

"When I was sick everyone thought I was going to die," she finally said. "I could tell. Even the nurses were crying and they never cry. I thought so, too. Then I didn't. I got well. It was...it was like magic or something."

Megan's voice dropped to a whisper.

"Maybe it was a mistake," she said. "Maybe I wasn't supposed to get well."

She looked at Lee as if he might know the answer. He wanted to tell her "No" and that everything would be okay. But he didn't know if that was a promise he could make. He didn't know enough yet. Lee didn't know what to say. After a moment, her attention went back to the chessboard. She moved her pawn.

"You know what was scary?" said Megan, looking up and with her voice back to normal. "The hurricane. Katrina. Now, *that* was scary!"

Chapter 34

IT WAS WELL past midnight. Novak had waited until Megan was asleep before telling his story to the reporter. A pot of coffee and a laptop computer sat between them.

"The body makes a lot of mistakes," Novak began. "Fortunately, it fixes almost all of them. It has safety systems built in at the cellular level that would make NASA proud. Redundancy after redundancy.

"A key one is a way to check on the new cells that your body is constantly creating. A quality control mechanism. It looks for any change in the chromosomes – mutations in the DNA really. If it spots any, quality control steps in and fixes the DNA, or that cell is eliminated.

"Another safety system is stopping the cell reproduction when enough is enough," Novak added. "It's why your skin isn't an inch thick. It's also why you don't have tumors and other strange growths popping out all over."

Lee couldn't help looking at his arms resting on the table. Normal. Nothing strange growing out of them.

"Thank, God, huh?" said the reporter.

"Well, thank someone or something," replied Novak. "Natural selection...God."

"Right," said Lee. "Another discussion, I guess. Okay. Go on."

"This leads us to cancer," said Novak. "You realize I'm vastly oversimplifying this, right?"

"Thanks," said Lee.

"But the typical case is that there is a two-step process," continued the scientist. "A genetic mutation occurs that blocks

132

the 'enough-is-enough' control mechanism. And then the protection that would detect and fix this mutation – the flaw in the DNA – fails as well.

"The result is uncontrolled cell growth – otherwise known as cancer. It competes for resources. It disrupts the normal operation of healthy cells and organs. And, of course, it can be terribly good at moving to new places in the body – from liver to bone to lungs to brain – and look quite different at each location.

"Much of the new cancer research going on now is to find these genetic mistakes and eliminate them – make the cells go back to behaving like healthy ones," continued Novak. "That's what the new generation of drugs is doing, tweaking the problem gene – suppress it somehow – so the original quality control system can get back on track."

"When you describe it this way," said Lee. "It's seems relatively simple. At least from the layman's perspective."

"Yes. Well, the devil is in the details as always," said Novak. "Many companies, thousands of careers and billions of dollars have been devoted to finding these genetic defects and figuring out how to fix them. There has been a lot of success."

"But...," prompted Lee.

"Yes...but one huge frustration is that the process often seems like a series of rifle shots," said Novak. "A drug only works for, say, breast cancer. But not all breast cancers. Only the 20 percent that have a certain gene mutation. Another one just works for lung cancer. But, only for the 15 percent with another certain mutation. A broad-spectrum genetic-based drug – something like antibiotics for cancer – has eluded us.

"Do you ever watch Cold War movies about nuclear war?" continued Novak. "The ones where a rogue submarine or a crazy general is about to launch a nuclear missile?"

"Um...sure," said Lee. "Changing the subject a bit, huh?"

"Not really. You know how they always have the scene where you need two people to turn their keys at the same time on opposite sides of the room to fire the missile?"

"You mean a fail-safe system?" said Lee. "So no one can launch on their own and start World War III."

"Exactly," said Novak. "Nothing happens unless both switches are turned on simultaneously. Well, when you look at the current cancer research you see that the problem genes – the rogue ones that disrupt the quality control system – often are present in healthy people. In fact, most people with the problem gene will never have cancer.

"So I went hunting," continued the scientist. "I started looking for a first switch, the one that must be turned on before the second one can have any effect. I looked for something general, that spanned many types of cancer. I had in mind an enabling mutation. Something that had to be there for all the other ones to do their damage."

"Like the first switch in the fail-safe scenario," said Lee. "A master switch."

"Exactly," said Novak. "A great analogy. And it's exactly what we found."

Chapter 35

"WE NEEDED A short hand for what we found, this 'master mutation,'" said Novak. "We just started calling it the 'C Factor' and the name stuck.

"We found it first in liver cancer cells. But once we knew exactly where to look, we also isolated it in most varieties of leukemia, melanoma, breast cancer, prostrate…and the list goes on and gets longer and longer.

"From there we had to understand the mechanism," Novak continued. "Exactly how the C Factor worked – at a cellular and molecular level – and devise a way to stop it."

Novak paused for a moment, deep in thought as he gazed the ceiling.

"Do you know when you travel internationally, how you take converters to match the local electrical outlets?" he asked. "So you can use your electric razor or charge your cell phone?"

"Tell me about it," said Lee. "I've got a drawer full of them. Every time I leave the country, I panic and buy another bag of them."

"Okay," said Novak. "Imagine the most elaborate of those converters."

"You mean the one with five prongs and they're all slanted every which way and it weighs two pounds?"

"Exactly," said Novak. "Now multiply that by a thousand and you begin to get a feeling for how the C Factor, or any other similar gene works. A train of complex connections. Molecular and chemical binding."

"All right," said Lee. "I think I get it. And how does Roxaten fit in to this?"

135

"Well, imagine your converter again," said Novak. "Suppose you change the shape of those prongs. Say, you slip a covering over some so they're twice as thick...or change the angle of their slant."

"They wouldn't work," said Lee.

"Yes. And that's one of the things Roxaten does," said Novak. "It blocks some of those points of connection. It also...well...to be honest, we're not sure of everything it does. We think perhaps it makes the C Factor more visible to the immune system. There is something in the C Factor that somehow convinces the immune system to stay away...not react. We think Roxaten suppresses this...this camouflage somehow. So, it almost acts like a flag, signaling the white blood cells to do what they do to foreign cells."

"Seek and destroy?" said Lee.

"Precisely," said Novak. "And the nature of these kinds of drugs is you don't understand everything. But you can measure the effects – good and bad. That's what the testing and trials are about. How effective. How safe.

"And, of course, the game changer is the number of cancers in which the C Factor is involved," he continued. "As I said, it becomes less a war of rifle shots and something much more broad in scope. And that changes the whole landscape in terms of prevention and, specifically, vaccination."

"How's that?" asked Lee.

"Well, if you can inoculate people to help them ward off cancer, it may not be very helpful if only five percent of the people carry the gene putting them at risk and only a fraction of them eventually get sick," said Novak. "It's just not practical to test millions of people to find and help those few.

"But suppose the C Factor is present in half of all cancers and a vaccination program stops it from becoming a problem in, say, 65 percent of those cases. Would you get in line for a shot that would reduce your cancer risk by a third?"

Lee thought for a moment. His mind flashed to his grandmother lying in her bed at the Chinese Hospital.

"Of course," he said.

Novak nodded.

"It changes the whole discussion," said the scientist. "And I'm confident that we have something close to that – a vaccine that primes the immune system so it will recognize the C Factor mutation when it turns dangerous. In our tests, it's been very powerful and effective. I'm convinced that in a few years you will, in fact, be standing in line for it. We all will."

Lee's head was swimming. He knew he would have to recite everything back to Novak the next day to make sure he'd gotten the basics right and understood them as much as he could without the relevant science background.

Novak's excitement about his work was contagious. Lee could almost see the lines of people getting their C Factor vaccinations. Who *wouldn't* opt for a shot that could reduce your cancer risk by a third?

But before it got much later and the fog of information and fatigue grew any more opaque inside his head, the reporter knew he had to get a better understanding of Megan's role in all this. Why were she and Novak hiding here? Was someone really after them? Why?

"Okay," said Lee. "I think I've got what you're saying from a high level – the scientific implications – at least all that I'm going to understand tonight. Why don't you tell me how Megan fits into all this?"

Novak paused. He stared at his hands clasped together in front of him on the table. Then he looked up at Lee. He had almost a defiant expression on his face.

"She is the only one to be treated with Roxaten," he said. "Actually, that's not entirely true. There was one other. Megan's marrow donor. Megan's ability to produce her own blood cells had been compromised by earlier treatments.

"Her donor was a retired school teacher in Michigan. She agreed to take the vaccine. Megan's resistance was so low. She needed the procedure anyway and I thought we could increase her chances by boosting her immunity at the same time. It was to help eliminate any residual pockets of the cancer.

"In both cases it was done without authorization," continued Novak. "There was no approved trial. There was no time. We still were testing Roxaten on animals."

"Okay," said Lee. "And what are the implications of that?"

"For me?"

"Yes."

"Professional disgrace," said Novak matter of factly. "Blacklisting by the pharmaceutical industry. Never working in drug research again. Never publishing a scientific article again. Maybe even worse."

"I get the idea," said Lee.

"And you're aware of my background...the other problems I've had?"

"Roxanne told me you were...at a psychiatric facility?" said Lee.

"Yes," said Novak. "I guess you'd call it a breakdown...whatever that's supposed to mean. It wasn't the first time but I had been well for a number of years. But, bottom line is 'crazy.' Now add to that, 'dangerous'... 'out of control.' You're a journalist, you can fill in the story.

"When I came back to Merrick from my...ah...hospitalization," Novak continued. "It was clear that something was wrong. They had stopped the trials. They were telling me about things that didn't make sense. Heart damage. I mean there's just no way it could happen. Not with Roxaten.

"That's when I found someone to look into the network...the computer network at Merrick. Someone who could see who had accessed the information about the trials. Anything unusual."

"Okay," said Lee. "And who was that?"

"I found him from a website," said Novak. "It was a site used by hackers and virus writers actually. I don't even know his real name. His screen name was 'Paul Revere.' He said he was a 'cyber sentinel'... warning the people when he found something evil or dangerous."

Lee looked dubious.

"I know," continued Novak. "I had no choice. I was desperate to find out what was going on. I brought him into the office with me a couple of nights. I gave him my passwords, let him use my computer. Here's what he found."

Novak opened the laptop sitting on the table between them. He hit a couple of buttons that brought the screen to life. Then he moved it so both he and Lee could see the screen.

"It's all in computer speak," he said. "But to an expert, it shows someone accessed the patient database for the Roxaten trial. And they went deep. They found the details of specific patients, the most seriously ill – who they were and where they were located.

"They copied names of hospitals," Novak added. "The floors. Exact room numbers. And these patients were the ones who had the health problems that stopped the trial. Within ten days after taking this data, every one of them had some problem. I'm convinced it wasn't a coincidence."

"And who was this?" asked Lee. "Who looked up this information?"

Novak shook his head slowly.

"They hid their identity," he said. "It was quite clever really. They ran it through *my* computer and used *my* access codes. It looks as if I did it but I was in a hospital at the time in Arizona...perhaps the only place on earth with no computers. And I believe that they *poisoned* those people. It had to be that. Roxaten couldn't have caused the damage. One of them died.

"And while we were doing this we caught them in the act," continued Novak. "They went after the files about Megan and her marrow donor. And that took some effort. They were breaking the passwords...encryption...everything. They took all the data. My private notes. Then they came back. A new session that seemed to have only one purpose – finding their home addresses. That's when I began to worry about their safety.

"The medical information about Megan is something that I don't believe I could ever publish," the scientist said. "It's the result of unauthorized treatment. But on another level, she is the proof of everything I hoped to accomplish."

"How's that?" said Lee.

"Well...Megan's alive, isn't she?"

Chapter 36

IT WAS ENZO Lee's second day in Savannah but his body clock still was operating on California time. He had slept late into the morning after the long session with Novak. It was overcast and muggy. Finally, the skies opened up after noon, flooding the streets. The rains continued into the night, tapering off finally to a light drizzle around midnight. Even with the light rain, it was warm enough with the humidity to keep the window cracked in the living room.

The reporter couldn't sleep. He tried to read a book but his mind kept circling back to what Novak had told him. He tried to make sense of it all and figure out what he could do about it. How could this help his grandmother? Was Novak a complete paranoid or did he have reason to worry? Was Megan truly in danger?

It was the sound of footsteps on the front steps of the house that caused him to peer out the window. Through the blinds, Lee could see the top of someone below. The man wore a trench coat. Lee saw a streak of white in an otherwise dark head of hair.

The man backed down the steps and stood on the sidewalk for a moment as he surveyed the building. Then, he walked across Chippewa Square. Lee saw him lean against the driver's door of a dark car that had its parking lights on. He saw another car idling two spaces behind the first.

Lee walked down the hall in the third-floor flat to Novak's room. He knocked once and opened the door.

"Walter," he said. "There are people outside. They're checking out the house."

Novak rubbed his face and gave himself a moment to completely wake up.

"Okay," he said finally. "There's a set of stairs down the back. Wake up Megan while I get dressed."

Lee went to Megan's room and shook her by the shoulder.

"Wake up, Megan," he said with urgency in his voice. "You need to get dressed right away. There are people outside. We're going out the back way. Hurry."

Within three minutes they were heading down the stairway. It was enclosed and opened onto an alley. When they reached the alley, Lee could hear loud pounding on the other side of the house. Then he heard a crashing noise and the sound of wood splintering.

"Christ," he thought. They must have brought sledgehammers or something. Talk about prepared.

Walter led them down the alley and out to the street. He looked both ways.

"What do you think?" said Lee, coming up on his shoulder.

"There's more activity near the river," said Walter. "There might be police around. Or even just people. Enough of a crowd might scare them off."

Lee wasn't sure that the people who had just busted their way into the house behind them would be scared off by anything. But he had no better idea. In the dim light of a distant street light he nodded his agreement.

They came out on Drayton Street and Novak guided them left, heading north toward the river. After two blocks, he took them left again.

"Let's stay on smaller streets," he said. "We'll be more difficult to see."

They came to another small square and cut across it, keeping in the shadows created by the towering oak trees above. They left the square and ran another three blocks to the next one. Lee slowed his pace. Megan was tiring. He thought he might have to put her on his back in another block.

As they came to the next square, they heard a car moving fast in the street off to the side a block away. Lee knew they'd been spotted.

They were half way through when they heard the car screech to a stop behind them. A door opened. Then gunshots. One. Then another.

"Go! Go! Go!" urged Lee, leading the way and weaving to the left to put the statue in the middle of the square in the line of fire behind them. He heard the car door slam again behind them, and then the noise of the car accelerating, then stopping, then accelerating again. The streets here were full of dead ends. Their pursuers had to figure out the detours to get to them.

Lee stopped. He bent down and gestured for Megan to climb on his back. She jumped on without hesitation. He stood, grabbed the backs of her knees to hold her on as she hooked her arms around his neck. Lee took off at a jog behind Novak and they continued toward the river.

What had he gotten himself into? What was he doing running in the dark while someone fired shots at him? But Lee knew the shots and the bullets were real. He could worry about how he'd gotten here later. Right now he had to figure out how to keep himself and the girl on his back alive.

Lee focused on keeping his footing, finding a pace he could maintain and keeping his breathing deep and steady. He could see a small golden dome ahead of them. He knew it was a building on the river not far ahead. A landmark of some type.

But behind them he also heard footsteps running after them. They were distant. Maybe two blocks away. But they would close quickly. Already he was tiring from carrying Megan.

They came out finally on the street above the river front. There was no one around. The rains had driven everyone inside. A ramp in front of them led down to the river. As they hurried down, Lee watched his step even more carefully. The roadway was lined with round cobblestones worn smooth and made even more treacherous by the rain.

When they came out on the river walk itself, Lee saw that it was deserted as well. But he also spotted in the promenade a sandy area, an oversized sand box for kids to play in. In the middle sat a small tug boat maybe 12 feet long and painted red, white and blue.

"Quick...the boat," said Lee panting hard. He dropped Megan onto the asphalt of the street and motioned for the two of them to go to the boat.

"Hide," said the reporter, pausing a moment longer to catch his breath.

He saw Megan and Novak reach the boat and dive inside. Perfect. He couldn't see them at all. He continued up the promenade, staying on the single-lane roadway. He heard footsteps again behind him. The men had reached the river front.

Lee made no effort to run quietly. He let his feet slap the pavement, leading his pursuers away from Megan and Novak. He heard them following along the river front. Then he cut right through one of the gaps in the warehouse row. When he got to the back of the buildings, he turned left and moved down a tunnel-like corridor that ran behind them.

It was very dark. Even if they heard his footsteps they wouldn't be able to see him or know that Walter and Megan were no longer with him. He was settling into a steady rhythm now, his running regimen paying off. Unless one of his pursuers was a dedicated runner, they wouldn't be able to keep up with him for long. But he knew he had the cars to worry about as well. They could be out there, waiting for him to get back to the street level. Maybe they were communicating with the people running behind him and knew exactly where he was.

He must have run the equivalent of three long blocks along the back of the buildings. He worried now about reaching the end of the corridor. He didn't want to hit a dead end and be trapped. When he reached another gap in the tunnel-like pathway and saw a staircase to his right, he didn't hesitate. He would get back to the street level and take his chances there.

He ran up a ramp and then up the 15 steps to the street. The uphill stretch slowed him but he kept moving at a jog, away from the river now. He crossed one street, ran down the next block and came to another street.

Suddenly, a car pulled up in front of him, coming from his right and going the wrong way in the divided roadway. It braked in front of him with a loud screech, forcing him to pull up before he slammed into it. The driver's window was down right in front of him. Lee thought about trying to dodge around the car. But something about the driver made him pause. He was balding and had his elbow resting on the opened window. And he was smiling. Then Lee noticed the heavy bar of lights – all darkened – running across the vehicle's roof. A cop car.

"Mister Lee, I presume," said Chief Cliff Davidson in his slow drawl, looking out from the car's window and behind Lee to see if anyone was coming. He flicked a switch on his dashboard and intense blue lights atop the car suddenly filled the darkness. They were painfully bright, flashing in a quick staccato rhythm that was visible blocks away.

Chapter 37

THE BRIEF PHONE call Chief Davidson had received from Lee around noon earlier in the day had been more than enough incentive to launch him on the eight-hour drive from Bayou La Batre to Savannah.

Megan Kim was fine, Lee had assured the police chief. He was staying with her and Novak next to one of the squares in the central core of Savannah. Davidson knew the city. His boyhood friend was a deputy chief on the city police force. He was confident he would find Megan, bring her home and reunite her with her mother.

The chief had been dozing in his car a few blocks from Chippewa Square, waiting for the morning, when he heard the unmistakable sound of gunshots. Then he saw cars burning rubber as they headed toward the river front. The lone figure he saw jogging away from the river fit the quick description of Lee that Det. Bobbie Connors had given him a couple of days earlier.

Chief Davidson was determined to take Megan back to Bayou le Batre and he convinced Lee and Novak that he could keep them all safe together in his patrol car.

He must have called in every chit he had acquired in his long career in law enforcement in order to have two Georgia State Patrol cars escort the four of them along the 140-mile run down the Georgia coast through thick pine forests and across the many coastal streams on the way to Jacksonville. Then the Florida Highway Patrol took over for the 350 miles across the Florida panhandle. Outside of Pensacola two cars from Davidson's own force picked them up for the last hour.

146

With Megan in the car, Lee had only given Davidson a partial explanation during their long drive of why Novak had tracked down Megan at her school more than a week earlier and why they had been running for their lives through the streets of Savannah in the early morning hours.

"There'll be time for all that later," the police chief said. "I know how a bullet sounds when it comes out of a gun. Occupational necessity, you might say. You're on someone's hit list. That's enough for now."

They came in from the southeast – the "scenic route," according to Davidson – following the roads close to Mobile Bay until they hit Shell Belt Road leading them into Bayou La Batre. The remnants of piers ruined by Katrina – pairs of pilings jutting through the ocean water 70 yards out into the bay – ran off to their left. The houses on the right were either perched high atop stacks of concrete blocks 10 feet high, or had been washed away entirely by the hurricane, leaving only traces of their foundations.

As they drove up along the river mouth that cut northward through the town, Lee saw the tops of the shrimpers and fishing boats tied up together with their long outrigger booms pointing skyward.

"Got most of 'em back in the water finally," said Davidson, nodding toward the boats. "Should have seen 'em right after the storm. Like the water drained out of the bathtub and left 'em wherever...maybe in your backyard."

He drove them over the trestle-style bridge in the center of town and a half mile north up Wintzell Avenue to the 22-unit Gulf Coast Inn. The town's only hotel was small enough to guard with a patrol car on each side, explained Davidson. There were plenty of open rooms to accommodate Novak, Lee, Megan and Megan's mother who met them at the hotel. Lee wondered if Mary Kim would ever let Megan out of her grasp again after their tearful reunion.

147

"Unless those boys send a tank after y'all, you should be safe here," said the police chief. Davidson left them in the hands of his deputies, one of whom took everyone's dinner order up to a Wendy's by the interstate.

"Right now, I got a hot date with a king-sized bed," he told Lee and Novak in the hotel parking lot, promising to meet them for breakfast the next morning.

The first thing Enzo Lee did after he took a shower and put on clean clothes was call Lorraine Carr in New York.

"Bayou where?" she asked.

"La Batre," said Lee. "It's on the Gulf of Mexico. It's the land of shrimp and crab. And, oysters, too, I guess, judging from the piles of shells I saw on the way here. Mountains of them."

"Sounds yummy," Carr said. "And why are you there? Are you okay? You sound exhausted. I can hear it in your voice."

"Yeah," said Lee. "It's been a long couple of days. And it's a long amazing story. But first I wanted to ask you something."

"Fire away," said Carr.

"Who do you know at the National Institutes of Health?"

Chapter 38

LORRAINE CARR WAS waiting just outside the jet way from his New Orleans flight, having arrived at Dulles an hour earlier. She was standing next to her rolling bag, arms crossed, toe tapping in feigned impatience with a smile breaking through a cool half pout. She was a shade under 5-foot-three with the carriage of a former ballet dancer and medium length black hair that framed her pretty heart-shaped face.

Their kiss and embrace was sweet and long, so long that when they came up for air, Lee had a question in his eye. Something had changed. But she gave up nothing. And they both knew they were pressed for time to get to the taxi line and make it to the Maryland suburbs outside Washington in time for their late afternoon appointment.

The National Institutes of Health office was in a hospital complex in Bethesda in an eight-story building with a cavernous lobby. They waited along with another half dozen visitors scattered among the orange and chrome sofas and armchairs.

Dr. Bernard Winthrop was in his late 40s, lanky and had a droopy mustache beneath his wire-rim glasses. Winthrop was the special assistant to the NIH deputy for cancer research. He sat in an end chair while Lee and Carr occupied the sofa in his office.

"Walter Novak," said Winthrop pensively. "Of course I had heard of him. But it seems as if his name is everywhere the past two weeks or so. I must have had a half dozen people I know mention him...and not favorably."

"What exactly are they saying?" asked Carr.

"He's lost it. Gone off the deep end," said Winthrop. "Unstable. A breakdown."

"I know he's had some problems," said Lee. "And he's spent time at a psychiatric facility. But I've spent the past four days with him. He's seemed pretty normal to me the whole time. And he prepared the file I sent you."

"Right," said Winthrop. "And *that* was interesting. Quite interesting. It's just that...ah...well...this whole situation is bizarre. Even the one case he's pointing to...totally outside normal protocols. I mean anyone in this building who did what he did – an unauthorized human trial – they'd be run out on a rail."

"But if there was something of value there...something to advance cancer research, you'd want to know what it is, right?" said Lee.

"Of course," said Winthrop. "But you have to understand there are scores of people out there clamoring for our attention. They have the support of their companies...legitimate studies...no controversy."

The three of them sat silently for a moment. Carr had set up the meeting. One of her sources had given her Winthrop's name. Her clout as a Journal reporter had gotten them the appointment on short notice. Lee gave her an almost imperceptible nod.

"I think we understand that NIH may need to have some...um...distance from Novak at this stage," said Carr. "But is there someone out there, perhaps a private party, who could take an initial look? Someone whose work you trust? And what would the first steps be for them?"

"Well, the obvious first step would be the one case...the girl," said Winthrop. "Someone would need to confirm the background, the pretreatment data from Tulane or wherever. And then they'd want to do a complete diagnostic battery. PET scan. Blood work. Lymph node biopsy. Marrow sample.

150

Everything. If she's acquired the resistance Novak claims, the story should be there as well. Certain proteins would be off the charts. We'd do assays. Eventually, you'd try to isolate the antibodies and test them against a battery of tumor samples."

"And who can do this?" asked Carr.

"I can think of a half dozen people at the top of the list with the lab facilities and lots of expertise," said Winthrop, staring off into space. "Folks I trust to do it right. Here. Boston. Durham. San Francisco."

He refocused on Lee and Carr sitting on the sofa.

"Listen," he said. "I can only go so far as to tell them...informally...that this is something that may be worthwhile. That will pique their interest. Whether they have the time...and funding...to do this, I can't say."

"I think there may be a way we can help cover that cost," said Lee, thinking of the millions that Novak had casually mentioned receiving when he sold his company to Merrick & Merrick.

"And perhaps San Francisco is the way to go, if there is someone there who is willing to do this," said Carr. "I'll check back with you for names after you've had a chance to contact them?"

Winthrop nodded and made a note on a legal pad in front of him.

When the elevator doors closed on their way back to the lobby, Lee encircled Carr with his arm and pulled her hard against him. Her return hug was almost fierce as she pressed herself against him.

"Hmmm," he said. "You were great."

"Just one of the services I provide," she said, pushing herself back and slyly, batting her eyelashes at him before laughing. "And, actually, this could turn out to be a hell of a story."

"Yeah," said Lee. "And now I have to figure out how to start leaking it."

"After what we just told Winthrop?" said Carr.

"Right," said Lee, ruefully. "I'm sorry about that. But I've got a kid to save."

* * *

"So, what's up?" said Lee.

He was standing behind Carr in their hotel room at the Intercontinental. They had finished a quick dinner in the hotel restaurant 20 minutes earlier. Her coat was off and she looked cool and crisp in her white blouse as if it was early in the morning instead of at the end of the busy day. He put his hands on her hips and pulled her back against him, resting his chin on the top of her head. They watched each other in the mirror.

Carr grabbed his hands and pulled them across her front so they rested along her ribcage with her hands on top of his. She leaned her head back harder against his chest and sighed loudly.

"It's another guy, right?" he said.

She nodded once.

"Yes, dammit," she said. "He's asked me out...I don't know how many times. I lost count. But I'm going to say, 'Yes.'"

'Well, I guess it was a matter of time," said Lee. "I'm sure all the single men at the Journal perked up when you walked in. One was bound to break through eventually. Like the egg and the sperm, huh?"

She turned in his arms and pushed him back a bit.

"You," she said it without anger but in admonishment, as if she still was his supervising editor at the San Francisco News. She held his forearms and shook them as she spoke.

"You know I would have stayed in San Francisco if you had asked me," Carr said. "Or even acted as if you wanted me there instead of ushering me out the door."

Lee nodded his head.

He could have said that he desperately wanted that as well but thought about the opportunity she would have to give up.

And there were all the future opportunities open to her as well by being on the East Coast and having a great job at a top national publication. In the current state of the profession, it meant the difference between having choices and perhaps not working at all.

And he could have added that the responsibility scared him. What could he and should he provide in return? What if things didn't work out for them? What would happen after the first blowout argument when one of them stalked out in anger? Sometimes he felt that he was just hanging onto his job and current life by his fingernails. Could he still hang on if anyone else's life was tied to his?

"I'm a big girl," said Carr, as if reading his mind. "I can take care of myself. I can make decisions for myself. I can carry my own weight and balance career against personal choices. And I think a lot of life is about taking chances at the right times and for the right reasons. And not being afraid to do that."

Lee looked at his feet and nodded.

"I'm sorry," he mumbled. "I guess I am who I am."

Carr sighed in exasperation. She leaned into him until the top of her head rested on his chest. She beat her head against him several times as if she were ramming her head against a wall. She started gently but hit harder each time. He had to restrain her finally before she hurt one of them.

"Men," she whispered after she stopped.

"Look," said Lee. "I can get another room if you want."

She stared at him for a moment.

"Don't be stupid," she said. She turned and walked toward the bathroom. "I'll be out in a minute."

She came out ten minutes later wearing only her panties and Lee watched her from the bed walk over to the dresser, take off her earrings and lay them down. He admired her from the back - the strong compact body of a former dancer turned bicycling enthusiast, athletic but with the curves that triggered a testosterone surge just by thinking about her.

"What?" she said when she turned around and saw his stare. She gestured down at herself. "You've seen all this before."

"God, you're beautiful," he said. "It's been so long I'd almost forgotten."

Carr smiled at him as she flung back the sheet and bedspread. He was wearing his boxers. She climbed into bed and kissed him as she pressed her body hard against his. She rubbed her breasts against his chest and slid her hand down his stomach and inside the boxers.

"Mmmm," she said. "God, I've missed this."

Chapter 39

MEGAN SWAM ALONG the bottom of the hotel pool, picking up the smooth black rocks that her best friend Lucy Quan had tossed in for her. When she surfaced, she held them triumphantly in both hands.

"Got 'em!" she said, water streaming down her arms and face. Holding on to the side a few yards away in the deeper water, Lucy jumped outward and had time to clap her hands twice in appreciation before sinking beneath the surface.

On the steps, Megan's two-year-old cousin sat and splashed the water while he shrieked. He was stark naked. Megan's mother sat beside him on the edge of the pool. She wore shorts, a button-up shirt and floppy hat. She dangled her feet in the water as her eyes tracked Megan.

Enzo Lee and Walter Novak sat at a black metal patio table that stood in the shade of the hotel at the other end of the pool. They saw Chief Cliff Davidson open the gate to the pool area and let it clang shut behind him. He grinned and nodded at the kids in the water as he skirted the pool and made his way to Lee and Novak. He set a shopping bag on the table as he relaxed into one of the patio chairs.

"Homework," the police chief said in explanation. "Her teacher's not too worried about Megan missing class. Says she's one of her brightest kids. But doesn't want her to fall too far behind."

Lee nodded his understanding.

"I wish I could come out there with y'all," said Davidson. "Never been to San Francisco. Course I'd mainly like to know those sons of bitches aren't messing with you."

"Well, between Bobbie Connors and Walter writing some checks for some off-duty help, I think we should be okay," said Lee.

"Happy to do it," said Novak. "I'd return all the money if I could stop what's happening."

Lee shrugged.

"Add it to the long list of things we can't undo," he said.

As Lee watched the kids playing in the pool, he thought about how much he was looking forward to getting back to San Francisco. It was his home turf. He felt more in control there. Plus, he needed to get back to his grandmother. He'd decided he would get her Novak's Roxaten somehow...even if he had to learn how to give her an injection himself. He'd become a believer in the few days he'd spent with Novak. Besides, she didn't have many good options at this stage. It felt like her only hope and he didn't want any more delays.

"You mind telling me again what exactly your theory is now," said Davidson, interrupting Lee's thoughts. "How does this stop those bastards from trying to kill Megan...and maybe the rest of you for that matter?"

The police chief was watching Lee carefully, his eyebrows arched in query. It was a good question. Lee wished he had a better roadmap carefully connecting all the dots. He didn't.

"It's pretty obvious that someone or some group is trying to bury Roxaten," said Lee. "They want to suppress it...keep it off the market. Maybe we can make some guesses about who it might be. But we don't have the resources to find out, and certainly we couldn't prove it."

"If we can get the story out...let Roxaten have its day," he continued. "Whether it's a miracle or a bust. Whatever. Just get it out in the open and let scientists debate it. Let real trials and experiments determine what happens. As long as it stays in the shadows, these goons with guns have leverage.

"The bigger the story," said Lee. "The more everyone knows about Roxaten and Megan, the safer she'll be. The scrutiny...the outrage. All the stakes will be higher if we can just get this public in a big way. And suppose we get the trials going again. If we can get a hundred patients – or even a thousand – in a Roxaten trial – then she'll truly be safe. They all will be potential Megans."

An hour later, Davidson had left them to tend to his police chief responsibilities. Lee and Novak still sat at the patio table, half watching the kids who were winding down their pool activities. Megan and Lucy drifted together on two air mattresses pointing out the various cloud shapes above them. Rabbit ears here. An ice cream cone there. A small order of French fries on the right. Come to think of it, they were more than ready for lunch.

Lee had his laptop opened. The medical reporter at the News had given him the name of an editor at the prestigious American Review of Medicine. Lee had just sent an email that introduced himself to the editor and asked for a phone call later in the day. Novak was jotting notes on a pad in front of him. From what Lee could see, it was all numbers and rough diagrams. Circles. Lines. Arrows. Boxes.

"Walter," said Lee. "There's something I need to talk to you about. The whole idea of getting publicity about this...about Roxaten. I want to start it now. It could take weeks for the results to filter back to NIH and for anything to happen. That's too long. Too long to keep Megan – and maybe all of us – safe. We need to speed everything up. Get things going at double-time...triple-time speed. Take the offense."

Novak nodded his agreement.

"It has an effect on you," added Lee. "I've been in this business for a long time. I have a pretty good idea of what makes a story...what gets an editor excited."

"Okay," said Novak. "And what is that?"

"Well, the testing itself isn't enough," said the reporter. "There are thousands of drugs being tested every year. Another one doesn't stand out. Maybe the results will eventually...but that could be months in the future."

"I understand," said Novak.

"But what will sell the story is you," said Lee. "The 'brilliant but...ah...controversial scientist.' The same facts that probably made you worry if you and Roxaten would get a fair hearing, will sell the story."

Lee put his hands in front of him, thumbs and forefingers creating brackets in the air.

"Let's be honest," he said. "The headlines will read something like this: 'Novak Goes Rogue With Roxaten. Cancer Cure or Fraud?'"

"A little over simplified, don't you think?" said Novak.

"Sure," said Lee. "The hallmark of journalism. The point is that we've got serious people – scientists – taking a look at this now who don't have a vested interested in the outcome. A lot of that is because the Journal is involved. It's out on stage now. So, let's light a fire under it. Force it onto the fast track. We want reporters calling the researchers and NIH every day. If the results are exciting, let's get it on the evening news."

"Okay," said Novak. "If you think that's the way to go, I won't argue."

"I won't lie to you," said Lee. "If we go this route, there will be people out there who will want to crush you. Some may have good intentions. Others will just make you a distraction. Either way, they'll be on you like a ton of bricks."

Novak exhaled slowly. He sank back into his chair as if already shouldering half of those bricks.

"If this is what it takes, then there's really no choice," he said.

* * *

The sun had been down for almost an hour when Mary Kim returned to the hotel. They were leaving for the New Orleans airport early the next morning for the flight to San Francisco. The researchers at the University of San Francisco Medical Center wanted Megan available for at least a week of tests. They had arranged for her to stay at their hospital where all the test and diagnostic equipment was close at hand. The schedule gave them time to duplicate any procedures in case they encountered problems along the way.

Mary Kim had agreed to the trip only grudgingly. She didn't understand why Megan needed to have more tests when her cancer was gone. Lee and Novak...with Megan's help...finally convinced her. She decided to stay behind. She said she couldn't get so many days away from her job. But Lee sensed that perhaps she was intimidated by the idea of traveling to a strange big city and being surrounded the entire time by doctors and scientists.

Chief Davidson also had shared his belief that Mary was torn between her concern for Megan and her own immigration fears. As a reporter in a city full of new immigrants, Lee understood the special fear carried by anyone with unsettled status or who had fudged the truth to get here. The public spotlight was exactly what they wanted to avoid.

This evening, Mary Kim had brought with her to the hotel a Winn Dixie grocery bag that held combs, beautician scissors and a white cotton cape. She sat Megan on one of the patio chairs, fastened the cape around her neck and trimmed her hair. The pair kept up a quiet murmur of conversation during the entire haircut. It was a warm evening with a light breeze coming off the gulf that carried the smell of the ocean. It felt like summer couldn't be far behind.

Lee was back at a table on the other side of the pool with his laptop opened. He was composing a detailed memo for the editor at the medical review. It covered the basics – the promise of Roxaten, Novak's treatment of Megan using the drug and the ongoing review commenced with the helpful nudge from the NIH. Lee assumed the editor would use his own contacts to confirm the key elements and fill in gaps.

When she was finished with Megan's hair, Mary took off the cape, shook it out and sent her daughter off to her room where Lucy was waiting for her to watch a video while they ate dinner. Mary Kim walked over to Lee and sat in the chair next to him.

"Her hair looks very nice," said Lee, looking up from his laptop and searching for something to say.

"Before...before Megan sick, her hair long. Like Lucy," said Mary Kim. "I ask. 'Why keep it short now?' She say it easier if she need to cut it again. Be bald. Not mind so much."

She was quiet for a moment but was looking intently into Lee's face.

"You take care her. You take care of Megan," Mary Kim said.

"I will do everything I can to make sure she is safe," said Lee. "To get her back to you."

"No," said Mary. She held the edge of the table and Lee could see her grip was so tight that the muscles in her forearms stood out. "You take care her. You promise. You promise."

Lee could see tears in her eyes. She gritted her teeth. She stared intently at Lee. He realized that she was a mother whose only child had nearly died a little more than a year ago. And now her daughter was under attack again by forces that must seem just as mysterious as the disease that had attacked Megan from within. Of course Mary Kim was desperate.

Lee slowly lowered the screen of the laptop in front of him until it latched with a click.

"Okay," he finally agreed. "I promise you. I'll get Megan back to you. Safe."

Chapter 40

CHIEF DAVIDSON DROVE them to the New Orleans airport with two deputies escorting them in a second car. They had stayed with them until Novak, Lee and Megan boarded the non-stop flight to San Francisco.

Det. Bobbie Connors was waiting for them at the end of the flight with two uniformed cops in tow.

Enzo Lee gave Connors a hug when he saw her just inside the terminal. He handed her the key lime pie packed in a cardboard box tied with twine that Davidson had entrusted to him.

"From Cliff Davidson," he told the detective. "He said to tell you, 'Greetings from New Orleans...and thanks.'"

Connors gave him a small smile. She wore a dark brown pants suit, a silver chain around her neck with a cross and the ever present profusion of braids.

"And I've got something for you," she said. Connors handed him a single sheet of paper. Lee let the others go past him and followed behind with Connors. As he walked he read the printout. He saw it was a story from the Ann Arbor News in Michigan. The story had appeared a week earlier.

Retired Teacher's Death Appears Accidental

ANN ARBOR — Preliminary autopsy results indicate a woman whose body was found in her bathtub died of accidental drowning.

Ann Arbor Police Lt. Lawrence Pellam said 63-year-old Nancy Johannsen of Ann Arbor probably slipped in the bathtub, hit her head and was knocked unconscious.

Pellam said Thursday that bruises on the body are consistent with a fall. Drowning was the cause of death. Her death is not considered suspicious.

Johannsen worked as a school teacher for the Ann Arbor School District for 36 years prior to her retirement three years ago. Johannsen's body was found Tuesday night by her niece.

Lee looked at Connors. He had given the detective the name of Megan's bone marrow donor to whom Novak had given the Roxaten-based vaccine in the hope that a strong resistance would be transferred to the sick girl along with the marrow transplant. Lee had left several unreturned messages for the retired teacher using a telephone number Novak had given him.

Connors gave him a shrug conveying the same sense of helplessness he felt.

"I've asked them to take another look," said Connors. "And I've arranged for the guard you wanted outside Megan's room...around the clock. Your friend pays the off-duty bill, right? Looks like a good call."

Lee folded the paper and put it in his back pocket. He would tell Novak about it later when Megan wasn't around. He looked warily around him at the bustling crowd in the airport terminal. They were surely safe with Connors and two uniformed cops as escorts. And it was unlikely anyone with a weapon could have gotten into the secure part of the terminal. Still, he recalled that night in Savannah, being chased in the darkness with the noise of the guns being fired at them. He had felt their pursuers' determination when they shattered the door of the flat. They would have been caught there – trapped and killed – but for the luck that Lee was jet-lagged and awake when they came.

Now they would be desperate to get to Megan.

* * *

Troy Axmann sat in his office with a view of downtown San Francisco. He was busy preparing his presentation for the next month's international sales meeting in Hawaii. The banana splits had been so successful with the MBA interns that he planned to use the same trick with the 200 or so salesmen to whom he would proclaim the benefits of Morceptin. It would be preaching to the choir. Sales of the drug were climbing steadily and the skies ahead looked clear and trouble-free.

Then his laptop made a loud ping. His assistant had just sent him an instant message with the highest priority setting. All it said was, "Look." It was accompanied by a link that the Merrick vice president quickly clicked open.

A webpage from the American Review of Medicine appeared on his computer screen with an online article bearing the current date.

Scientist and His 'Cure' Face Scrutiny

By Jason Rosenthal
An experimental drug administered to a patient in clear violation of rules governing human medical trials has attracted the interest of cancer experts and the National Institutes of Health.

Roxaten, a drug developed by Medvak Technology and its founder Walter Novak, gave early indications that it might be a powerful anti-cancer medicine useful against an array of cancer types. Animal tests also suggested it could form the basis of a general cancer vaccine, according to sources.

But recent human trials of the drug by industry giant Merrick & Merrick, which acquired Medvak early last year, were suspended due to unexpected side effects. At the same time, Novak came under scrutiny for administering the drug to a young cancer patient prior to approval of the human trials, say Merrick insiders. Such unauthorized use of the drug would breach many ethical and legal rules and possibly violate criminal laws governing the improper practice of medicine.

Researchers are reportedly intrigued by the drug's effectiveness as an anti-cancer medicine and are examining whether the limited use of the drug so far, while improper, may also provide evidence of Roxaten's potential. The inquiry will include tests on the patient, now 10, who received the medication and survived a particularly aggressive and usually fatal form of leukemia.

Sources say key NIH officials have requested regular updates on the ongoing research into the drug which is being conducted at the University of San Francisco Medical Center.

Troy Axmann sat perfectly still. His phone rang but he let it go to voicemail. He stared out his window which had a view of the neighboring small office buildings, a small park in the middle crisscrossed by paths and pedestrians scurrying across on their way to lunch. He suddenly wished he was out there with them. He would walk and walk and avoid the maelstrom that he knew was coming.

Chapter 41

EDWIN MERRICK REREAD the medical review article for the second time, using his ball-point pen to underline one particular sentence: "*Such unauthorized use of the drug would breach many ethical and legal rules and possibly violate criminal laws governing the improper practice of medicine.*"

He picked up the phone and dialed Troy Axmann's extension. The Merrick vice president's only contribution to the conversation were his two words uttered upon picking up the phone: "Troy here."

"Call our attorneys," ordered the CEO. "Have them terminate Novak. Tell them to figure out every possible way to go after him. Go over his published work for the past five years. Ask every publication to review his work for possible fraud and scientific misconduct. Call the Louisiana state police and tell them we think one of our *former* employees may have deliberately injured a child in their state and misrepresented himself as a physician.

"Get public relations started on a press release covering all this. I want to see it in the next hour. Tell them not to pull any punches. I'm going to pound this son of a bitch into the goddamn ground."

* * *

Jason Rosenthal was exhausted and worried. His mood had shifted in less than 24 hours from exhilaration to dread.

The article about controversial scientist Walter Novak and his possible miracle drug, Roxaten, had seemed like the highlight of his six years at the American Review of Medicine.

His usual job was ushering into print articles written by others – usually scientists studying the effectiveness of some new drug or medical device. He would find other experts to review the articles to ensure the research was good and significant. At most, he might offer a minor edit or two.

But the Roxaten story was legitimate news. And he could put his byline on it for once. He'd even fantasized about the follow-ups. If Roxaten proved to be truly important, he could ride the wave of a big story. It would give him bragging rights at his next journalism grad school reunion – finally some ammunition to use against the hotshots who had gone on to the big newspapers. He had fought hard to get the Roxaten story into print.

But now the suits were huddled together in the main conference room. Two were his bosses. The other two were lawyers and they were doing the good-cop, bad-cop thing.

Rosenthal had been in the room for the first 20 minutes.

The bad-cop lawyer had spit out the allegations like bullets from a revolver.

Why was the publication jumping the gun and speculating about a drug still in early clinical trials? Why was the review using Merrick & Merrick's internal private information? Why was it exposing its trade secrets? How could they give credence to a scientist who had violated basic ethical guidelines and possibly even criminal laws? Why should this go outside the normal FDA process where it was now?

Rosenthal had watched his bosses shrivel under the assault. He knew they saw that much of this was just a smokescreen. But he also knew that the mere mention of a lawsuit – the "L" word – would ruin their day. Just making the most bullshit legal filing go away would take – what? – a week of lawyer time? Forty hours at $400 an hour...$16,000? Christ. That was a quarter of his annual salary. It was enough to put the review into the red for the quarter. And Rosenthal knew that

Merrick & Merrick could easily keep a lawsuit going long enough to put the publication out of business. It would be like flicking a beetle off the sleeve of the drug giant.

They sent Rosenthal out of the room before the groveling began. But he could read the body language from his desk. And when his bosses did look out the big window separating the conference room from the office area where Rosenthal sat, he saw their anger. He was the reason they had to sit there being raked over the coals by those jerks. The lawyers were no smarter than the editors. They had just opted for big-time lawyer money and the clout provided by clients like Merrick & Merrick. It made it that much worse – being punching bags for those pricks.

How bad would it be? Rosenthal doubted he'd be fired. He was cheap and worked hard. And, after all, he hadn't really done anything wrong. But they would be pissed at him all the same. And as far as the follow-ups? Forget it. It would be a mistake to do anything that would dredge up the memory of what was going down in the conference room.

Rosenthal stared at his computer screen. The email had been waiting for him when he got back to his desk from the conference room. It was anonymous. The sender described an illicit meeting in Macau of Big Pharma executives involving price fixing, bribery of government regulators and suppressing Roxaten. Rosenthal felt sick. He stared at the words until they blurred in and out of focus.

He glanced up at the conference room. Everyone was standing. They would walk out in a couple of minutes. Rosenthal hit 'reply,' typed "try Enzo Lee at the San Francisco News" and clicked on the 'send' button. His relief was instantaneous. He inhaled deeply. Had he actually been holding his breath? Rosenthal grabbed his jacket off the back of his chair and headed out the door. He wanted to avoid his bosses for at least another hour or two.

He decided on his way down in the elevator that he would treat himself to a fabulous lunch. He would start off with a very cold vodka gimlet.

* * *

The first television van arrived while Novak and Lee were inside the scientist's two-story Edwardian in Lower Pacific Heights. After getting Megan settled into her room at the San Francisco medical center, they went to pick up extra clothes for Novak who had agreed to stay in Lee's North Beach flat. Between his sudden notoriety and the possibility that Megan's pursuers had targeted him as well, it seemed the safer course for Novak to avoid staying in his home for a while.

Within 15 minutes, two more television crews and a couple of print journalists were assembled outside the house. Stuffing the clothes and a few other items into duffle bags, Lee and Novak made a dash for Lee's Spyder.

"No comment. No comment. No comment," said Lee as he pushed Novak ahead of him toward the car.

"Hey, Enzo," one of the television reporters that he knew yelled. "Enzo...hey."

"Sorry, Scott," said Lee. "Got to go."

As they drove away, Lee looked over at Novak. He was shaken.

"You okay?" he asked. Novak nodded his head.

"Yes...I guess," said Novak. "I didn't expect *this*. I mean what have I done to deserve this treatment? Do they think I'm a mass killer or something?"

Lee shrugged.

"They don't know what to think," he said. "Savior or sinner. I told you I know what plays in the media. They just know you're a story...however it plays out. Merrick & Merrick is just pouring gas on the fire."

Lee thought back to his own time in the media glare. That was when he was a reporter in New York. An investigative story about a supposedly corrupt detective backfired. His key source – also in law enforcement – had fabricated the evidence. Before it was over, the innocent target almost died in a suicide attempt. Lee became the poster child for bad journalism as his editors abandoned ship and shifted all the blame to him.

He survived the storm but it led him to move back to San Francisco and change his focus to light frothy features where the only controversy was how many puns he could squeeze into a sentence. But he recalled how hot the spotlight could be and how helpless it felt to be buried under a mountain of shame.

"This will all pass, Walter," he said. "You've done something that matters. Remember that. Otherwise, no one...including the Merrick's of the world...would give a damn."

Novak nodded his head in silence. Then he reached into his pants pocket and pulled out a small vial. It was clear with fluid inside and a white sticker on the outside that bore a handwritten label. Novak held it between his thumb and forefinger, rocking it slowly left and then right.

"We need to get this into a refrigerator," said Novak. "It's the last that I have. The rest of it...Roxaten...is locked up inside Merrick. If you decide to give it to her, it's the beginning of your grandmother's treatment."

"The beginning?" Lee said.

"Our tests show that leukemia patients need sustained exposure to Roxaten," said Novak. "At least for 15 days and preferably 20. Less than that and it isn't able to reach enough of the problem cells. Reservoirs of the cancer survive and it comes back...with a vengeance. So there may not be a good second chance."

"So how far does this get us?" asked Lee.

"The doses should be given every fifth day," said Novak. "There is enough here for the first two. So, after the first dose, the second is given five days later."

"Then what?" asked Lee.

"Then…you'll need more," said Novak. "Ten days after you begin."

Chapter 42

LEE SLOWED HIS step and tiptoed as he entered his grandmother's hospital room. If she was sleeping, he didn't want to wake her. It had been almost a week since his last visit – before he flew out to find Walter Novak and determine whether the scientist offered any alternatives to the cancer medications that were failing to halt the march of her illness. He prepared himself in case she appeared even weaker and more emaciated than he remembered.

He stopped just inside the door. He saw an old Chinese man sitting in the chair next to the hospital bed. His right hand rested on the bed. He spoke in a low voice to his grandmother, but her eyes were closed and she looked as if she was sleeping.

After a few seconds, Lee moved to his right and cleared his throat.

Master Chu turned slowly in his chair, saw Lee behind him and gave him a small nod.

Lee had known Chu for several years, ever since the elderly man had called him over during one of his early morning runs through Chinatown and had introduced him to tai chi, the martial art that focuses on slow controlled movements and balance. They had become friends and Lee had incorporated Chu's training into his weekly workout regimen. To Lee's surprise, Chu and his grandmother – both well into their 80s – had become fast friends after he introduced them and had married 18 months earlier.

Chu stood and moved to the foot of the bed next to Lee.

"She sleep," he murmured.

"How is she?" asked Lee. Chu shrugged.

"Same," he said. "Sleep a lot. Wake up for meals. Not eat much. I try to help her."

Lee nodded. He had witnessed the meals shared by the pair. Invariably, Chu ended up consuming most of the meal as he tried to encourage his wife to eat more herself by setting a good example. Lee concluded that Chu at least was benefitting from the steady flow of hospital food. Whenever he could, the reporter added some extra dishes he thought Chu would enjoy when he filled out forms for the next day's fare.

"What were you talking to her about?" asked Lee.

"Just telling stories," said Chu. "Old stories. Ones I remember...growing up. Maybe she know them, too. Old memories best."

Lee nodded his head. They both watched his grandmother as she slept, her breathing barely causing any movement in her tiny bent form.

He heard footsteps entering the room and turned to see Dr. Choy sweep in. Her lab coat was open and she wore a purple dress cinched in folds in the middle that displayed a hint of cleavage and an athlete's tanned legs from the lower thigh down.

She nodded at Lee, smiled at Chu and stepped to the head of the bed. She watched his grandmother for a moment and checked a few of the machines before turning back. On her way out, Choy beckoned Lee with her right forefinger and he followed.

"Wow. You've certainly been busy," she said, facing him in the hallway.

"I found Novak," he said. "And got the story of his drug, Roxaten."

"So I've read," said Choy. "It's created quite a stir. And not just in the exciting world of oncology. Although my colleagues are also quite appalled at what he's done."

Lee shrugged.

172

Since the media scrum outside of Novak's home, the circus had continued unabated. Merrick & Merrick had released a stream of damaging disclosures about Novak. The climax was a blistering press release announcing Novak's termination and accusing him of conducting medical experiments on unsuspecting children from poor families in the South. Bloggers eager to jump on any controversy were comparing him to Josef Mengele, the notorious Nazi physician who performed medical experiments on children at the concentration camps.

"Well," said Lee. "Novak is in the middle of a...of a..."

"Shit storm?" said Choy.

Lee laughed. Her precise Hong Kong accent made the vulgarity sound almost polite.

"Well, I guess that's one way to put it," he said. "And listen. I've spent a lot of time with Novak now. I know I'm not a doctor...or a scientist..."

"But you want to give Roxaten a try," Choy interrupted him.

"Yeah," he said, nodding.

"Because you're desperate," said Choy. "You want to save her. You think it's her only chance."

Lee just nodded his head silently.

"Five minutes," he finally said. "I'd just like five minutes alone with her."

Choy looked at him closely. He might have been a lab specimen she was closely studying.

What he wanted to say to Choy was: "Please, don't fight me on this. It's something I need to do for her. At least give her a chance."

But he didn't. Instead, he put his hands in the pockets of his windbreaker and remained silent, returning her stare. He'd decided to ignore any trouble this might create for him – giving his grandmother the unapproved Roxaten. He'd accept whatever happened. But he knew Choy, as a licensed doctor, could be severely punished. The medicine had even been withdrawn from trials. He would try to deflect any fallout away from her. But he didn't want to ask for her help. It would just make her more complicit. The less said, the better.

Finally, Choy turned and walked into the hospital room. She asked Master Chu to come out and join her in Choy's office so she could update him on his wife's status. After they left, Lee walked into the hospital room. He stood on his grandmother's left side next to the stand that held the bag of intravenous fluid that was slowly dripping through a long tube into a vein on the back of her hand.

Several years earlier – after his mother had died followed a few months later by his grandfather – Lee's grandmother had sent the message to him that she wanted to meet. He had been prepared to be angry at her for the decades of family exile that he and his mother had endured when, as a young woman, she had taken a non-Chinese husband in open defiance of her father.

Instead, Lee quickly realized that his grandmother had been caught between the stubborn, unbending wills of Lee's mother and grandfather. The family schism had hurt her as much as anyone. She showed him the scrapbooks she had kept of Lee's mother growing up – the achievements and milestones of childhood. She had hidden them from Lee's grandfather. And she had also secretly saved articles her relatives sent her of newspaper stories Lee had written earlier in his career.

He came to view her as a fellow survivor of a family war. And his grandmother became his silver lining – a new piece of family to help fill the huge void left with his mother's passing. He had treasured her ever since.

He pulled the vial of Roxaten out of his windbreaker pocket along with the hypodermic syringe that Novak had given him and showed him how to use. This was after the scientist had reviewed the medical files for Lee's grandmother and confirmed that her type of leukemia was one his research had identified as having the C Factor mutation that Roxaten would target.

Lee uncapped the syringe, inserted the needle into the vial and pulled back the plunger until the vial was half empty. He found the medical port of the IV bag and inserted the needle into the end of the short tube. He depressed the plunger steadily until the hypodermic was empty. He massaged the half-empty bag a few seconds to disperse the medicine. Then he capped the syringe and put it back into his pocket.

He stood watching his grandmother's slow breathing and the equally slow, steady dripping of the IV solution dropping from the bag into the clear tube that led to her hand.

After a few minutes, Lee heard Choy and Master Chu reenter the room. Chu resumed his position on the other side of the hospital bed.

Choy stood next to Lee. After a moment, she put her hand into his. He kept his eyes on his grandmother but smiled as he ran his thumb along the back of Choy's hand. They both listened to Chu murmur in the sing song cadence of Cantonese as he told another story from his youth. Lee watched his grandmother's face twitch into the barest trace of a smile.

In his head, an internal countdown began. Tomorrow would be Day One. He had 10 days to somehow get inside Merrick & Merrick and get more vials of Roxaten.

Chapter 43

ONCE EDWIN MERRICK made clear his ultimate goal of demolishing Walter Novak's standing in the scientific community, several of his prominent lawyer friends highly recommended local attorney Henry Roth and his law firm for the job.

After six years as a prosecutor, Roth had joined George Weiler's 12-lawyer law firm with the tacit understanding that the 60-year-old Weiler would retire within five years and leave Roth free to remake the litigation boutique in his own image.

Weiler had happily held up his end of the bargain, retiring to tend his money-losing vineyard outside of Healdsburg. Meanwhile, Roth doubled the size of the firm, changed the name to Weiler & Roth and gave it a cultural makeover. From gentlemanly and collegial, Roth sharpened the firm's edges and instilled in his troops a love of combat. Like him, most of the attorneys were thin and wore black.

Roth entered Edwin Merrick's office at 8 a.m. the day after the Review of Medicine's article had run. He wore an impeccable dark business suit, carried a sleek Italian leather briefcase and had his black hair slicked back. He was a lithe 6-footer who ran at least six half marathons every year, placing well in his age group. Merrick & Merrick's general counsel had already given Roth a thorough memo on Novak and Roxaten. Roth's firm had spent a busy day researching relevant law and finding every relevant piece of information available online as well. Troy Axmann was waiting along with the Merrick CEO.

"I've been a manager for more than 30 years," Merrick told Roth. "I believe that proper incentives are crucial to getting the results you want. The rest is talk.

"For example, I can tell you that our goal is to destroy Walter Novak professionally and personally. In three months, I want his name to have the same meaning in scientific circles as Charles Ponzi's does in the financial world. I want his sole aspiration in life to be never to hear the name 'Roxaten' again or set foot in a laboratory.

"But to really get the point across to you," continued Merrick. "I can tell you that I will pay your law firm a $250,000 bonus if Novak declares personal bankruptcy in the next 90 days. The same amount applies if he spends a month in jail or you send him back to a psychiatric facility. The trifecta is worth $1 million which I'll gladly pay."

Roth flashed a bemused smile.

"I believe I get the point," he said. "You don't really care about the ultimate outcome of these cases then."

"Correct," said Merrick. "It's irrelevant what a judge decides in a year or two. I want unrelenting pressure and public humiliation, whether it's through the courts, the media or even personal friends if he has any. Troy will coordinate our side – press releases, scientists' statements about the improper testing and whatnot. I want you both to squeeze this guy until his head pops."

The campaign against Walter Novak reached a fevered pitch the next day. It began with a morning press conference that Troy Axmann organized. It featured six luminaries in the biological sciences, including two Nobel laureates.

"This type of unauthorized experimentation conducted by Walter Novak is reprehensible," said the chairman of the West Texas State University biology department who was also on an annual retainer from a major drug company that paid him more than $100,000 each year. "It smacks of exploitation of minorities and poor refugees who don't understand the language or the law. Anyone involved is a disgrace to the scientific community."

Merrick & Merrick's employment-related lawsuit filed later in the day didn't stop at the more or less routine allegations that Novak was improperly using the company's trade secrets and intellectual property. The Weil Roth lawyers accused Novak of stealing computers, lab equipment and medicines that belonged to Merrick.

Henry Roth used his old law enforcements contacts to get the San Francisco County Sheriff to initiate a criminal investigation into the theft charges against Novak. He had one of the most conservative Superior Court judge in San Francisco rubberstamp a search warrant. The 5 p.m. news shows featured live video feeds of sheriff deputies carrying boxes of files and computers out of Novak's home. The two-story home with its gingerbread details was festooned in enough yellow crime-scene tape to qualify as public art.

A second lawsuit was filed in Delaware where Merrick & Merrick was incorporated. It asked the court to reverse the sale of Novak's Medvak company to the pharmaceutical giant on the grounds that Novak had failed to disclose problems with Roxaten, including harmful side effects and flaws in the drug's patents.

But the key to the Delaware lawsuit was the judge's agreement to immediately freeze all of Novak's assets so he couldn't move or hide any proceeds from the Medvak sale. Unless his own attorneys could reverse the initial order, the move would force Novak to live on the cash in his pockets and his credit cards, at least until those maxed out.

Chapter 44

WHEN MEGAN KIM woke up she felt like someone big and strong had punched her hard, first in the middle of her chest and then in her right hip. She walked gingerly when she got up to use the bathroom because her hip was so stiff. She was glad they had put her to sleep when they took samples of her bone marrow. What had they done to leave her feeling like this?

Before she returned to her bed, she stood in front of the mirror and lifted her gown. She saw six small band aids – a pair under her arms, two more on her stomach and the last two near her ribcage. Lymph nodes, they said. She wondered what they were and whether she had any left.

It was the end of her second day at the hospital and Megan had stopped counting the vials of her blood that had been taken. She wondered at what point she would feel the effects. What would happen then? Would she faint? She had been introduced to the gigantic machine with the circular tunnel that made such a huge racket all around her while she lay there, trying not to move and listening to the technician ask her every few minutes, "How are you?"

"Okay," she always replied. But, she wasn't.

She heard the sound of someone walking briskly and looked up as Dr. Choy entered her room.

"*Jóusàhn. Megan.* Hello, Megan. *Néih hóu ma?* How are you?" said Choy.

"*Hóu* Fine," said Megan. "*Hóu.*"

Choy sat down on the bed next to the girl.

"No you're not," she said. "What's wrong?"

Megan began crying. It surprised her as much as Choy. The doctor moved closer and hugged the girl until Megan rested her head on Choy's shoulder. She was sobbing and Choy rubbed her back. She could feel the muscles in Megan's small back tightening and then releasing as the sobs continued.

"It's pretty horrible, isn't it?" said Choy. "All the tests. Are you sore from the bone marrow biopsies?"

Megan nodded into her shoulder.

"And does this place...the hospital...bring back a lot of memories?" said Choy. "Maybe some bad ones, huh?" Megan nodded into her shoulder again – harder this time.

Megan wanted to add that she knew her fear was crazy. But she kept thinking about how hospitals were full of germs. It was true that everyone around her was sick. But she knew cancer wasn't like, say, the measles or the flu. Still, she couldn't escape the scary thought that the cancer might come back. There were reminders everywhere. And not having her mother here made it that much worse.

Choy had visited Megan for the first time the previous day. She was immediately charmed by the poised and capable 10-year-old. And Megan's humble background reminded Choy a lot of her own.

She remembered when she was a school girl roaming the busy streets of Hong Kong filled with the kinds of shops like the ones Choy's father had owned. He had started at the lowest rung of the tourist trade, selling fans, key chains, post cards and porcelain cats. From there, he moved up the product chain to leather luggage knockoffs and, finally...electronics. Along the way, Choy's father had scraped and saved to finance his brilliant daughter's education.

Had she met Megan when she was 10, thought Choy, they probably would have been great friends.

"Megan," said Choy. "My niece is a little older than you. She's 12. And she lives just a few miles from here. I bet she has time this afternoon to come and visit. She has a lot of magazines. And I'll tell her to bring her iPod. She's a bit crazy about music. Does that sound good?"

Megan pushed herself back, wiped away the worst of her tears with the palm of her hand. She nodded excitedly.

"Does she like to play cards?" she asked.

* * *

Wrinkles. That was why the tiny vial of clear fluid that he held in his hand had come into being.

It had arrived at John Average's home in an overnight FedEx package. The vial had no label. Its inspiration was curare, the South American poison that had been used for centuries by indigenous tribesmen who coated the tips of their arrows and blow darts with it.

Scientists had created this synthetic cousin of the paralyzing agent. Like curare, it worked by paralyzing the voluntary muscles. In animals – and people – a sufficient dosage of curare was lethal because it immobilized the muscles used for breathing. Victims simply suffocated although they could remain otherwise alert and conscious, their hearts never missing a beat until asphyxiation stilled them forever.

This highly concentrated derivative was 50 times more powerful. It had been developed by scientists searching for alternatives to botox, the cosmetic toxin which temporarily reduces wrinkles by paralyzing facial muscles with injections.

The amount he held in his hand – less than a teaspoon – could kill upward of a dozen people, he had been told. Also in the overnight package was an ingenuous delivery system based on a design conceived three decades earlier by a spy agency in the former Eastern Bloc. It looked like a nice piece of jewelry – a man's ring with small silver nuggets embedded in the setting. But a sharp, almost invisible point protruded less than a quarter inch from the middle of the ring setting. Pressed into someone's skin, it felt like the sting of a small ant – and would inject a lethal dose of the drug. A tiny bladder inside the ring held sufficient fluid for five mini-injections.

Within four seconds of receiving the tiny injection, Average had been told, a victim would be unable to speak, stand...or press a hospital call button to ask for help.

Average added the FedEx package to his overnight bag. Already in the bag were four sets of hospital scrubs in shades of blue and green and a white plastic clipboard. He zipped it up. Then he picked up the telephone and called the taxi service that would take him to the airport.

Chapter 45

SHERIFF JULES DUPONT from Orleans Parish in Louisiana was as big a horse trader as Edwin Merrick. As soon as he picked up Henry Roth's phone call, he knew he had something that the quick-talking San Francisco lawyer was desperate to get. He knew within two minutes exactly what it was. He also understood that Roth was just an intermediary. The key to any negotiation was getting the decision maker in the room – or at least on the phone.

"So," said the sheriff on the private phone call with the drug company CEO. "Ya'll want my help on something, huh?"

"I assume Mr. Roth has explained the situation," said Merrick. "This man – Walter Novak – has presumably practiced medicine without a license in your fair state. He also gave an experimental drug to a child while it still was waiting to be approved for human trials. Mr. Roth tells me that amounts to battery, potentially a criminal felony."

"I see," said Dupont. "So tell me. Exactly how is that little girl doin' today? She still sufferin' from what that man did to her. What's his name?"

"Novak," said Merrick.

"Right...Novak," said Dupont. "Got a history of messin' with children, does he?"

"Well...uh, no," said Merrick. "Look. The point is that technically he committed these...uh...crimes. And we'd like you to..."

"I see," interrupted the sheriff. "'*Technically*' he committed these crimes. And you jus' hopin' I see that justice is done in this case, huh? Doesn't matter that he maybe cured this girl and is causin' trouble for y'all?"

Merrick was silent for a moment.

"Sheriff," he finally said. "Changing the subject for a minute, what's going on with you down there? What matters are occupying your interest these days?"

"Funny you should ask," said Dupont. "Y'all know, of course, that sheriffs are elected here in Louisiana. Got a tough one comin' up. These liberal soft-on-crime types, you know. Hate 'em. Just as intolerant as the KKK in they own ways."

"I would hazard a guess that it is expensive running such a campaign there, as it is everywhere," said Merrick.

"You have no idea," said the sheriff.

"Well," said Merrick. "I've got some experience helping people run for office – all the way from national to the very local. I'm sure I've got some ideas that could help you with your election."

"How many?" said Dupont.

"What?"

"How many ideas exactly would you say you got?" said the sheriff.

"Ah...well...I'd say...um...25," said Merrick. "About 25 excellent ideas."

"Hmmm. Okay. That's good," said Dupont. "But could always use more. 'Bout 50 real good ideas would help us out a lot. Go a long way down here."

"I see," said Merrick. "Well, sheriff, let me get working on those right away. And, shall we continue our conversation afterward?"

"No need for you to be on the call," said Dupont. "I know you're busy. I can work with your lawyer. What's his name? Roth? I'm sure we can make some...ah...progress on the...um...charges and that extradition request. I mean if that's okay for y'all."

"Works for me, sheriff," said Merrick. "Works fine for me."

After he hung up, Merrick placed an internal call to Troy Axmann.

"Listen," he told Axmann. "Look up the campaign for this sheriff – Dupont – in New Orleans. Get the information for contributions. Account numbers. Give them to my secretary. She'll wire the funds. Get the transaction number from her.

"Then, compile a list of 50 people – members of the management team down to the director level," continued Merrick. "Include our subsidiaries and international offices if you need to. Draft a letter to Dupont's campaign that says the payment – it will be $50,000 – represents contributions of $1,000 each from those on the list.

"Right after those go out to Dupont's campaign, call Henry Roth. Tell him to call Sheriff Dupont again. And that if he isn't completely cooperative, let me know…immediately."

Three hours later, the Orleans Sheriff's Office issued a press release announcing that criminal charges had been filed against Walter Novak for practicing medicine without a license and committing battery against a child. The office was commencing extradition proceedings to have Novak arrested in California and transported to Louisiana.

The news came out just in time to be carried on the 5 o'clock news by every television station in Northern California.

* * *

The panic attacks were coming back. As Walter Novak lay in the second bedroom in Lee's flat long after midnight, he could scarcely breathe. His chest hurt and his skin tingled. His body was rigid under the sheet. He couldn't move. He imagined people staring at him. Just outside the building. Maybe outside of the room, on the other side of the door. He thought he could *hear* them. The whole world looking at him…watching…waiting to destroy him.

He thought back to the relaxation techniques he had been taught to use at the clinic in Arizona.

Start with the fingers. Move them up and down. Let them drum the mattress. Bury the wrists in the softness. Let the hands lay there sinking down. Then forearms, elbows, shoulders. Let them sink down as if weights were sitting on them to hold them deep in the bed.

Then he moved to his toes. Felt them flex, point toward the bottom of the bed. He pressed his heels down. Then he moved up his legs. He felt the weights on his legs pressing him down. Holding him in place.

On to the head – eyelids, nose, lips, cheeks, forehead. Everything relaxed, held down by gravity. He felt the back of his head...his back. Everything sinking deeper into the bed...every muscle. Relaxing. So relaxed. And so heavy.

It was working. His breathing slowed. He was pulling inside of himself and not thinking about the dangers and pressures outside of him. He felt heavy. Like a body on Jupiter with the extra gravity making him unable to do anything but lie immobile.

It was when he was in this state – deep, meditative and far within himself – she sometimes came to him. Twelve-years-old and, strangely, with blonde pigtails. It was as if she waited in that deep place until he came.

She lay in his arms quietly. He watched her while he rocked slowly. It was very peaceful. It was just as it had happened.

Finally, she opened her eyes. She looked deep into his. She was perfectly lucid.

"Don't worry," she said. "Don't worry."

And then she closed her eyes, turned her face against his chest and struggled through three or four breaths until, finally, she wasn't breathing anymore.

Chapter 46

JOHN AVERAGE HAD driven past the emergency room entrance at the USF Medical Center before parking three blocks away from the hospital on a quiet side street. Through the sliding glass doors in the fluorescent lighting of the lobby he had seen a young man pushing a wheelchair. He wore light blue scrubs. Average had the same shade of blue in the small pile of clothes behind him in the backseat. He pushed the driver's seat as far back as it would go and slid the scrubs over his jogging pants and light sweater.

He opened the small black plastic box that sat in the cup holder of the center console and carefully pulled out the ring studded with small silver nuggets. He slid it over the middle finger of his left hand. It caught the light from the bright Halogen street lamp 20 yards in front of his windshield. Average rolled his hand right and left. The light bounced off the rough silver and flashed in his eyes.

This would be his last job. It was dangerous. The stakes were high. But the payment – $250,000 – was high as well. It would give him a lot of options. He could buy into his brother's successful restaurant if he wanted. There were plenty of businesses he could buy that – with a little elbow grease and smart management – would generate a decent income for the rest of his life.

He walked into the main lobby of the hospital with his white clipboard in his hand. He went straight to the bank of elevators. He had been given a floor plan in advance. He knew exactly where he was heading. Fifth floor.

It was a little after 2 am. Dead time, he thought, chuckling silently at the inadvertent pun. Very dead time. He took a few deep breaths on the way up the elevator. When the doors opened on five, it would be time. Show time. Dead time. It would be time to act, not hesitate.

They opened now. He stepped out and looked down to his left. Far down the hall, he saw the cop. He sat in the chair looking outward in front of him. He was moving a little, sort of bobbing up and down.

Average walked toward him.

Average speed. One...two...three...four. One...two...three ...four.

He went by the nursing station without looking at anyone. He kept moving. When he was close to the cop, he saw he had earphones on – tiny ones. He was young, probably early 30s. He was Hispanic and looked fit. He was moving to the beat of whatever tune was playing on some music device, an iPod or something. Average couldn't see it.

When he got to the cop, Average bent down to him and gently touched his upper arm with his fist. He made sure the ring and its tiny needle went through the shirt and into his arm.

"Look out," he murmured to the cop. "Spider. Nasty looking."

"Ouch!" said the cop, jerking away. He put his hand over the spot where he had felt the pain. He rubbed it and looked at his arm. He twisted it a little to see if a spider was still on him. After reassuring himself nothing was there now, he looked up at Average. Then he started to topple off his chair.

"Ahh...ahh...ahh," he said. Average could see his jaw go slack. He set his clipboard on the floor and held the cop in place, pressing him back against the chair and the wall behind it. The cop's eyes fluttered and then closed. Average held the cop in place until there was no movement at all. When he backed away and let go of him, the cop stayed sitting in the chair.

Average walked another 15 feet to the door of the room the cop had been guarding.

* * *

Enzo Lee sat with his back toward the door. He was hidden by the larger of the two chairs he pulled together in the corner of Megan's hospital room. He sat in the larger chair facing the corner with his legs propped on the smaller one.

He had sent Novak home after dinner. The man was clearly exhausted, nearly falling asleep on his feet. Lee was worried about him. Three days of media attention was taking its toll. The scientist seemed more distracted than ever. Lee hoped he was getting a good night's sleep back at his flat.

Something alerted the reporter. Afterward, he wasn't sure what it was. Maybe it was the light footfall on the linoleum. Or perhaps the faint rustle of the scrubs, one leg brushing against the other.

When Lee looked behind him, he saw a figure of a man wearing hospital scrubs who stood over Megan who was sleeping in the hospital bed. She was facing away from the man. He was average height and weight. He was poised over Megan, as if unsure exactly what to do next?

"Hi," said Lee softly.

It was his reaction that told the reporter something was wrong. The intruder was surprised. He obviously hadn't expected anyone other than Megan to be in the room. But rather than return Lee's greeting or laugh at having the crap scared out him, he moved back a step and scanned the room quickly as if to ensure there were no other dangers. It took less than a second but Lee saw his fear very clearly in that instant. He was like a cornered animal. Then it was gone, replaced by a slight smile and the bored expression that a hospital worker might have in the early morning hours.

Lee pushed his chair back a few inches, stood up and moved around until he was on the same side of Megan. The man in scrubs moved to the machines at the head of the bed and off to the side. He bent over and started checking the wires and tubes. He fingered the gauges and control panels.

"What are you doing?" asked Lee, moving forward until he was between him and Megan.

"Just checking the machines," said the man. "Routine maintenance. Making sure everything is working."

After a few more seconds, he straightened up. He looked at Lee and then over his shoulder at Megan still asleep.

"I should adjust her blankets so she stays warm," he said, moving toward the head of the bed and to Lee's side where he could move between the reporter and the girl.

"I don't think so," said Lee. He stepped sideways half a step and rested his hip against the bed. He blocked the man with his arms crossed in front of him.

Chapter 47

IF THE GUY had come at him with two hands to push him out of the way, or even swung with a fist, Enzo Lee would have reacted differently. But John Average stepped back and then reached out his left hand at Lee's chest. It was as if he was wielding a knife. Nothing was there, though, except his closed fist with something on his middle knuckle that looked like a ring. But he held it in front of him as if it was a dagger.

Lee grabbed his left wrist and then the right when the guy brought his other arm up to push the reporter away. He held on and walked Average back a couple of steps and then shoved him backward toward the door. Lee was taller and heavier. The guy stumbled back and caught himself against the wall. Then he started moving toward Lee again.

"Stay away from her," the reporter said almost in a whisper as he lowered his shoulder and took the two steps to hit the man in scrubs in the midriff. He felt him start to buckle and he wrapped his arms around his knees and lifted up, determined to put him down on the floor hard this time. He'd had his chance to back off.

When they hit the floor, Lee heard the intruder's pained grunt and felt the fight leave him. But as he lay on top of the man, he felt a sharp prick in his back. He lifted his right arm, threw out his elbow and the pain was gone. Lee stood up over the man who was lying on his back halfway out the doorway into the hall now.

He was deciding what to do next when he felt himself sway. Lee grabbed the doorway with his right hand first, and then both hands as he slumped against it. He tried to move his legs to regain his balance, but they wouldn't obey him. He felt himself lean all the way against the doorway and start falling forward. It was all he could do to shift his weight sideways so he slid down to the floor rather than fall face first.

As he sprawled face down with his left cheek and nose mashed into the linoleum, Lee heard the intruder get to his feet and run down the hallway. Then he heard Megan screaming at the top of her lungs. And he realized that he was having serious trouble breathing. He fought hard to get more into his lungs. But all he could get was a sip of air. Then another. Then a third. Then one final small breath that felt like it would be his last.

* * *

John Average calmed his heart and breathing while he waited for the elevator to take him down to the lobby. He was extremely thankful no one was in the elevator and no one stopped it in the five floors down. When the doors opened, he would walk normally through the lobby, past the automatic doors and out to the street. He would be in his car and moving in four minutes, maybe less.

The elevator stopped. After a couple of seconds, the doors slid open with a perfunctory "ding." But instead of an abandoned lobby, a security guard stood in front of him. He was hugely overweight and looked both confused and annoyed.

Average guessed he'd been taking a nap in a back office 30 seconds earlier.

"Uh...sir," said the guard in a deep voice. "There's something happening upstairs. And...uh...we have to keep people here. Maybe...uh...just for a few minutes."

He paused with a questioning look on his face.

Average quickly assessed his situation. He felt the underside of the spiked ring on his middle finger with his thumb. He was ready to use it. He thought that if he moved quickly enough, he could hit the guard fast, bounce off him and keep on going.

He had taken his first step toward the guard when a second one appeared in front of him beside the first. This one was thin, moved like a whippet and had his gun out.

"Down! Down! Down! On the floor! Now!" he screamed. He was waving the gun wildly at Average and looked as if he might blow his head apart at any moment, intentionally or not.

"Okay...okay...okay," said Average. "Just take it easy." He got to his knees with his arms outspread, palms facing forward at head level.

"All the way! All the way! Face on the floor!" said the second guard.

Average did as he was told. He lay face down, arms outstretched above his head with his palms flat on the lobby carpet.

"Move an inch and I'll blow you the fuck away," said the guard, more relaxed now but speaking with enough conviction that Average guessed that he probably would do what he threatened.

"He might have a weapon or something, man," the guard told his companion. "He did something to someone upstairs. The cops are on their way."

The elevator doors closed, bumped against his thighs, and opened again only to close on him a second time after a long pause. John Average closed his eyes.

"Shit. Shit. Shit. Shit," he muttered softly to himself. The cop. If he died, that put him in line for death row.

He'd already contemplated what he might do if he got caught. He'd snitch. Of course he would. He damn sure wasn't going to the gas chamber if he had anything to say about it. Maybe...if he were lucky...he'd eventually get out before he was truly an old man.

* * *

Enzo Lee couldn't open his eyes or make a sound. He was completely aware of everyone around him, what they were saying and what was happening to him. He heard the nurse who reached him first tell everyone – very quickly, thank God – that his heart was pounding like a jack hammer but he wasn't breathing. He probably was turning blue by that point.

"I'm not dead!" is what he screamed inside his head. "I can hear you. I know everything that is going on. Get some goddamn air in my lungs!"

He felt the device they inserted into his mouth and then could hear and feel the air being pushed into his lungs every few seconds. When they moved him to a gurney, one of his eyelids opened just long enough for him to see a clear tube maybe two feet long reaching from his mouth to a plastic bulb attached to the end. The hand on the bulb belonged to a young nurse. She gave him a quick smile and then his eye closed again. He'd never felt so helpless. Lee prayed that the woman holding his life in her hands wasn't the type to get bored.

Chapter 48

IT TOOK THREE hours for the paralyzing poison to work through his system enough for Enzo Lee to resume breathing on his own. It happened quickly. He could feel himself trying to breathe for himself. Three or four tries and it was back. They switched off the automatic ventilator they had put him on and then pulled the plastic tubing out of his throat.

His eyes opened fully. He was staring at the ceiling of the hospital room enjoying for the moment being able to see again and breath on his own. Lee knew that in a few minutes he would take it for granted – being able to breathe again. But for now, he luxuriated each time he deeply inhaled. One. Two. Three. Four. Ahhh. Breath. Life.

He looked gratefully over at the nurse smiling at him who was the same one who had held the breathing bulb in her hands. He was thinking 5 pounds of Godiva chocolate might just begin to express his gratitude.

"Thank you," he croaked through a throat that was dry and sore. She smiled back.

"You're welcome," she said. "You've given me a great story. Top Ten. And a full recovery to boot. That's a good day for me."

"Makes two of us," said Lee. She handed him a plastic cup with water and Lee drank it gratefully. He put the cup down on the table to his side and looked down at the foot of his bed where he saw Bobbie Connors and Ming Wah Choy standing on either side.

Lee lifted his hand up and gave them a weak wave.

"Your fan club is here," said Connors. Choy gave her a quick smile.

"And how is Megan?" asked Lee.

"The little girl is fine," said Connors. "Aside from worrying about you."

"They called your grandmother," said Choy. "I came to let her know how you're doing. And I see you're doing very well. Your doctors think you'll be fine. Apparently, your oxygen levels stayed at a safe level throughout. They watched it very closely."

"Right," said Lee. "They were all over it. I could hear it all. It was an amazing feeling. Totally conscious but helpless. I kept thinking of those stories of people being buried alive. You know. Inside the coffin while the dirt is piled on top."

"Well, a little better outcome," said Choy. "I'm glad you're fine. I've got to get back. I have *my* patients to take care of. I'll tell your grandmother you're fine." She grabbed Lee's right toe through the hospital blanket and gave him a squeeze before walking out.

Connors watched Choy leave. She turned back to Lee and raised her right eyebrow.

"Cute," she said. "And she wasn't that cool when she came in and saw you livin' through a tube." Connors raised her left eyebrow in question.

Lee was quiet for a moment.

"Getting complicated," he finally murmured.

"Life is, ain't it?" said Connors. The two friends stared at each other for another couple of seconds.

"All right," said Lee. "Am I going to have to ask you 20 questions or are you going to tell me what the *hell* is going on?"

"Okay," said Connors. "Here's *my* story. We got the guy...the one who put you to sleep. But he took out Mendoza...our guy who was standing guard. He wasn't as lucky as you. They got to him too late. Couldn't revive him.

"So I'm asking *you* what the *hell* is going on," she added. "I need to know everything. They take down one of our guys and...well...now it's war. I am *going* to find out who is responsible for this. And when I do...let's just put it this way. They gonna be in a universe of pain."

* * *

Gray Axmann was eight over par, a lousy round for him. He usually didn't make excuses. He always felt that a golfer who made excuses was deluding himself. He just wasn't as good as he thought...or hoped...he was.

This time, though, his thoughts had been far away from the game and he was neglecting the other member of his twosome as well – the majority owner of the largest casino in South Korea who was a potential whale of a client.

He knew that around the time they had made the clubhouse turn, his lawyer was scheduled to meet the man on his payroll who had been arrested overnight in the lobby of the University of San Francisco Medical Center with a ring full of poison on his left middle finger. Axmann had been waiting for the past 90 minutes for the call that would tell him the outcome of that meeting.

The call came just after he teed off on the 17th hole, lacing his drive down the right side. He watched it gain altitude slowly like a fighter jet lifting off the tarmac. Then it drew left just before it descended, hit the fairway and rolled another 30 yards. A perfect drive.

"He won't see me," said the lawyer. "The son of a bitch won't even see me. He's insisting that he get a public defender. A goddamn public defender. Can you believe it?"

Gray Axmann believed it so completely that he immediately climbed into his golf cart and drove to his car in the parking lot, leaving the cart there in the late afternoon sun. He abandoned on the 17th hole both his ball nestled dead center in the fairway

280 yards from the tee box and the prospective client from South Korea.

When your business is helping casino interests solve their most sensitive problems, your transformation from a valuable asset to a dangerous liability can occur in an instant. The sudden attention that Walter Novak and Roxaten were receiving was bad enough. The failed attempt to kill Megan Kim was a disaster. The assailant's refusal to meet with Axmann's attorney was a red flag that he was ready to flip and cut a deal with the authorities. Axmann had tried to shield his identity from the man who seemed able to slip in and out of the hospital rooms of patients in the Roxaten trial like he was death himself. Axmann never gave his real name. He used temporary, prepaid cell phones. He routed money through impenetrable entities. But had he slipped up somehow?

Gray Axmann had a little time. The people who employed him were busy running their empires. They didn't spend time reading medical journal blogs or paying attention to local crimes in San Francisco. But they weren't dumb. If he couldn't put out the fires quickly, they would soon know that he was in serious trouble. And a man in serious trouble who had handled their most delicate security matters for years made him a threat. They were accustomed to eliminating threats. Now he needed to figure a way out of this mess and do it fast.

Chapter 49

WHEN BERNARD WINTHROP, a long-time professional acquaintance at the National Institutes of Health, called Miriam Pastor to talk about Roxaten and Walter Novak, she was intrigued. At 64, the petite feisty researcher had recently retired after a long career at GenenMed where she had shepherded a long parade of medications through the lengthy FDA approval process.

In her semi-retirement, Pastor had taken a research fellow position at the University of San Francisco Medical Center. A highly respected microbiologist, her grants from government and foundation sources more than paid for the cost of her research. The university had the potential upside of prestige from any work that Pastor might publish since it would be under its auspices. The arrangement let Pastor do whatever she wanted.

She would have been interested in the science of Roxaten alone – the potential of a broad-based cancer treatment plus a possible general vaccine. Pastor knew it could revolutionize cancer treatment if it really worked.

But the real bonus was Winthrop's off-hand comment relaying Novak's allegations that Merrick & Merrick was suppressing – and perhaps even sabotaging – the Roxaten research.

The allegation didn't surprise Pastor. She knew that when the drug companies encountered a tradeoff between increased profits and improved public health, profits won out more often than not. She had been in boardrooms when executives negotiated "pay for delay" deals. They wrote checks to the generic drug manufacturers so a popular medicine could continue to be sold at $10 a pill rather than the 50-cent price competition would bring. It worked well for everyone except consumers.

Everyone in the industry knew that drug companies bought companies with drugs that might compete with their best selling products when they could, even if just to bury the possible competitor. And the manipulation of the patent system to gain an extra year or two of protection for a hot-selling medicine was legendary.

Just that week, Pastor had heard how a major drug company was trying to stop European doctors from using a cancer drug that had astonishing results keeping elderly patients from going blind. The small amounts used – mere drops – were too cheap. The drug company wanted to force doctors to buy a repackaged form of the drug at many times the cost.

So the prospect of a fight like this one spilling into the open was enticing. She hadn't seen this in a while – a public, no-holds-barred clash of scientists, doctors, egos and Big Pharma corporate interests. Profits vs. health. And Winthrop was offering her a ring-side seat. Was she in? Of course.

Pastor agreed to coordinate the samples and tests during Megan Kim's stay at the medical center. With the physicians at the hospital, she would make sure that they got all the blood, tissue, marrow, lymph node material and anything else they might need. Then, she would ensure that Megan was screened, scanned and tested in every way possible to determine if any hint of malignancy remained in her body.

The key work would be the analysis of Megan's resistance to the cancer that had once run rampant through her blood and whether that resistance extended to other types of cancer as well. This would let her assess Roxaten's potential as a broad-based cure. It also would tell her the likelihood that Novak had actually found a general vaccine that would dramatically reduce cancer risk.

Pastor would give Bernard Winthrop and the NIH her assessment of Roxaten and Novak's research. And she would suggest the next steps for the drug – including whether it deserved a place in national health policy or should be left in the hands of private industry.

The call from a partner at the Weil Roth law firm came after the third day of getting samples and tests from Megan Kim. With the barest of introductions, the lawyer launched full bore into threat mode on behalf of Merrick & Merrick.

Pastor was interfering with the drug giant's contractual relationships. She was gaining access to Merrick's confidential information and misusing the company's trade secrets. What right did Pastor think she had studying the effects of Roxaten when the drug was the property of Merrick, protected by patents and Merrick was developing and testing the drug in accordance with FDA regulations? Did Pastor want to wind up in court to fight a cease and desist order?

Pastor waited until the attorney had a chance to wind down, finally exhausting his litany of threats.

"Megan Kim and her mother have given us their written permission to perform the tests and take the samples we're taking," she told the lawyer. "The last time I looked, people still owned their bodies and everything that's inside of them.

"As far as I know, independent study of drugs and their effectiveness is legal and not patent infringing so long as I'm not making money from actually selling it. I have no intention of doing that. Look at any medical journal. Half the articles are reports of independent studies of drugs owned by Merrick and other drug companies.

"You come after me and I will call a press conference and say that Merrick is trying to intimidate me and suppress independent research into Roxaten," she continued. "I will support everything Walter Novak is saying. If you want that, go ahead."

She hung up the phone without waiting for a reply. After a moment, Pastor suddenly punched the air with her right fist, putting all of her 110 lbs. into it.

"Hah!" she said. She couldn't resist a satisfied smile. The only thing more exhilarating than witnessing a good fight was being in one.

Chapter 50

BY THE TIME that Enzo Lee was released from the hospital, it was late in the afternoon. He had had a small lunch at the USF hospital, headlined by chicken noodle soup and strawberry jello. Although he felt fine, the doctors were cautious, wanting to ensure whatever paralyzing agent had been used on him would have no delayed effects.

On his way out, Lee stopped at Megan Kim's room. He introduced himself to a patrolman sitting outside. The cop made him find the head nurse on the floor to confirm his identity. He then explained that Megan had been taken into the hospital basement for X-rays or some other scanning procedure. Another officer – a police woman – had accompanied her. Megan now had at least two – and sometimes more – SFPD officers assigned to her at all times. After the death of a colleague, Lee guessed that the level of police vigilance would be at an all time high.

Although Megan was gone, Walter Novak was sitting in her room waiting for her return. The scientist sat staring out the picture window at the residential district beyond, sloping down toward the San Francisco downtown skyline in the distance.

"Walter," said Lee.

Novak slowly turned toward him. His face was slack. Eyes dull. His hair was even more askew than normal. He had shaved unevenly.

"Are you okay?" asked Lee.

"Am I okay? Am I okay?" said Novak. "How are you? After your close brush."

"I'm great...now," said Lee. "I was very lucky. But you look like...well...you look like crap, Walter."

Novak stared down at his hands.

"I'm tired...just so tired," he said. "Haven't been sleeping well. I'd been talking with my lawyers. They are keeping up this...this unrelenting assault. I've lost track of the lawsuits. The press conferences. They're threatening...I don't know. Criminal charges. They're talking about forcing me to go to Louisiana."

"They're desperate, Walter," said Lee. "They're losing control. They're lashing out however they can at this stage. I told you this would happen. We need to stand up to them. Otherwise, they'll crush you. They'll crush Megan. We're in a war here."

Walter nodded. He glanced up, held Lee's eyes for a second, and then looked down at the floor again.

"I know...I know...I know," he said, his voice trailing off.

Lee left Novak to await Megan's return, picked up his car from the hospital garage and drove the few miles to his home. He parked in the street-level garage at the bottom of the double-decker Victorian that held his flat. He was starving, so he walked the three blocks to his favorite take out place on the edge of Chinatown.

He ordered wonton soup with shrimp, snow peas, chicken and barbecued pork. He also got an order of sliced beef with broccoli, water chestnuts and black mushrooms as well as a box of steamed rice. He recognized his desire for the comfort food of his youth after a day that had come perilously close to being his last on earth. He also needed to regroup and get his head around everything.

Lee let himself into the stairwell that led up to his flat. He pushed his cat, Max, back inside the front door and put the bag of Chinese food on his dining table. He fed Max first and then got out a plate, fork and a big spoon. He ate the soup directly from the container, barely looking at it as he stared at a wall that still held the framed poster of a ballerina in mid-spin. A peasant's skirt billowing around her. It had been Carr's. She gave it to him when she moved back East.

Novak had looked shaky. Lee felt sorry for the scientist and he understood the intense pressure he felt. But the last thing he needed was to have the man whose brilliant research had set everything in motion flame out at this stage. He needed to help him however he could. Try to shore him up somehow.

And then there was Lee's grandmother. She was part of the mix now. The clock was ticking. He only had eight days to get more Roxaten for her.

If the drug was effective in halting her cancer, his grandmother would be the second person to receive the course of treatment. If Megan was Exhibit A in the story of the medicine's effectiveness, his grandmother could soon be Exhibit B. He knew Ming Wah Choy would not tell anyone about his grandmother's treatment and he would keep it quiet as long as he could as well. But there was no doubt that the treatment that might save her life could also endanger her. The stakes kept getting higher.

Now there was a dead cop, killed while trying to protect Megan Kim. That totally changed the dynamic. No one could view this now as just a scientific debate or corporate intrigue, and dismiss his and Novak's fears as paranoia. He was sorry about the patrolman, Mendoza, but the total involvement of Connors and the rest of the SFPD would help. It might be decisive. But the wheels of justice often moved slowly. The criminal investigation could take a while. And Lee didn't have the luxury of time.

He set down the won ton soup, now half gone, and left the rest of the food sitting on the table. He picked up the telephone, consulted his reporter's notebook on his nearby desk and dialed a number.

"Hello?" said Roxanne Rosewell.

"Roxanne. This is Enzo Lee."

"Yes. Hello. You've been creating quite a stir, I see."

Lee breathed out a long sigh. Total exhaustion was setting in.

"You don't know the half of it," he said. "Listen. I think…I think Walter needs you. Can you come over right now?"

"Of course."

Chapter 51

ENZO LEE WAS working on his second cup of coffee when he heard the door to the second bedroom open, footsteps walking down the hall, and then the door to the bathroom click shut.

He had gotten up an hour earlier. He bought croissants and scones at Café Trieste and a dozen eggs at the corner convenience store on the way back. The pastries were on the dining table. The eggs sat in a large bowl on the counter next to the stove. With a wooden spoon, Lee pushed sliced onions and mushrooms sautéing in olive oil and wine around a frying pan.

He heard Rosewell behind him and he turned to see her.

She had on the same thick button-up sweater and long skirt she had worn when she arrived the previous night. She carried herself with the same elegance he remembered from their first meeting at her house and that he now realized was her natural state.

"Coffee?" he said, nodding to a pot filled with strong, black Sumatra.

"Perfect," she said.

"And scrambled eggs if you're game," he added.

"Yumm."

Lee cracked the eggs, scrambled them and poured them on top of the onions and mushrooms. He took a block of aged Parmesan out of the refrigerator and grated a small mound on top of the eggs. Rosewell stood quietly with her arms crossed. She held a mug of coffee in one hand and watched Lee continue to work the eggs.

"How is he?" said Lee finally.

"He's sleeping…which is good," she said. "When he gets this way and he stops sleeping as well, everything is compounded. He can spiral very quickly."

"I noticed," said Lee. He sprinkled some pepper over the eggs, carried the frying pan over to the table and spooned the contents onto two plates. He put the pan back on the stove and they sat down at the table. They ate in silence for a minute.

"He didn't ask you to call me, did he?" asked Rosewell.

"No."

"Why did you?" she asked.

Lee shrugged.

"The man names his life's work after you, I figure that means something," he said. "And just things you and he said. I think he said you were his 'contact with reality' or something like that. Plus I was desperate."

Rosewell smiled.

"I'm glad you did," she said. "I wish he'd call me when he gets this way. If I'm around to see it, I can help. If I'm not…well he can go somewhere deep and scary. It can be hard to reach him."

Lee nodded.

"You know," he said. "I like Walter. I mean obviously he's a smart guy and impressive. All of his work and all that. But he seems…I don't know…like a real *mensch*. You know?"

Rosewell suddenly burst into tears. Lee grabbed a box of Kleenex and put it in front of her.

"I'm sorry…I'm sorry," she said, grabbing a handful of tissues and blowing her nose. "Dammit!"

"It's okay," said Lee.

"A 'mensch,'" she murmured. "He is. He truly is. God. I should have married him 12 years ago."

"Really?" said Lee. "You were close to that?"

Rosewell nodded. Her gaze shifted away from Lee and out the kitchen window.

"Engaged...or agreed anyway," she said. "It's not as if he got down on his knee. But, we were going to...and...and I couldn't go through with it. Got cold feet. He'd had some episodes. Like this or worse. And...I just couldn't. I was afraid to commit...to commit to dealing with that."

"That's understandable," said Lee.

"But I didn't realize how much I loved him," she said, looking back at Lee. "And that I would be with him anyway. I should have seen it. Instead, it was as if he was close...coming into shore finally. And then I pushed him back out...back out into... Oh, God."

Rosewell was in tears again. She grabbed another handful of tissues.

"I'm sorry," she said. "I know you've got a tremendous amount on your plate. And...uh...you don't need a woman in tears."

"Listen," said Lee. "I hate to think how he would be without you. From what I've seen, he's lucky to have you in his life. I mean marriage...who knows how that would have gone?"

Rosewell nodded as she politely blew her nose again.

"Thank you for saying that," she said. "Well, it's done now. All we have is the here and now...not what might have been."

"Right," said Lee. "Let's be honest, Roxanne. We've got a 'situation' here. It's a bad time for Walter to check out of it. I don't think he has to be out in public defending Roxaten. But he should be available if questions arise over Megan's tests or anything of that sort. And, let's face it, a lot of this rests on him. If he appears unreliable, it makes it hard to overcome the doubts about Roxaten."

"He's overwhelmed," said Rosewell. "There is so much coming at him and with the publicity, the condemnation, all the nastiness...it's no surprise that he's breaking down. Let me take him to stay with me. I can deal with everything for a while. The lawyers. The researchers. Doctors. He trusts me.

I've been doing this for a long time…being the buffer between Walter and the world. Let's give him a couple of days. I think he'll be better with some rest. This kind of battle…it's not his strength."

"Yes. I know that," said Lee. "If I could speed it up or bring it to a close somehow, I would."

Chapter 52

TAKEO HAYASHI WAS worried about his nerves so the Kimura Pharmaceutical executive didn't leave the Tokyo restaurant where he was sipping green tea until he knew the Shimbashi station on the Ginza subway line would be jammed with the rush-hour crowd.

On his way, he passed a sliding-glass doorway off the sidewalk with yellow plastic flowers in boxes outside. The facade around the doorway was designed to look like Roman columns and also was painted a rich yellow – the color of gold. Through the opened door, he heard the bells, electronic pinging and rattling of the balls ricocheting inside the banks of pachinko machines.

Even how, he felt an urge to walk in and down the center aisle bordered by the rows of machines. This is how it had all started for him as a teenager. All the hours in the neighborhood parlors. Racking up the points. The excitement and adrenaline. Winning and losing. Losing and winning.

He forced himself to continue on. He reached the subway station and dropped down inside. It was as he had expected.

The platforms were packed with people. Any relief when the crowd jammed onto a train after it rolled into the station was short lived. Within a couple of minutes, new waves of humanity replaced the old, pouring down from the street-level entrances and surging over from the other lines that intersected there with the Ginza.

He positioned himself toward the end of the platform where the Ginza train would arrive. He wanted to make sure it was moving at maximum speed.

211

First, he felt the vibrations in his feet. Then the sound – a rumbling that he knew would soon be overwhelmed by the squeal of the brakes. Then the wind as the air in front of the train was pushed forward in the tunnel and out onto the platform area.

He only had a few seconds.

He pulled out his phone. The email he had composed to the reporter in San Francisco was ready. He clicked on the button that instructed a huge email server somewhere to send it out – but only after a delay. A "send" date a few days from now seemed safe. Then he reached into his right coat pocket and found the subway card. It showed he had entered the station here rather than arriving on his usual train for the transfer home. He let it flutter to the ground.

He walked along the edge of the platform with his back toward the oncoming train. He went to a clot of people crowding the place where a door would soon open. The squeal of brakes was loud behind him and getting close. He deliberately walked into a man, said, "*Abunai!* Watch out!" and flung himself off the platform.

As he hung for a moment in the air, he said silently, "I'm sorry."

He was sorry for the massive gambling debts he had incurred as he doubled up and redoubled up in an effort to dig out of his financial woes. He was sorry he would miss seeing his children grow up and have lives and families of their own. He was sorry to leave his wife alone. Most of all, he was sorry that the terms of his life insurance policy cheated him of what he would have traded for almost anything – the chance to say 'Good bye.'

* * *

"Enzo!" said Lorraine Carr when Lee picked up the telephone in his flat. "Are you okay?"

212

"I am," said Lee. "But it's been a rough couple of days. So you heard about what happened in the hospital."

"Well, yeah," said Carr. "I mean it was in the newspaper. Plus Ray Pillman called me." She referred to an editor at the News.

"Well, still alive and kicking," said Lee. "And trying to figure out how I got in the middle of this and how to get out of it."

"You'll find a way," said Carr. "At least you usually do. And how is Grandma?"

"Not too much change at the moment," said Lee. "But I'm hopeful. Very hopeful."

"Good," said Carr. "Give her a big hug for me. And...uh...I gotta go. But...uh...I just have to say. I miss you, damn it!"

"Me, too, Lorraine," said Lee. "Me, too. And...uh...listen. If this guy...Billie Bob...Willie Joe...or whatever his name is..."

"Barry," said Carr.

"Right. Barry. If he's not good to you, tell me and I'll come out there and beat the holy crap out of him. He's not very big is he?"

"He's huge," she said.

"Oh, shoot," he said. "Well...doesn't matter. If he's big, he's big."

Carr was silent for a moment. Lee thought maybe he'd lost the connection.

"I love you," she finally said in a whisper so soft that Lee almost wasn't sure he'd heard it.

"Lorraine?" he said.

But she was gone.

* * *

Novak and Roxanne Rosewell had barely settled into her home when the San Francisco Sheriff's deputies came for him.

Two were in uniform and two wore plainclothes. They were polite but adamant. One of them immediately placed a steel-toed boot in the open doorway in case Rosewell tried to close the door.

Then, when they saw Novak watching them from the living room, they marched right in and surrounded him. They insisted on handcuffing Novak and would not let him change out of his tattered sweatpants, white T-shirt and sandals.

One of them read Novak his Miranda rights and then they were out the door, back into the two cars they had left sitting outside. Novak was alone in the back seat of one of them, slumped behind the metal grill that separated the back seat from the front.

Of course, the media had been called to witness Novak's arrival for booking into the county jail where he was formally notified of the charges – four counts of theft of trade secrets and office supplies from Merrick & Merrick. The evening news footage showed a gaunt, aging man who stared into the cameras as if hypnotized by the bright lights. The chaos around Novak confused him – the photographers jostling for position and reporters shouting questions. He plodded numbly in wherever direction the deputies steered him, an old, defeated bull being led to slaughter.

At the same time that Novak was being paraded before the media in handcuffs and sweatpants, the lawyers that Roxanne Rosewater had sent to defend him from Merrick & Merrick's legal assaults in other parts of the country weren't faring much better.

The Delaware courts – always reluctant to give up a case that has any connection to the state – denied his lawyers' efforts to have the lawsuit attempting to reverse the Medvak acquisition transferred to California.

And in Louisiana, Novak's lawyers lost their first attempt to stop the extradition proceeding, arguing that since Megan's mother had given her permission for the Roxaten treatment it could hardly be considered criminal battery. They had no idea the Louisiana judge in the case was the second cousin of Sheriff Jules Dupont who had filed the extradition request immediately after the deposit of Edwin Merrick's 50 "good ideas" into his campaign coffers.

But it was the arrest, of course, that made the biggest splash and dashed any hope that Novak could rest, recuperate and gain some distance from the raging controversy.

He spent less than an hour behind bars but was exhausted by the time Rosewell got him back to her house. He slouched in a chair. Then he began to weep. He couldn't stop. Only after he took a powerful tranquilizer could Rosewell lead him into a back bedroom, tuck the blankets around him and put an end to the tumultuous day.

Chapter 53

THE TABLE AT Greens Restaurant was right up against the bank of windows that looked out over the adjacent marina. The bright white of the boats against the deep blue of the ocean water was almost painfully blinding in the crystal clear noon sunlight.

Bobbie Connors and Enzo Lee took a moment to enjoy the view while the waitress put their menus in front of them.

"I assume this is just dabbling on the vegetarian side of life, huh?" said Connors.

"Well, a few times a year I like to remember that there is life beyond meat," said Lee. "I don't think you'll miss it. If I could eat here for every meal, I might actually consider it – going vegetarian."

"You can actually say that with a straight face," said Connors. "I'm so impressed I'm going to let you order for me."

"Well, okay," said Lee. "The only provision is that we share everything. That way you can get a better feel for all the options."

They started with a salad that had Chioggia beets, grilled artichoke, spring peas, tiny carrots and sliced radish in a dressing of olive oil flavored with lemon, mint and chunks of bleu cheese. Then came spring rolls with green papaya, red cabbage, jicama, sautéed tofu, cilantro and rice noodles served with fresh peanut sauce. Lee ordered them two glasses of a dry Austrian Veltliner.

"I just love it when you pump me for information," said Connors when she paused for a moment between bites of the spring roll.

Lee shrugged.

"Well, you rarely disappoint," he said. "Plus you said maybe I could help you out somehow. So, I'm all ears."

Connors finished chewing while she pondered what she would say next.

"Okay. This is off, off, off the record," she began. "As in career-changing off the record."

"All right," said Lee. "I assume this has to do with the guy who put me to sleep for half a day."

"It does," said Connors. "Michael Leonard. It turns out he has so many aliases I'm surprised he remembers his real birth name.

"He actually refers to himself as 'Mr. Average,'" she continued. "As in being anonymous by not standing out. Blending in. Anyway, the brain trust at the department has adopted that name for him – Mr. Average. Seems to fit. The man is very eager to cut a quick deal. His court-appointed attorney is dangling all sorts of stuff in front of us – glittery prizes that are looking very tempting. All we've got to do is take his deal – 20 years."

"Okay," said Lee.

"And that's the problem...for me at least," said Connors. "Guy killed a cop. Probably killed at least one other person. Maybe more. Plus hurt lots of people. Look what he did to you."

"Let's see," said Lee. "What does 20 years mean in real time?"

"Good question," said Connors. "Of course that's part of the deal. We can't mess with the 'good behavior' formula and whatnot. Let's say he gets out in 15 years, maybe even a couple less."

"Yeah," said Lee. "That does seem pretty light."

"No kidding," said Connors. "Don't get me wrong. I'll do the deal to climb the ladder and get the top guys if I have to.

But it hurts me big time. I went to Mendoza's home. You know. Visit the widow. Let her know we'll take care of her and all that. We're all a big family at a time like this. It could have been any of us. He's got a couple of kids. Two and four. Boys. They wore department T-shirts. It...it just broke my damn heart."

Lee nodded his understanding.

"And so, Mr. Average and his attorney have raised their skirts a bit," Connors continued. "They gotta give us the peek so we know what we're paying for. Just part of the dance."

"And how does it look?"

"Oh, it looks real," said Connors. "He poisoned the patients. Eight total. We matched his travel...plane flights...with the list you gave us from Novak. The people in the medical trials who got sick. Mr. Average will tie it all together.

"And his boss did a pretty good job of hiding his identity – no names, changing phones, running the money off shore," Connors added. "But he made a mistake." The detective paused for dramatic effect.

"Okay," said Lee. "*Ta-da.* Any time now."

"He called once on a land line," said Connors. "It shows up on Mr. Average's phone records. He'll confirm this and tie it all together, too. Came from the Palladium Casino...Las Vegas. Odds are we'll be able to trace it to a specific extension once we have a subpoena, which would be easy to get after Mr. Average signs on the dotted line...or maybe I should say 'if' he signs on the dotted line."

"If?" said Lee.

"And here is where you come in," said Connors. "What do you think about writing a story that covers most of this, attributing it to 'anonymous law enforcement sources'?"

"What I think is...are you kidding me? I'm all over it," said Lee. "But how does this work on your side exactly?"

"It's a calculated risk," said Connors. "Maybe we tip off the target. But I'm betting he's already on high alert. If they can run, hide, destroy evidence, whatever...it's already been done. My plan is to launch an unofficial rocket up their tailpipe – with your help. My guess is we'll see a couple of people come flying out the window...or at least something interesting will turn up.

"Of course the whole reason we do this is so we don't have to cut a deal," she added. "So Mr. Average goes directly to Death Row, which is only right."

"And how could this go wrong and what happens then?" asked Lee.

"Yeah...well, my ass is on the line big time with this," said Connors. "His defense attorney will go nuts. He'll make sure the judge pees her pants when the story hits. But at least I don't have to start drafting my apology to the Mendoza boys. Not yet, anyway."

Chapter 54

THE DOCTORS, NURSES and technicians finally seemed to have run out of new things to do to Megan Kim.

The previous day, they had started with the ultrasound of her heart. They let her watch the beating and the ghostly fluid moving around from chamber to chamber while they rubbed the metal head covered with goop around her chest. Then she ran on the treadmill with a dozen wires attached to her to see how her heart behaved. She rode the bicycle with a mask on with the tube attached to see how she used oxygen. She'd blown into various devices. Long, deep and slow. Then fast and explosive.

In the afternoon, she was in the operating room again and one of the doctors put something into her IV line that quickly put her to sleep. They had told her they would insert a tube down her throat and into her lungs. Then they would squirt liquid deep inside her lungs that was then sucked out. The cells that were washed out would be carefully studied. They also planned to take some tissue from her liver and some fluid from around her spine.

When she woke up, her throat was very sore and she had more small band aids on her side.

Now, they said she needed to stay for at least one more day – maybe two – to make sure her liver wasn't bleeding.

Thankfully, Dr. Choy's niece, Karen, had continued visiting every afternoon. She brought her magazines. Science articles for kids. Glossy gossip magazines about pop singers and young celebrities. Some Megan knew and other she didn't. Megan taught her how to play poker. They watched shows together on the Disney Channel. Karen brought an extra pair of headphones so they both could listen to the music she was constantly adding to her iPod.

Megan was enjoying Dr. Choy's daily visits as well. She was the best at explaining everything that was happening to her. She told her that what Megan was doing might help a lot of people in the future. Maybe even millions over a long, long time. And she told Megan that she believed the girl would not have to worry about leukemia any more. Megan smiled for about two hours after she heard that.

When Walter Novak shuffled into her room, it was a surprise. She hadn't seen him for two days. And even after that short time, he seemed thinner and grayer than the last time she'd seen him. And the words struggled to leave his mouth.

"Come...come on now," he said. "It...it...it's not safe here anymore. Nuh...not safe."

"I brought...I brought your clothes," he brandished a small backpack.

"Where are we going?" asked Megan. "They said I was supposed to stay here for a while so they could watch for bleeding or something."

"Th...th...they want you to believe that," said Novak. "They want to hurt you. But I won't let them. Nuh...no. No way. I won't let them. C'mon now."

So, they walked out of the room and down the hall.

"Ra...radiology," said Novak to the pair of cops who sat just outside of Megan's room in the hallway. "De...Detective Connors said you should stay here. Sh..she'll meet us there."

On the bottom floor, Novak sent her inside the women's restroom with the pack full of her clothes. She came out into the lobby happy to be out of the hospital gown.

They crossed the parking lot outside of the hospital and got into the car Novak had driven there.

"So, where are we going?" asked Megan.

"Did...did I tell you I own a sailboat?" said Novak.

"No. Really?"
"Yes," he said. "I…I'll show you."

Chapter 55

Cop Killer Suspect Linked to
Medical Tests, Vegas Casino

By News Staff Writers
San Francisco News
   Law enforcement officials believe that the killing of a San
Francisco police officer at the University of San Francisco
Medical Center last week is linked to the poisoning of multiple
patients involved in the medical trial of the controversial new
cancer drug Roxaten.
   Michael Leonard of Waltham, Massachusetts was arrested
and charged with the first degree murder of Patrolman Louis
Mendoza who was killed while on an off-duty assignment.
Mendoza was guarding Megan Kim, the 10-year-old girl who is
undergoing tests at the hospital as part of a scientific
investigation into Roxaten's potential as a ground-breaking
cancer treatment.
   Law enforcement officials who spoke to the News on the
condition that they not be identified also said that they are
investigating a possible link between Leonard and personnel at
the Palladian Casino in Las Vegas.
   Kim is the only known cancer patient to have received a full
course of Roxaten treatment which she was administered while
she was critically ill with leukemia more than a year ago. At the
time, Roxaten had not been approved for human trials. Rights
to the drug were acquired by drug giant Merrick & Merrick but
initial medical trials were suspended after one patient died and
several showed signs of liver and heart damage, according to

ROBERT B. LOWE

the company. Kim has apparently fully recovered from advanced stage leukemia.

The drug company yesterday declined to comment on the report that participants in the Roxaten trials may have been deliberately poisoned during the drug trial.

Merrick & Merrick has terminated Walter Novak, the scientist who developed Roxaten and administered the drug to Kim without authorization. The drug giant acquired Novak's small drug development company and the rights to Roxaten early last year for $80 million. The drug giant has sued Novak for fraud in connection with the sale of his company and alleges that he has stolen assets of the company and misused its private, proprietary information. Novak denies the allegations.

* * *

ENZO LEE HAD collaborated with the reporter at the News covering the Roxaten story to get the article into the newspaper. It was the solution he had worked out with the editors. They desperately wanted the story – a timely inside scoop that advanced the reporting on both the cop killing and the ongoing saga over Walter Novak and Roxaten. But Lee was clearly a participant in both stories so the newspaper had another experienced journalist vet the reporting with an objective eye.

It was still quiet in the newsroom the afternoon after the story ran. But Lee knew the piece could be a time bomb. In places he could only guess about – perhaps within the inner circles running the Las Vegas casinos, at levels high within the drug industry or even inside the federal NIH bureaucracy – the implications and natural next questions stemming from the article would be crystallizing.

Back in his investigative reporting days, he compared the best stories to opening the shades in a dark room full of rats. As the sunlight hit, the rodents would scramble desperately to find

224

the shadows again, crawling over anyone and everyone to save themselves and regain the safety of darkness.

It worked the same way in the human sphere, just slower and with more calculation. How far would the exposure reach? Who needed to be sacrificed to save those higher up the chain? How would this all end and what was the best way to limit the damage? He guessed that Bobbie Connor's hunch was right. Other shoes would start to drop – soon.

When his telephone rang, it was Roxanne Rosewell on the other end.

"Do you know where Walter is?" she asked, worry clearly in her voice.

"I have no idea," said Lee. "What happened?"

"I had to leave," she said. "I had an appointment at work I couldn't cancel. Oh, God. Oh, God. I shouldn't have left."

"Look," said Lee. "Let's not panic. Maybe he just went for a walk or a drive. Maybe he just wanted to get out."

"I hope so," said Rosewell. "He was in such bad shape. The arrest. The booking. The whole thing. You could see him crumble under the pressure. He was saying things that didn't make sense. He was a mess, Enzo. I'm worried."

"Okay," said Lee. "How long has he been gone?"

"Let's see," said Rosewell. "I guess I left about four hours ago."

"Okay. Why don't we give him until dinner time?" said Lee. "Take a few minutes and think about where he might have gone. Make sure he didn't leave a note somewhere. The last thing we want to do is start a police or public search for him if we don't need it. That just feeds into what Merrick & Merrick is trying to do to him – make him out as crazy, a criminal or both."

"Okay," said Rosewell. "Let me go over things here and think of where he might have gone. I'll check back with you."

Ten minutes after Rosewell hung up, Lee's phone rang again. This time it was Ming Wah Choy.

"Megan's gone," said Choy.

"What happened?" said Lee. "Wait. Let me guess. Walter?"

"Yes," said Choy. "He lied to the officers about where he was taking her. She wasn't released. They were keeping her here for at least another day."

"All right," said Lee. "Look. The thing he cares about the most is keeping Megan safe. I can't imagine him doing anything deliberately to endanger her. Roxanne is trying to piece together where he may have gone. Let's let her do that."

After he hung up the phone, Lee leaned back and stared out the bank of windows at the end of the newsroom. This was just what they didn't need – to have the next chapter in this saga be a manhunt for Walter Novak. They needed to avoid that if at all possible. He could imagine the headline: "Mad Scientist on the Loose." It would be an utter disaster.

When the telephone rang again, Lee answered quickly. It was Rosewell.

"There are some things missing," she said. "His big raincoat. He had it on his bed this morning. I didn't think anything about it. Some special shoes. And the other set of keys. They're for his boat. It's all for his boat."

"His what?" said Lee.

"The sailboat," said Rosewell. "It was his one indulgence. After the sale he bought a used sailboat and got someone to teach him how to sail it. It's at the San Francisco Yacht Club. It's called the *Oblique*."

Chapter 56

CAPTAIN NICK AND Enzo Lee stared at the glowing green scope that showed what the marine radar unit circling above their heads atop the *Red Snapper* could see. Lee saw the rough outline of the San Francisco Bay he knew well. A glowing line emanating from the center of the screen swept around in a complete circle every three seconds.

"This is set to pick up anything of size on the Bay," said Nick. "But most boats have at least a transponder and all commercial ships and a lot of pleasure craft transmit an AIS signal as well. That will tell us everything but the amount of beer on board."

The *Snapper* belonged to Nick Sokolov, otherwise known as 'Captain Nick.' He was a burly man with long blonde hair and most of a PhD in Comparative Literature which he had abandoned in favor of running a daily fishing boat. Every day, the *Snapper* took up to 30 fishermen out through the Golden Gate in search of salmon, snapper, bass and whatever else they could find off the Northern California coast.

Lee had immortalized Captain Nick in an article about the former academics in the Bay Area who had become overqualified gardeners, plumbers, cabinet makers and...boat captains. Ever since, Nick had been his go-to source for everything nautical.

After a quick call to Nick, Lee had picked up Choy on the way to the *Snapper's* berth in Emeryville.

"Ah ha!" said Nick as he stuck his finger at a blip on the radar southwest of Alcatraz Island. "Thar she blows!"

Nick fiddled with the screen, pushed a button and the name *"Oblique"* appeared on the screen along with details of the craft's location, speed, heading and even the size and type of boat – a 27-foot Catalina.

"So he's heading for the Golden Gate?" said Lee.

"Yep," said Nick. "Sure is. Straight for the open ocean and straight into a 20-knot wind. See his angle? He's gotta tack all the way out. Slow going for a sailboat. C'mon. Let's go get her."

Nick started the *Snapper's* engine, yelled down to one of his helpers on the pier to let loose the lines holding the fishing boat in place and slowly eased toward the opening to San Francisco Bay.

They were a mile past the Golden Gate Bridge when the *Snapper* caught up with the *Oblique*. The sun had already set and the late afternoon winds were blowing hard. Whitecaps were everywhere and the rolling swells were lifting up the *Snapper* as it plowed forward, slamming down into the following trough before being lifted again by the next swell.

Once they passed under the bridge and hit the open ocean, the *Snapper* had closed quickly on the *Oblique*. Nick ran the *Snapper* along the sailboat's starboard side. Novak was at the wheel in the back and Megan sat on the port side bench near him. The wind came off their port bow and pushed the sailboat onto its starboard side. They wore yellow rain gear. Megan's jacket was huge for her and hung down to her knees. She wore no life vest.

Lee left the enclosed bridge and stood along the railing on the upper deck. He waved his arms up and down as if he was shaking sand out of a towel, trying to get Novak to slow the *Oblique*. Megan gave him a small wave. Novak just glanced at Lee and then turned his gaze forward, over the bow of the sailboat and the ocean beyond.

"How can we stop them?" Lee asked Nick back inside the bridge.

"There is no way without doing something pretty crazy, not to mention dangerous," said Nick.

"Explain," said Lee.

"Well, we've got the speed," said Nick. "We could just cut them off. Force them to turn away or run into us."

"Then what happens?" asked Lee.

"One, he turns to avoid us," said Nick. "He's not that experienced a sailor. It'll take him a while to get sorted out. Hopefully, he'll be dead in the water. You should have a chance to talk to him, at least.

"Two, he runs into us. I'm not too worried about the *Snapper*. Some patching and paint. But, his damage could be anything from minor to massive."

"Life threatening?" asked Lee.

"Shouldn't be," said Nick. "I can nose over so it won't be a direct collision. We'll be right there if they have to abandon. I've got life vests…even inflatable rafts. We can come to a dead stop pretty fast."

"Okay," said Lee. "I think we need to do it. It's getting dark. The wind is picking up. Walter doesn't know what he's doing. It will be life threatening if we *don't* do anything."

Nick nodded his head solemnly.

"If you're right and he doesn't have any open ocean experience, he might not survive the night," Nick said. "These winds can get vicious and he's got to manage the boat alone. That's tough. One mistake. One misjudgment. It's all over."

Lee nodded his head and he picked up a handheld radio that the *Snapper's* crew used to communicate on the boat.

He descended the stairway to the lower deck where he joined Choy at the stern. He pulled out a couple of orange life vests from a white storage compartment. He put them on the deck near where he took a place on the portside rail. He gave Choy a donut-shaped float with a rope attached to it that was hooked on an exterior wall. She wore one of Nick's sweaters and a long rain jacket over her dress. He told her the plan and then called Nick on the radio.

"We're ready," he said. "Let's go."

The *Snapper* drifted over closer and closer to the *Oblique*. Lee waved at Novak, urging him to pull his boat toward the port side away from the *Snapper* which must have appeared like a huge wall of moving metal as it shifted almost on top of the sailboat.

Lee saw Novak turn the wheel hard to the left. The *Oblique* shifted quickly away from the *Snapper*. It lost momentum suddenly as the sailboat turned into the wind, the big mainsail flapping and swinging loosely. Nick throttled back the *Snapper*. In the relative quiet, Lee yelled across the water.

"Walter," he shouted. "Go back. You've got to go back. It's not safe out here." Lee pointed back to the Golden Gate Bridge in the distance.

Novak looked at Lee. His white hair splayed out in all directions in the wind. His face was flushed. He shook his head, leaned down and picked something off the deck near his feet. He brandished it up in the air. It was a spear gun. Novak waved it in Lee's direction and then put it back at his feet. Then he reached behind him and pulled on a line that yanked the *Oblique's* mainsail tighter until it stopped fluttering and filled with wind again. The sailboat picked up speed, heading off toward the left on its new tack.

Lee felt the engines of the *Snapper* pick up in pursuit. He clicked on the handheld radio.

"See that?" he said.

"Right," said Nick. "He is nuts. What now?"

"Can you do that again? Make him turn and stop for a minute?"

"I can try," said Nick. "What does that get us?"

"I think I can get aboard if you stop him," said Lee. "He's got a fender on the left...port side. It's almost in the water. I can pull myself up."

"You're more nuts than he is," said Nick. "You have any idea how hard that is?"

"If you've got a better idea, let's hear it," said Lee. "I'm not going to let him drown Megan out here."

Silence.

"Okay," said Nick. "Look. Wait until I've throttled down. If he starts up again, I'm not following. I'm staying put until we get you back on board. I've got a rope ladder down there. You can swim, right?"

"Water polo team. Lowell High School," Lee said. He didn't add that he dropped out after two weeks when he nearly drowned during the high school team's first scrimmage. He wasn't going far. He swam well enough.

The *Snapper* was churning forward again, closing the gap on the *Oblique*. Nick pulled up on the port side to repeat the previous maneuver but from the opposite side. Lee and Choy moved to the opposite side of the *Snapper* as they drew closer. He explained his plan to her. She shook her head.

"I wish I had a better plan but we left our grappling hooks back in the car," he said. "I think I can do this. And if I can't, you're going to have to save me, okay?"

"We can get you out of the water," said Choy. "I'm more worried about you getting crushed or your head getting laid open. Be careful. Don't make things worse. We're a long way from a hospital." Lee nodded.

As they came up close to the sailboat, Lee undressed quickly. He dropped his jacket and sweater on the deck. He was glad he had worn a white T-shirt. It would give Nick and Choy a good visual if they needed to fish him out of the water. He kicked off his shoes and stepped out of his jeans. He stood

231

on the cold deck in the chilly wind in his bare feet, boxer shorts and T-shirt. He smiled at Choy as he tried not to shiver.

Choy shook her head. She wasn't happy about this.

Lee had an orange life vest in his hand as they pulled even with the *Oblique*. They edged closer and closer, giving the sailboat time to change directions. Lee figured Novak would be quicker making the direction change the second time. He'd probably tack without stopping completely. But, if the sailboat slowed just for a few seconds and he was in the right position, Lee thought he could manage it.

Nick swung in tighter, forcing the *Oblique* over until it was once again heading straight into the wind, its mainsail fluttering. Lee moved to the front of the *Snapper*. He wanted to be a way in front of the fender – a white rubbery cylinder dangling parallel to the ocean surface with a rope passing through it. It protected the sailboat from banging against other boats. Novak must have forgotten to haul it on deck.

Lee needed time to position himself while the sailboat continued to move past him in the water. He found his spot. He was just ahead of the *Oblique's* bow. He felt the *Snapper's* engine throttle down. He guessed he would hit the water 10 feet away from the sailboat.

Lee abandoned the life vest at the last second, tossing it to Choy. He needed to swim and climb as fast as possible without any hindrance. The vest would just impede him. He climbed over the railing and hung off the outer side of the boat for a moment facing inward. His legs were bunched under him. Then he pushed out to get some distance from the *Snapper's* hull and dropped down into the dark water below.

"Oh, no." He heard Choy's voice as he dropped toward the water.

Chapter 57

LEE SCISSOR KICKED and flung his arms down as he hit the water. He didn't want to lose time by sinking far below the surface. His head just barely went under and he was back up in a moment, taking a few quick overhead strokes toward the sailboat and trying to judge how close he was as it began to pass almost directly over him. Lee ignored the cold of the water although he knew it would rob him of his strength and coordination even after just a couple of minutes.

The *Oblique* was almost on top of him when a big swell passed under her so the sailboat was suddenly high above him. It looked as if it might slide down sideways on Lee. He backpedalled furiously. Then the swell was past the boat and lifted him upward. He was briefly high enough to see inside the boat. He saw Novak in the back, one hand on the wheel while the other reached behind him. He guessed he was pulling in the mainsail. That would transfer the force of the wind to the *Oblique's* forward movement. It would soon be moving far faster than he could ever swim.

As he dropped down on the other side of the swell, Lee moved another stroke closer to the boat. The port side of the sailboat slid past. He saw the fender hanging from the middle of the boat coming at him above his head. As it reached him, Lee pushed down with his arms and began the eggbeater kick, the one move he remembered from water polo. It elevated his body a few extra inches for a handful of seconds and left his hands free to block a shot on goal...or to grab hold of a sailboat sliding past.

His hands hit the fender. He held it as if he was hanging from a log overhead. But, it was wet and slippery. He felt it slipping away from him as it dragged him along while the ocean resisted, holding back his lower torso and legs. Finally, just before he lost his grip Lee kicked one last time, twisted his body hard and grabbed desperately with his right hand. He found the rope and gripped it, holding on as he lay with his back against the fiberglass hull of the *Oblique,* his legs streaming behind.

Then Lee felt the *Oblique* surge as the sailboat completed its turn across the wind and the breeze filled its sail. The sailboat heeled over on its starboard side, lifting Lee farther out of the water. He hung down almost vertically now with only his legs in the water up to mid-thigh, leaving a white wake behind him.

He had to get his other hand on the rope.

Lee flipped over onto his stomach. He kicked, half hitting water but also getting some traction from the side of the *Oblique.* He reached with his left hand and now had both hands on the rope.

The angle of the boat was an asset now. He used his hands on the rope and his feet on the side of the sailboat to crawl up. It was slick and his bare feet slipped. But, he pulled and scrambled, hauling himself higher. Finally, he got his elbow hooked over the fender. He kept working his way up until he got his left knee on the rubbery cylinder.

Lee clawed himself higher still until he finally got his fingers over the edge of the cockpit. With a final pull and a barefoot push off the wet hull, he tumbled into the cockpit head first. He slid past the bench and onto the steeply canted deck and kept on going until he found himself wedged head first in the right corner of the cockpit next to the hatch that led down into the *Oblique's* small cabin. He was exhausted and in a helpless position for the several seconds it took to untangle himself and flip over until he was at least sitting.

234

Finally able to look up and back toward the stern, Lee saw Novak holding the wheel with his left hand while he aimed the spear gun at Lee's face. The black rubber tubing stretched tight and the silvery point of the spear dipped and wavered in small jerky motions as Novak adjusted his weight to keep his balance in the moving sailboat.

"Walter...wait," Lee said.

"You aren't going to get her," said Novak. "You...you aren't going to get her."

"Walter," said Lee. "I'm on your side. Remember? I want to help you." Novak's expression didn't change.

Then Lee saw a bundle of yellow come flying from the opposite corner of the cockpit toward him. It was Megan, launching herself along the tilted deck. She half fell and half ran toward Lee. He caught her before she crashed onto the bench and inner wall of the cockpit. The top of her head hit his cheek and he held her in his right arm while steadying himself with his left.

Novak moved a half step as if trying to catch Megan as she flew in front of him. But he was much too late and his hands were full anyway. He lost his grip on the wheel for a second and the *Oblique* spun to the right. She dipped more deeply on the starboard side for just a moment before righting herself. Novak fought to keep his balance. The spear gun waved wildly, pointing skyward, then down and finally back at Lee's head when it went off with a soft click and the slick sound of metal sliding against metal. Lee cringed as the shaft passed over his head and just cleared the top of the cockpit. A few inches lower and it would have hit him in the face. A foot lower and it would have impaled Megan. He looked up at Novak, summoning all the anger and disgust he could muster.

"Damn it, Walter," he said.

Novak looked at him for a moment and then his eyes dropped down and he let the spear gun fall. He turned the wheel until the *Oblique* was heading into the wind and came to a stop. He sat down on the seat behind him and buried his face in his hands. Hunched over, he was a beaten man.

Lee helped Megan to her feet.

"Are you okay?" he asked. Megan nodded.

Lee pulled himself to his feet and moved to the stern, using the mainsail boom that was waving in the wind over the cockpit for support in the rocking sailboat. When he got to Novak, he pushed him on the shoulder to get him to move to the side bench. He wanted him away from the wheel. Lee picked up the spear gun and dropped it over the stern. It bounced once before plopping into the ocean.

It took him a minute to figure out how to drop the sail and several more of scrambling around to finally get it down. He wrapped a loose line around it to keep it from flapping.

The *Snapper* had been slowly circling the *Oblique*. With the sail down, Lee waved at Captain Nick and he brought the fishing boat closer. As it passed by, Choy threw a line toward the sailboat that uncoiled in the air until it landed almost in Lee's hand.

Lee tied the end of the line to a cleat in the *Oblique's* bow. Soon, both boats were heading back to the bay, the fishing boat steadily towing the sailboat as the swells pushed them along, rolling past from stern to bow. Lee realized he was shivering uncontrollably. His teeth were clattering. He dropped down the hatch and rummaged around inside the cabin. He found Novak's bag and put on a pair of sweatpants and a heavy sweatshirt.

Back topside, Megan sat next to Novak on the side bench. Lee took a seat on his other side even though it left the *Oblique* tilting to port. Novak stared over the opposite cockpit wall at the dark ocean and the half moon now fully visible. After a moment, he looked over at Lee.

"I'm sorry," said Novak. "I don't know. I just...I don't know."

Lee nodded.

"It's okay, Walter," he said. "You've done a lot. I think we can take it from here."

He looked across Novak at Megan whose eyes flicked up into his for a moment. The rest of the trip in, they held Novak between them while Lee told stories about the bay, the red-orange bridge they passed beneath and the city that glittered brighter and brighter.

Chapter 58

IT WAS IMPOSSIBLE for Miriam Pastor to say with absolute certainty that Megan Kim was free of cancer.

The tests had been exceedingly thorough.

Her lab had studied Megan's blood carefully. It had collected and examined multiple tissue biopsies from the young girl. She had undergone PET scans using different radioactive tracers to isolate metabolic activity unique to cancer cells. Everything came back negative.

But who could say there wasn't a tiny handful of cancer cells too small or too inactive to show up on the tests? You can't check every cubic centimeter of someone's kidneys, lungs, skin, skeleton or brain.

Within that limitation, though, the petite, gray-haired microbiologist believed that Megan Kim was clean. Given the records and tests from Megan's period of illness more than a year earlier, either Roxaten had cured Megan or a spontaneous miracle had coincidentally occurred at the same time.

Pastor believed in singular miracles. She had seen them, giving patients life when it should have been taken away. That's why she and scientists like her repeated experiments over and over and over again. She didn't believe that miracles occurred on demand and in bunches.

But Pastor didn't have the authority or time to retest Roxaten on another 50 patients – or even on five for that matter.

She had no more patients. The lab would have to suffice.

From the many vials of Megan's blood, she converted a small amount into blood serum. She further refined the serum to isolate several types of antibodies that she believed were the most obvious candidates to have attacked Megan's cancer. They probably were what had kept Megan's cancer from reappearing.

The antibodies would be treated to bind with a fluorophore, a chemical compound designed to emit a florescent green light when exposed to light of a certain frequency. It was the laboratory version of the black light.

Small amounts of Megan's treated antibodies would be applied to 86 separate slides holding a range of cancer types – thin slices of tumors preserved in paraffin. Pastor had collected the specimens from colleagues from the Mayo Clinic, Sloan-Kettering, Dana Farber and other research centers. Many of the slides came from patients having cancers in the same location – say lung cancer – but the cancer cells themselves were different types. There were six varieties of melanoma alone.

The overall goal was to see how well Megan's antibodies could bind to the antigens present in the different cancer cells on the slides, surviving the rinses that would otherwise wash them away. In real life, such strong binding would typically be a death grip – marking the cancerous cells for destruction by the body's white cells.

Roxaten's potential would be measured by color. The more slides that contained the glowing green after the processing, particularly if it was of high intensity, the greater would be Roxaten's potential as a broad-based cancer cure. It also would provide a measure of how widespread and effective the C Factor-based vaccine could be.

Pastor couldn't sleep the night that the slides trays were left inside the Ventana autostainer at her lab. She knew that while she tossed and turned, the slides would go through nine separate processes over an eight-hour period, all of them with much greater precision than anyone could achieve by hand.

Pastor was in the lab by 6:45 a.m., long before anyone else. When she set the tray holding the first 40 slides on the table in front of her, she imagined a green glow emanating from them. She laughed at herself. It wasn't possible. She knew her mind was playing tricks.

One by one, she placed them on the Leica MM fluorescent microscope. A lighting source underneath the slides excited any fluorophore on a slide, causing it to glow green. She zoomed in on single cells and back out to see big clusters. She recorded the images as she methodically worked her way through the tray.

When she finished, she threw up all the images on a wide computer display and scrolled through the collection.

There was green that looked as if it might be the ocean observed from far above with white lines of waves passing through. There was a field of light green with darker nuggets attached together in small clusters. There was forest green in slender stalks with a horizontal row of white filled with lime dabs in the middle, resembling a Van Gogh painting of wildflowers. And there were blobs of deep green against black that might have been some interstellar plasma in remote outer space.

Pastor saw green everywhere in a wider variety of shades and hues than she had seen the previous summer on her first trip to Ireland where the palette of green had seemed inexhaustible. The shades and shapes differed, depending upon the vagaries of the different tissue samples and the degree of magnification she had used.

Only a few of the slides contained no green at all.

Pastor's heart was pounding as she slid the second tray of slides next to the microscope. She would finish the initial survey and then go back to methodically measure the amount of color she saw on each slide. She would repeat the process on the control slides derived from a blood sample taken from a normal healthy volunteer. Her assistant would duplicate each step later in the day as a further check.

But Pastor knew what she was seeing was huge, unprecedented and would likely alter the course of cancer treatment – perhaps even within just a few years. She was both humbled and amazed by it. She doubted that she would be any more affected if she had witnessed Krakatoa erupt or seen a star explode.

Dazed, she stood up and walked into the small kitchen off her lab where she filled a mug with hot water on top of a bag of chamomile tea. She stared out the window at the neighboring buildings, trees and streets. She blew across the top of the mug.

Pastor contemplated the email she would compose to Bernard Winthrop at NIH at the end of the day. Roxaten was the real deal, she would say. The C-Factor discovery opens a whole new front in the cancer wars, she believed. This was far too important to leave in the hands of one company motivated more by profits and share price than public health.

Then Pastor smiled at her reflection.

In the past she'd always paused in indecision whenever someone asked for her favorite color. Not anymore. From now on it would always be green.

Chapter 59

ENZO LEE HEARD the voices before he reached his grandmother's hospital room. He stopped just outside the door, folded his arms and leaned against the wall. He closed his eyes and listened.

He heard his grandmother and Master Chu chattering in Chinese. And then she laughed. It was her shrill, high pitched giggle that she invariably covered with her hand. It brought tears to his eyes.

He took a moment to compose himself. Then he knocked on the doorjamb and walked into the room.

She was sitting up with a partially eaten tray of food sitting in front of her. The second bed was empty. Her eyes sparkled. Her skin was full of color.

"Grandma," said Lee. "Master Chu."

"Enzo," she said, holding out her hand to him. He sat down on her left across from where Chu sat. He held her hand for a moment and then leaned over to give her a hug. After a moment, she pushed him away, a little embarrassed but still with a big smile.

Suddenly, she pulled off her cap to reveal a thin and very short growth of white hair covering her skull.

"Look," she said proudly. "Coming back."

"Wow," said Lee. "Time for the hair dresser."

She laughed, covering her grin.

"Not yet," she said. "White...for now." She ran her hand wistfully through her scalp.

The sound of quick footsteps from the outside hall got louder and then Dr. Choy walked through the door in a swirl of white lab coat, green dress and tanned legs.

"Look," she said, coming up to the bed. "It's Superman. Or are you Clark Kent today?" She said it with a smile. "How are you today, Mrs. Chen?"

"Good," said the patient. "Hungry."

Choy busied herself checking the machine settings, the IV bag and the chart that hung at the foot of the hospital bed. Then she caught Lee's eye and nodded quickly toward the hall. He followed her out.

"God, she looks great," said Lee.

"She's doing wonderfully," said Choy. "Since yesterday. I can hardly believe it. Her blood work. It's almost normal."

"Yes!" said Lee, presenting a fist. Choy rolled her eyes, then presented hers for a dignified bump and allowed herself a smile.

"Let's be happy but cautious," she said. "These things rarely progress in a straight line."

"I know, I know," said Lee. "But Jeez. It feels like the sun came out."

He put his arms around Choy's waist and pulled her toward him. She held herself stiffly at first but then softened until she embraced him back and allowed her body to settle fully against his.

Then Lee pulled back a little, put his hands on Choy's shoulders and kissed her. He could see her eyes widen at first and then felt her smile as she enjoyed their first kiss for several seconds. Lee realized then that he had been dying to try those lips for weeks. They were, indeed, perfect.

When they stopped, she quickly looked around them to see if anyone had seen them. No one was there. She looked back at Lee pushed some loose hair behind her ear.

"Quite unprofessional of me," she said.

243

"I won't tell anyone," said Lee. "I never kiss and tell."

"Hmm…we'll have to see about that," said Choy. "Meanwhile, I have some business to discuss with you."

"Okay," said Lee. "Business."

"Yes. I wanted to ask you about Megan," said Choy. "She's ready to be released. Today. Tomorrow at the latest."

"I heard," said Lee.

"Is she going home?" said Choy.

"I was going to call her mother and Chief Davidson back in Alabama," said Lee. "I don't think it's safe. I'd like to keep her here a little longer."

"Well, my sister lives near here," said Choy. "In Burlingame. You know her daughter has been visiting Megan every afternoon."

"I know how much she's enjoyed that," said Lee.

"I asked Megan if she'd like to stay with them…for a few days anyway," said Choy. "She said, 'Yes.'"

"Okay," said Lee. "Let me talk to the police. There must be some way to get the coverage that makes sense. And let's keep it totally quiet. This is like the witness protection program. The safest thing we can do is to hide her."

"You like her don't you?" he added.

"Yes," said Choy. "I do. To be honest, she reminds me a lot of myself at that age."

Lee stepped back a step, looked at Choy and imagined Megan standing next to her. He nodded and smiled.

"I can see it," he said. "And I can see her growing into you one day. May need to get her out of small-town Alabama though."

Choy gave him a mischievous smile.

"I'm already working on that," she said. "Just give me time."

"All right. I'll just get out of your way. Is there anything else?"

"Yes," said Choy. "She asked if she can see Walter again."

Lee nodded.

"Sure," he said. "That can be arranged. I'll call Roxanne."

The sound of laughter came out of the hospital room.

"She seems great," said Lee, nodding toward his grandmother's room.

"It's very exciting," said Choy. "I mean from an oncologist's point of view. Very exciting."

Lee nodded pensively. The clock ticking in his head suddenly became louder. It was Day Six. The Roxaten that Novak had given him was gone, used up for the first two doses. He had four more days to get more of the drug locked away in the Merrick & Merrick labs.

He still had no clue how he would get past the drug company's small army of security guards, a battery of video cameras and a sophisticated access system that used pass codes and fingerprints. Both Novak and Roxanne Rosewell were now locked out of their lab. Lee had brainstormed and rejected a half dozen plans. Now he was getting desperate.

Chapter 60

THE EMAIL THAT arrived in the middle of the day had an unassuming subject line.

"*Pharmaceutical Industry Meeting,*" was all it said.

But once he clicked it open, Enzo Lee sat transfixed in front of his laptop sitting at the dining table. Half way through it, he paused and clicked the mouse twice to send it to the printer in the second bedroom that doubled as his office. He half expected the email to disappear if he blinked. He wanted to make sure he had a copy he could hold in his hands that no computer virus, power surge, hard-drive crash or second thoughts could erase.

Lee leaned back in his chair and listened. He heard the rubber rollers picking up the paper. The gentle churn of gears. The smooth ejection of the finished pages into the tray. His HP LaserJet had never sounded so sweet.

* * *

Walter Novak was on his knees planting a kumquat tree on the far side of the yard when Megan walked through the backdoor of Roxanne Rosewell's house and into the enclosed area. Every square foot had been utilized to produce a verdant garden stitched throughout with a wandering chain of gray paving stones the size of dinner plates.

Megan stepped on them carefully and quietly until she came up behind Novak. She paused for a moment, hands clasped in front of her. Then she placed her hand on the man's shoulder.

"Hi, Walter," she said. "It's me. Megan."

He turned on his knees slowly toward her, his trowel still in his hand. He put the tool into the dirt, placed his hand on her shoulder and used her for support as he pushed himself to his feet.

Although he smiled at her, it seemed distant as if it could vanish in an instant. She was reminded of their first day together, the long drive through Alabama when Walter had stared out the windshield absorbed in his thoughts and she had wondered if he remembered she was there sitting next to him.

Novak walked a few steps to a small bench that stood along the back fence and looked over the garden and toward the back of the house. He sat down. Megan sat next to him. They both studied the yard. Megan swung her legs back and forth, trying to think of what to say.

"They finally let me out of the hospital," she said. "I'm staying with Dr. Choy's niece."

Novak nodded.

"I'm glad," she added. "They were nice. But it was *so* boring."

"All the tests," said Novak. "They weren't much fun, huh?"

Megan shook her head.

"No," she said. "Not very." They studied the yard again.

"Megan," said Novak. "The day in the sailboat...you know...I just got...I don't know. I was a little...um...upset, you know?"

Megan nodded her head slowly.

"It was pretty out there," she said. "I'm used to the ocean, you know. I wish I had taken a picture of the Golden Gate Bridge...to show my mom."

Novak looked down at the ground in front of him.

"The food was pretty good at the hospital," said Megan. "But one day I ordered the fish. It was terrible."

He glanced at her and gave her a small smirk.

"Not as good as ours?"

"Not close," she said. "I wonder if the ones we caught are still in that freezer. They probably wouldn't be very good now."

"We should catch some more one day," he said.

"Someone told me they catch salmon here," said Megan. "I've never caught one. I don't even know if I've seen one."

"They are amazing fish," said Novak. "You know how they return to the stream of their birth? They will do anything to get there…lay their eggs. They die after that."

"They die?"

"Unfortunately, yes," he said. "When they've finished their important work. Before that they do whatever it takes. Very tough. Even heroic."

Megan nodded.

"Do they taste good?"

"Very," said Novak. "Delicious."

She nodded again and waited.

"Do you remember the girl you told me about?" said Novak. "The one in your dreams?"

"Yes," said Megan.

"Have you seen her again?"

Megan shook her head and waited. Novak looked as if he was going to say something else but didn't.

"Do you know who she is?" asked Megan.

Novak shrugged.

"I had a…um…I had a sister," he said. "She was much younger than me…10 years. My senior year in college, she got very sick. I came home early…to be with her. To help my mother. She looked like the girl you described. Blonde pigtails. But that was before…"

"…before the chemo?"

"Yes," said Novak. "Before the chemo. I dream about her, too. Quite often sometimes. She always has her hair."

"Can you share dreams?" asked Megan.

Novak pondered the question.

"I suppose so," he said. "Or something similar."

"I liked her," said Megan. "She...I don't know. She made me feel better. Not so afraid."

"Hmmm," said Novak. "Me, too."

They were quiet for a minute.

"Are they big?" asked Megan. "Salmon."

"Um...yes," said Novak. "Quite. The boats from San Francisco catch them off the coast. They go up to 20...maybe 25 pounds.

"And...uh...if you wanted to, we can get some," he added. "We can't catch one, of course. But I know where we can buy some."

"Really?"

"Sure. Still know how to cook a fish?"

"*Yes.* Of course," said Megan. "I'll never forget that."

Chapter 61

AFTER RECEIVING THE email, it took Enzo Lee the rest of that day and half of the next to do the research. He got the basic background on a half dozen of the world's largest pharmaceutical companies and their key officials. He called one of his old newspaper colleagues who had fashioned a career out of covering Congress and got a half hour lesson on the House Ways and Means Committee and the names of several key staff members.

Then he called Roxanne Rosewell and met her at a café near her home. Over cheddar cheese scones and strong coffee, they spent an hour devising a plan. They moved to an outside table and spent the second hour eating oatmeal cookies and tracking down Novak's lawyers.

Lee then placed a call to Merrick & Merrick and asked for Edwin Merrick. His call went through to a young man who identified himself as the CEO's assistant. Lee guessed Merrick had several assistants and wondered how this one ranked. But it didn't matter much. He just wanted to ask for a meeting. He knew that one of Novak's lawyers would call Merrick & Merrick's general counsel within 20 minutes and set the ground rules for the meeting. By the time he dropped Roxanne back at her house, he had a confirmed appointment for the following afternoon.

Back home, Lee fed Max and poured himself an ice-cold Stoly from the bottle he kept in the freezer and squeezed the juice of an entire lime into it. It took him a few minutes to print out both documents he wanted to take with him and place them all into a manila folder that he left on his desk. Then his phone rang.

"It's Roxanne," said Rosewell.

"Hey," said Lee. "Everything okay?"

"Yes," she said. "It's all as we discussed. There's...uh...just one thing."

"All right."

"I discussed this all with Walter, as I said I would," said Rosewell. "And he wants to come with you."

Lee was quiet for a moment.

"How is he?" he said finally. "What do you think?"

"He's much better," she said. "You know that whole episode on the boat. It was...it was like a fever that broke. He's been subdued...and embarrassed. But on the whole, quite good."

"Is he there?" asked Lee.

Instead of answering, Lee heard Rosewell hand the phone over to Novak.

"Enzo," he said.

"Hi, Walter," said Lee. "Look. I can't tell you not to come. You've got a lot at stake here. But we only get one shot. If we show weakness, they'll try to exploit it."

"I...I understand," said Novak. "I'm sorry. I'm sorry about what happened. I need to stand up. I need to finish this."

Lee sighed heavily into the phone. He didn't mind if the scientist heard it. He wanted him to hear the ambivalence. A strong Novak in the room determined not to break would be a big asset. A crumbling, unstable Novak would be disastrous. He needed five aces in his hand to win this. Not four aces and a weak card they could exploit. And he was running out of time. Only two more days to get his grandmother more Roxaten.

But it was all about Novak's discoveries. And now the drug giant was bent on personally ruining the scientist and destroying his reputation as a means of discrediting Roxaten. Even with the others at risk – his grandmother and Megan – could Lee really deny him a place at the table?

"Okay, Walter," said Lee. "I'll pick you up at 1 p.m. tomorrow. It's early. But I want to talk about the ways this might go so nothing will be a surprise, even if they come after you."

"I'll be ready," said Novak. "Thank you."

* * *

When Enzo Lee and Walter Novak entered the office of Edwin Merrick, the CEO was standing in front of the magnificent picture window that looked out over San Francisco Bay with the towers of the Bay Bridge in the foreground. Lee guessed it was the executive's standard opening posture whenever he wanted to preempt any question of status. Here was a man who had earned a huge office in a huge building with a huge view that would be the envy of all but a handful of humanity.

Lee knew Henry Roth by reputation. The slim lawyer with slick-backed hair stood respectfully to the side. But he shifted his weight almost imperceptibly from the ball of one foot to the other. It was a fighter's dance, as if he harbored a welter-weight boxer in his soul eager to get out. He was too dangerous to ignore.

"So," said Merrick after the initial introductions, hand shaking, and beverage requests were completed and the four men took their places around the coffee table. "Do we understand the ground rules here?"

Lee nodded.

"My understanding is that everything discussed here is off the record," said Lee. "Nothing gets into the newspaper and nothing can be used in litigation."

"Correct," said Roth.

Lee didn't need to add that although the actual words uttered in the 20 minutes would never be directly turned against their speaker, any hints they carried of strategy, weakness or fear would be ruthlessly exploited by the other side.

"You seem convinced you've got something to say that I'm interested in hearing," said Merrick, directing himself to both Lee and Novak. "I seriously doubt this is the case unless Walter wants to tell me he'll return the $80 million we paid for his company and admit that Roxaten is a complete and utter fraud."

Lee smiled.

"Not today," he said. "But I recently received an email that I think you'll find interesting. Let me read it to you."

Lee set the manila folder he was carrying on the coffee table, opened it and pulled out two pages. He began to read.

"We met in the basement conference room of the Florentine Hotel and Casino in Macau on April 21," he read. *"It was one of a series of secret meetings held at least once a year and included key executives at the largest pharmaceutical companies worldwide.*

"Mr. Merrick started the session by describing the Roxaten drug and the disruptive influence it could have on the industry by providing an inexpensive, more effective cure for many cancers as well as the possible basis for a general cancer vaccine. Participants agreed to cooperate in discrediting the drug as well as its discoverer despite its possible health benefits.

"Another topic at the meeting was an updated minimum pricing schedule for medicine organized on an ailment by ailment basis to avoid price competition. This arrangement has been standard practice within the industry for at least the last 12 years.

"Attendees also agreed to increase lobbying activities and expenses in a concerted effort to reduce the pressure to provide medicine at cost to impoverished regions for such diseases as

253

AIDS, tuberculosis, malaria and typhus. Cash payments directly to key officials in the United States and European countries were discussed that would constitute illegal bribery under the laws of those nations.

"I have included at the conclusion of this email a complete list of the attendees at the Macau meeting," Lee concluded.

He let the pages in his hand drop onto the coffee table between them. Merrick's and attorney Roth's eyes were glued to the white sheets of paper as they drifted down.

The room was silent for several seconds as everyone tried to get a read on the others' reaction to what Lee had just read.

"And who is the author of this missive?" asked Roth.

"It's anonymous," said Lee. "Unsigned."

"Hmm," said the attorney. "Even fiction usually is signed by the author. You can't run a story based on this."

"No," said Lee. "Of course not. There still is reporting to be done. Corroboration. Interviewing regulators to get their take on it. The usual beating of the bushes to see what comes out."

"These are vicious allegations," said Merrick. "If you bandy them about, you can expect to hear from Mr. Roth and other attorneys. I won't stand by and let you destroy my reputation."

"You do what you have to do and so will I," said Lee.

"And don't think for a minute that we will stop what we are doing," said Merrick, rising to the attack now. "We will continue to correct this...this swindle that Walter has perpetrated. The assault on the girl. Everything. You are mistaken if you think we will pause for an instant. You have not seen anything yet."

Merrick glared across the coffee table at Novak. His face was red. A muscle in his neck twitched. Lee half expected him to jump up or throw something. He pulled his feet under him in case he needed to get between the two men.

Novak cleared his throat. When he spoke it was ragged at first, as if he hadn't talked in a long time and was getting accustomed to hearing himself speak once again.

"You...you have taught me one thing," he said. "Along the way, I've sometimes been seduced by...by the signs of success. The money. Recognition. The trappings and...and accolades.

"You've threatened all of that," continued Novak. "You've forced me to remember why I started down this path. And it was for none of that. Thank you. Thank you for that...that reminder. What really matters."

All four in the room were silent for several seconds.

"Okay," said Lee, getting to his feet. He picked up the manila folder on the coffee table. He thought briefly about pulling out the second email but decided against it. Instead, he nodded at the two pages on the coffee table.

"That's yours," he said. "I've got the original."

Lee waited until the doors to the elevator closed before he spoke to Novak.

"Well done, Walter," he said. Novak looked down at his feet.

"I don't know that we accomplished anything," the scientist said. "Other than to make them mad."

"Oh, that was just our warning shot," said Lee. "I didn't think it would be enough. But we've got a few more cards to play. And these should cause some serious pain."

Back in Merrick's office, the CEO was staring out the window but paying no attention to the view.

"Outrageous," he murmured. Roth noted that the fire the CEO had shown moments before with his adversaries in the room was gone.

"Can I ask you..." Merrick continued.

"Before you do that," interrupted Roth. "There are a couple things I should point out."

"First, if anything in that email is true," continued the lawyer. "And I'm not saying there's anything there. But the allegations are serious and bring up questions of representation. Currently, I represent the company."

"You're politely saying I should lawyer up," said Merrick, turning away from the window.

"Yes," said Roth. "You really should even if there is no substance to it. There are potential criminal allegations. You should be careful.

"And the other thing," the lawyer continued, "is that it sounds great to threaten the press. But it rarely works. Papers as large as the News have been there before. In this country you almost need to find someone who intentionally prints a falsehood. Until they make a clear mistake, they're hard to fight.

"Finally," said Roth. "Lee has a reputation. He had trouble in New York before he came back here. A story blew up and he caught most of the flak. But before that he was considered a very good investigative reporter. And relentless. The kind of guy who digs in when he's under attack."

"You're saying this isn't over," said Merrick, turning back to gaze out his window.

"No," said Roth. "Not by a long shot."

Chapter 62

ENZO LEE'S FIRST fax to the other Big Pharma companies went out just after 1 a.m., ten hours following the meeting in Edwin Merrick's office. It was addressed to the vice chairman of Wyatt Healthcare and he faxed it to the main company number in London as well as the fax numbers for the public relations and sales departments. Those were the only fax numbers he could find on the Wyatt website. He timed it so the faxes would arrive at the beginning of the work day in England.

It included a copy of the anonymous email about the Macau meeting, the list of attendees with all the names blacked out except for the Wyatt vice chairman's. Lee's cover letter identified him as a reporter for the San Francisco News and asked for confirmation that the Wyatt vice chairman had attended the Macau meeting as well as an interview at the executive's convenience.

He slept a few hours and then sent out the second fax at 5 a.m. to the CEO of Rausch Laboratories in New York, again trying to time it to the beginning of the work day on the East Coast. He sent copies of the fax to the CEO's office as well as to the fax numbers listed for the general counsel, legislative liaison, human resources and building security. He found more fax numbers but figured those four were enough to ensure it reached the CEO and passed through a few other interested hands on the way there. The fax was similar to the one he had sent to Wyatt Healthcare except the only addressee not inked over was the Rausch Laboratories CEO. Lee hoped it would be the main topic of discussion that morning among the top echelon of executives at Rausch.

Lee prepared a third message to go out. This one would be an email rather than a fax and be sent to more than two dozen recipients. He used his scanner to convert the anonymous email into an image file. He did the same with the email he had held back from Edwin Merrick and Henry Roth the previous day.

Lee attached both of the image files to an introductory email that explained the significance of the attached documents. Then he prepared the list of recipients who would receive a copy of the electronic documents.

When he was finished, Lee pulled his hands away from the keyboard, put them on his knees and stared at the computer screen. He felt as if he had just put the finishing touches on a work of art. It was ready. One click of the mouse and it would go out. The nuclear option.

Lee hoped he wouldn't have to use it. If he did, he guessed it would be a bit like detonating a bomb. And he didn't know if he could control the fallout. He couldn't say if, after the dust settled, his grandmother, Walter Novak or Megan Kim would be better off. But he was running out of other options as well as time. His internal alarm clock was screaming. His grandmother was due her next dose of Roxaten. She needed it today.

* * *

"What the *hell* is he doing?" yelled Edwin Merrick in his 8 a.m. call to Henry Roth. "I got calls at six in the morning from London and New York."

"Do you have the email there?" said Roth. "The one he gave you yesterday?"

"Yes," said Merrick.

"Where are they on the list, the ones who called you?" said Roth.

"Let's see. They're one and two."

"Okay," said Roth. "It's pretty clear, right? He's working his way down the list. Top to bottom."

"Well. Make him stop. Damn it. Make him stop."

"How?" said Roth.

"What do you mean, 'How?'" said Merrick. "You're the goddamn lawyer. I'm paying you enough."

"If we sue them, it will take two days to get into court," said Roth. "The lawsuit itself will be headline news. And we'll lose. The only other way is…well persuasion. Either give him something or find some other reason for him to stop…even if it's fear."

"What?"

"Either way will involve a conversation," said Roth. "If you want, I can invite him in and convey the message that we hope he'll take a time out from these faxes. That will give us some breathing room. But we better see him today. And you can decide how you want to play this."

"Okay. Call him," said Merrick. "Now."

* * *

This time in Edwin Merrick's office, the four men remained standing. Lee could see that Merrick was fuming.

"Good," the reporter thought. He wouldn't be this upset if the anonymous email wasn't legitimate. After his many years in the business, Lee thought he could usually spot the true tips from the fakes. Merrick's attitude was telling. He glanced at Roth who was watching Merrick as well.

"Before we go any farther, let me show you another email that I've received," said Lee handing a page to Merrick and an identical one to Roth. "It's short. And this one is signed."

"Dear Mr. Lee," read the email. *"This is to confirm our conversation today in which I stated that the committee and its subcommittees have the power to subpoena non-citizens of the United States. In the past, our practice has been to invite their attendance and testimony. If they reside in this country or enter it on business or vacation, it is our view that non-citizens can be*

served and compelled to testify under the threat of contempt and related penalties.

"As I stated, the subcommittee would be interested in any information relating to systemic antitrust or corruption by or within the pharmaceutical industry. The extent of hearings or any Congressional investigation would depend upon the severity of the allegations."

The email was signed by the chief of staff for the House Commerce Committee's subcommittee for oversight and investigations. Lee noticed Roth look back at the beginning of the email, probably searching for the date. He'd see that it was dated two days earlier and know that Lee had withheld it at their first meeting.

"And," said Lee. "Let me show you two more things. First, here is an introductory email I've drafted. It will go out with the two other emails attached to it – the one about the Macau meeting and the one from the Commerce Committee.

"I also don't mind sharing a list of the recipients."

Lee handed both Merrick and Roth the list. It included the original list of Macau attendees as well as 12 others – key members of committees in Congress, regulatory agencies in Japan, England, Germany and the European Economic Community, and editors at the New York Times, the Guardian in England and Le Monde in France.

Merrick turned slowly to his picture window where no one else in the room could see his face and stared out in silence. The muscles in his neck and jaw were rigid and his face was turning a dark red as Lee watched.

"I will destroy you!" said Merrick, spinning suddenly toward Lee. Flecks of spit sprayed out from his mouth and onto the glossy sheen of the coffee table. "You send that out and I will take your job, your home, every dollar you have. You will spend the rest of your life…pumping gas and selling goddamn Slurpees at Seven Eleven. Do you understand?"

Lee didn't reply. Instead, he forced himself to wait eight seconds. There was more than anger and indignation in Merrick's outburst. Lee could feel fear beneath the bluster as well.

"What time is it?" he asked.

"What do you mean what the hell time is it?" shouted Merrick, spitting over the table again.

"It's 2:40," said Novak quietly.

"That email goes out automatically at 3 o'clock," said Lee. "Unless I stop it. And I'll need a computer and an Internet connection to do that.

"Here is what you need to agree to do before I do that," he continued. "First, call off the war on Walter. Dismiss the lawsuits. No more press conferences. Stop this nonsense in Louisiana. Get the extradition stopped.

"Then, announce the first Roxaten trials were flawed and start the process again. We're going to set up a non-profit foundation. Walter will contribute the first $5 million. We want Merrick & Merrick to assign all its rights in Roxaten to that foundation...everything. And your company will contribute another $10 million to it.

"Finally, Walter gets full access to his lab at your research campus immediately," Lee concluded.

"Fat fucking chance!" said Merrick. "God damned fat fucking chance."

Lee remained silent for a few seconds.

"We'll wait outside," he said. "You probably need a few minutes to think this over."

Without waiting for an answer, Lee signaled Novak and they walked out of the CEO's office to the waiting room outside, closing the door after them.

Novak looked shell shocked.

"He's not going to agree," the scientist said. "I don't think he can even make a rational decision."

"He's built Merrick & Merrick into what it is today," said Lee. "He's probably been in dozens of billion-dollar negotiations. If anyone can flip the switch and make a rational decision with a tight deadline staring him in the face, it's him."

Lee could imagine the scenario running through the CEO's mind. A Congressional committee investigation into the allegations of suppressing Roxaten, price fixing and bribery could run for weeks if not months. Politicians railing on their soap boxes for the heads of Big Pharma. Drug executives hauled before committees to testify. Boards of directors looking for scapegoats, desperate to escape the public scorn. Doing anything to dodge accusations of lining their pockets at the expense of millions of human lives. Multiply that by two or three as the international community piles on. As the Macau ringleader, Edwin Merrick could even be cast out of his company. His legacy would be disgrace.

At least that was what Lee hoped was going through his mind.

Ten minutes later, the doors to Merrick's office opened and Roth invited them back inside. Again, everyone remained standing.

"There is no fucking way I'm giving a dime to you," began Merrick. "And how do I know you won't send this out anyway...or leak it somehow?"

Lee shrugged.

"Because if I do, I assume you'll follow through and I'll be out of a profession and selling Slurpees or whatever," said Lee. "I'm sure you've got power and connections that I can't even dream about."

"You're damned right I do!" said Merrick.

"Look," said Lee. "There might be other copies of the Macau email out there. I have no idea. All this – the foundation...assigning the rights...a contribution – it's all stuff that a public relations consultant might suggest. Do it now before there's any whiff of scandal. Get ahead of it. Make Roxaten a gift to the world. Be proactive."

Lee looked at his watch. Five minutes to go.

"So, do we have a deal?" he asked.

"Yes, we do," said Roth softly. "You can use my computer." He pulled a laptop out of his briefcase. The screen lit up as soon as he opened it.

Lee sat down and pulled the computer close to him so Merrick and Roth couldn't see the screen. Then he pulled up Yahoo and navigated to the baseball box scores so he could see how the Giants were doing in their afternoon game. He punched a few meaningless keys.

When he had taken enough time, he closed the browser window and shut the laptop.

"We're going to Walter's lab now to get some of his notebooks," Lee said. "Will you call ahead so we can get in?" Roth nodded.

Lee didn't add that their first order of business would be getting another vial of Roxaten so he could give his grandmother her third dose.

"You know, of course, what will happen if you go back on any of this," said Lee. "Or I get any hint you're trying to block this email – get a restraining order or something. Bam. The whole thing goes out to everyone. It will only take me five seconds. I'll shoot first and ask questions later."

Merrick remained silent, staring at Lee with cold anger. Roth gave him another small nod.

On the way out to the elevator, Roth escorted Lee and Novak. They didn't bother to shake hands. Roth waited until the elevator doors were about to close.

"How are the Giants doing?" he asked without a trace of a smile.

"Tied," said Lee. "Three to three in the sixth."

Chapter 63

TROY AXMANN WAS surprised by Edwin Merrick's cryptic order to cancel that day's Novak-bashing press conference. A former U.S. Surgeon General – who had demanded a guarantee of six paid speaking engagements to attend – headlined the event. Other award-winning doctors and scientists had been flown in to fill out the program.

Equally mystifying was the message he received from his twin brother, Gray. Take the late Alaska Airlines flight from San Jose to Reno, said the email. It included instructions on how to get to a small warehouse in nearby Sparks a few miles east of the downtown area. Troy received no replies to his emails or phone calls to Gray.

It was past midnight when Troy Axmann pulled his rented white Malibu down the alley that led to the warehouse. He left the car idling along a chain link fence. Gray's email had provided the combination to the lock that secured the thick chain that held a pair of tall gates together. They blocked the opening to an asphalt parking area in front of a loading dock.

The gates fell open on their own once the chain holding them together was unlocked. Troy got back in the car and backed through the opening until the rear bumper of the Malibu was six feet from the raised loading dock.

He sprang up the stairs to the loading dock surface. A rollup metal door 20-feet across sealed the warehouse space from the outer loading area. A single floodlight provided enough illumination for Axmann to unlock the second combination lock. Troy made sure to use his legs when he lifted the door. Fortunately it was well balanced. But it still required a determined effort and the screech of the door rubbing against the tracks made Axmann wince.

Inside somewhere in the blackness was an office where Gray had said Troy should wait for him. But sitting just inside the opening on the other side of the rollup door and illuminated by the outside light were two suitcases. Troy used his phone to see them better. Matched black leather with a diamond pattern. Expensive. They had tags embossed with the initials "GRA." They were Gray's initials.

Alarms went off in Troy Axmann's head.

"What the hell is going on?" he wondered to himself.

He was staring into the black void wondering where a light switch could be to turn on the interior lights when a car drove into the parking area, blocking his rental. It was big and black, maybe a Lincoln. He saw two men get out while a third remained behind the wheel. He could only see the silhouettes as the pair mounted the steps. One was huge, the other average size. Neither was Gray.

They came up on either side of the pharmaceutical executive, each grabbing an arm.

"Whoa," said Troy. "I...uh...what is this?"

"Hi, Mr. Axmann," said the smaller man. Troy Axmann saw that he wore a leather jacket and jeans. His dark hair had a single white streak running through it. The other man looked as if he may have once played linebacker on a college football team. Big and powerful.

"Do I know you?" said Axmann. The man looked at him quizzically.

"It's Whitey," he said, stepping so the outside light could better show his face. "I last saw you...when? Was it Philly more than a year ago? I guess it's been all phones and email since then. But, you haven't changed much. The hair, of course. But they told me about that."

"Whitey? Oh. I know. Look. You think I'm Gray. I'm his brother, Troy. You know we're twins, right. Fraternal. You mentioned the hair. Can't you see mine's brown?"

"I'm sorry," said Whitey. "You need to come with us." He pulled his Glock 19 out from his shoulder holster. He held it in the light for a moment, making sure Axmann saw it. He wore an apologetic expression.

Axmann tried to pull away, taking a step backward. He pulled his arm away from Whitey but the ex-linebacker spun behind him and grabbed Troy's shoulders. He held him from behind by his biceps. He let go with one hand and ran it along the side of Troy's chest, then along his waistband, and finally along his leg outside and inside. The big man repeated the operation with his other hand. Then he grabbed Troy by both biceps again and marched him back down the stairs to the parking area.

"You're making a mistake," said Troy Axmann as he let himself be marched to the waiting car. "Can't you call Gray? He can explain everything."

The pair was silent. When they reached their car linebacker opened the back and pushed Troy's head down, cop style, to miss the door frame and climbed in next to him. Whitey went back up the loading dock and hauled down the two suitcases. He put them into the trunk of the car.

The four in the car rode in silence. Troy's mind was racing. What was going on? Were they taking him to Gray? Was Gray in trouble?

"Can you tell me where we're going?" said Troy. Whitey glanced quickly back from the front seat and then turned back to the front. He said nothing.

They passed through Reno's downtown casino district and then turned down a narrow alley that led to a parking garage. They went up several levels – Troy counted five – to the top, although the garage was empty. They took him into an elevator and went down a half dozen floors to the basement. It was bare except for pipes running overhead. They walked down a corridor and into a room with two desks and four chairs. They were old and solid. All metal.

Linebacker guided Troy to one of the chairs. He moved behind him and pulled Axmann's hands back until they poked through the slats that made up the back of the chair. Troy felt something being tightened over his hands. He looked back and saw they were black plastic ties. Disposable handcuffs. That was when the real panic hit. Until then, he felt as if a phone would ring and it would be over. Mistake resolved. There was something about the ties. He had visions of Polish Jews lined up along a freshly dug pit. Cambodians on their knees in the killing fields.

"Gray," he said. "Gray!" He said it louder. Finally, at the top of his voice. "Gray! Is he here somewhere?"

Whitey stood in front of him. He had the gun out again, an expression of pity on his face. He simply shook his head.

"Where is Gray?" said Troy. "You know I'm not him, right? I'm his brother, Troy. Can't you tell me what's going on here? There's a big mistake being made. A really big mistake. You've got to believe me."

* * *

The knock on the door was soft and unsure. Whitey opened the door a crack and murmured to the person on the other side. He opened it further and Eileen looked inside. Her eyes went instantly to Troy Axmann still sitting in the chair with his hands fastened behind his back.

He had been in the bare basement room for 13 hours. Twice they had cut the plastic cuffs, led him to a bathroom and fed him a sandwich before cuffing him again. He'd not heard anyone else pass by the room during his entire confinement. But he had overheard the one who called himself "Whitey" on his cell phone in the corridor.

"He was planning a trip," Whitey had told the unknown person on the other end. "A long one. At least $50,000 in cash and more in traveler's checks in his suitcase."

After a pause, Whitey added: "You know I just saw him a few times. We did everything by phone. Can't we do fingerprints or something?"

After that, Troy felt better. They were taking seriously his protestations that he wasn't Gray. This would work itself out after all.

The attractive head dealer wore a light trench coat unbuttoned over a short dress, black with lace on the top. It was what she had worn to work before receiving the short note telling her she needed to fly to Reno and watch for a man in baggage claim with her name on a sign. Eileen could feel the eyes of all three men in the room exploring her body and she pulled the edges of the trench coat a little closer.

She stepped into the room, studying Troy Axmann carefully, looking him up and down as he sat in his chair. Her gaze came back to his face as she moved across the room until she stood in front of him.

From high school on, Troy had been accustomed to seeing his brother with the best-looking woman in the room hanging on his arm. It was a given. He just hoped the woman in front of him was Gray's current girlfriend so she could get word to him quickly that Troy was in trouble. That should fix everything. Whatever was wrong, Gray would take care of it. He always had.

Eileen lingered in front of him, studying him. Delaying. Trying to decide what to do. Then the indecision on her face vanished. She knew. She stepped close to Troy, placed her finger under his chin and lifted his face. Then she bent down and kissed him. Hard. Troy was surprised but couldn't stop himself from returning it. He noticed how she smelled...a hint of cinnamon. Then Eileen pulled away.

"Good-bye, Gray," she said. Then she whirled and walked quickly to the door which she shoved open. She stalked quickly down the hallway back toward the elevator. The sound of her heels echoed in the basement corridor.

When she reached the elevator, she heard Troy Axmann yell.

"No!" he screamed. "No! No! No!"

She put her hands to her ears and willed the doors to close.

Chapter 64

Merrick Gives Foundation $10 million
Assigns Roxaten Ownership, Rights

By Staff Writers
San Francisco News
    Merrick & Merrick announced today that it will assign its rights to Roxaten, the controversial cancer drug, to a non-profit foundation created to speed FDA approvals of the drug as well as a related vaccine that scientists believe could dramatically reduce overall cancer rates.
    The drug giant's announcement came as it dropped litigation against the drug's founder, Walter Novak, and said it would donate $10 million to the newly formed foundation.
    In a related announcement, the National Institutes of Health revealed the creation of a scientific panel to review the effectiveness of Roxaten, study the appropriate uses of the drug and make recommendations for achieving the best public health benefits. One area of study will include the vaccine options based on the underlying scientific breakthroughs that led to the medicine's creation, said committee chairperson Miriam Pastor.
    "Merrick & Merrick believes the public deserves to have Roxaten thoroughly tested and, if appropriate, distributed to patients through policies adopted by the Roxaten Foundation in coordination with the NIH," said Edwin Merrick, CEO of the drug giant.
    Roxaten Foundation president Roxanne Rosewell, one of the scientists who worked on the initial research that resulted in

Roxaten, said the non-profit planned to make the rights to Roxaten and all related research that it supports part of the public domain.

"Roxaten is just the first step," said Rosewell. "There will be more research, more discoveries and more medicines in the next years and decades. The foundation's job is to help this process financially and to provide it with the strong scientific, legal and political infrastructure it deserves."

* * *

WALTER NOVAK DROVE into the Presidio through the gate just a few blocks from his home. He left the shops, interior design businesses and cafes of Pacific Heights behind as he began the curving descent down Presidio Boulevard through a thick grove of eucalyptus trees. It had rained in the early afternoon, heightening the fresh, piney smell that wafted through his cracked windows.

He passed by a row of tidy Spanish-style homes on his left – small apartments really with red-tile roofs, white stucco walls and long concrete walkways. He guessed they were built in the 50s, each large enough to house three or four military families. Anyone assigned to them must have felt as if they'd won the lottery.

After passing through the cluster of buildings that had been the headquarters of the old military base, the road wound past the cemetery. Endless rows of identically shaped white headstones ran up the hill in geometric perfection. Novak had an image of a thousand soldiers lying side-by-side beneath the earth attired in immaculate dress uniforms. They would be in exact alignment as defined by a team of surveyors, a formation more precise than any they had formed on the parade ground. An underground army at well-deserved rest.

He took the shortcut past more 50's Spanish-style homes and then parked in an empty lot. He walked the quarter mile down

271

the hill and through the two-lane tunnel that passed beneath the Golden Gate toll booths. He emerged at the tourist lot for the bridge. Bypassing the café and visitor center, he walked up the crushed granite path to the walkway that ran along the east, city side of the Golden Gate Bridge.

The rain had driven most of the tourists away. The traffic – still busy after the evening rush hour – was just a few feet away heading north toward Marin. It kept up a steady rumble accented by the metallic staccato of cars hitting the metal plates that joined the sections of roadway every 50 yards or so. After a while, the sound just became background, a steady loud buzz on his left.

After eight minutes, Novak stopped at a turnout that jutted a few feet out from the walkway just past the first gigantic tower in the middle section of the bridge. He faced east. In the waning sunlight, Alcatraz was in front of him. To the right was San Francisco, the beaches and the Marina district just off the water and the high rises further back.

Novak leaned against the rail. He could feel the vibrations of the traffic passing from the roadbed, through the bridge girders and into his body. It felt like the growl of an empty stomach, although he wasn't feeling hungry in the slightest.

Far below, the gray ocean was alive. White caps came, lingered and disappeared. Broken lines of surf moved slowly inward, pushed by the flood tide. It was still light enough to see a line of birds passing below, each one followed by its shadow just behind it on the water's surface. They were only a few feet above the sea.

After a long glide with wings outstretched, the birds took on an elongated shape with skinny necks outstretched, legs trailing behind and wings flapping hard to the sides. Ducks? No. At this distance they had to be larger. Geese then, probably passing through on the way to Canada.

The height made the tableau below surreal. It had a dollhouse quality. A toy world. It would be windy, cold and wet down there with the ocean and the force of its swells dominating everything. But he had no sense of that from the bridge.

Another line of geese flew out, just skirting Alcatraz. As they reached the bridge to pass underneath, Novak saw the last bird in line suddenly tumble into the ocean. It disappeared for a moment and then popped to the surface, flapping its wings and shaking to get the water off. It floated for a time. Then a wave broke over it and the bird disappeared only to surface after a few more seconds. From above, it looked like just a splash of water. Novak knew that down there, it would be a sizable wave perhaps even four or five feet high. He remembered how it had been when he passed under the bridge in the *Oblique*. He was seeing a life-or-death struggle.

Another half dozen geese were coming through. Novak could see the one in the water trying to get into the air and join them. For a few seconds, it matched the flapping of the others. Then it hit the water with a small splash, maybe using its feet to help propel itself forward. It flew a few more yards and then hit the water for a final time and remained floating helplessly.

Novak wanted to somehow reach down to help it. Dry it off. Give it a rest out of the tumult of the ocean. Maybe whatever was wrong could heal. It just needed a break from the incessant flying and, now, the chaos of the sea. How could it recover when its mission was traversing the thousands of miles between Latin America and Canada? That instinctual drive. The imperative. It was driving it to its death.

Then he saw the bird try again. It was alone this time. It flapped, got some air and headed west toward the open sea. It splashed a little again but kept going. This time it didn't stop. The wings kept moving. It continued flying until it disappeared from his view underneath the bridge.

Novak smiled. One day at a time, he thought. One mile at a time. Keep going and maybe you'll make it.

Novak lifted his eyes and scanned the horizon. It suddenly occurred to him why the bridge was such a magnet to jumpers. He knew the end-of-the-land theory. That looked at America as a box tipped westward. Those without roots or purpose holding them down rolled to the west coast. Once there – having run out of land, dreams and hope – only the ocean remained. The bridge became their gateway.

But he saw something else, too. It was mesmerizing on the bridge, almost mystical. The cityscape. The natural beauty. And the miniature ocean world below. It was God's view of the world. How easy it would be to seduce yourself into thinking that you could climb the railing, drop over the side and tumble down into that fantasy below. So easy. Become part of the toy world.

How long would it take to climb over the rail? Five seconds. How long to get your footing on the thin platform on the other side and take a deep breath. Nothing between you and the void. Three seconds. Close your eyes. Wait for her to come. A last time to say good bye...or hello. And then fall.

But the face that came to him this time wasn't the pig-tailed blonde girl. It was the girl with short black hair, bangs and an irrepressible smile. It was Megan.

It shocked him into opening his eyes. Suddenly he could feel the danger. His feet were on a beam four inches wide on the unprotected side of the railing. Had he just climbed over? A sudden gust would be enough to send him down. His legs shook. He staggered to the rail and clung to it, only then becoming aware that a half dozen people were staring at him from the safe side, their mouths wide open.

He pulled himself back over. His heart pounded like he had just run a race. He was covered with sweat, even in the cool wind.

274

It took him time to regain his breath. A minute or five. He wasn't sure. Then Novak reached into his jacket pocket. He pulled out the end of a pigtail – five inches long and held together by an elastic band. It had been yellow-white more than 30 years earlier. Was it his imagination or had it somehow faded? It seemed darker now.

Composed again, he looked at it closely, rubbing the hair between his thumb and fingers. He tried to remember how it had felt before it had been cut from the head of his dying sister. He slipped off the band and held the loosened hair in both hands, one palm pressing down on the other. Then he lifted his top hand and extended the lower one out past the railing, tilted downward.

Separating into strands, the hair slid down to his fingertips and then was caught by the strong ocean breeze. The hair swirled up, away and then down until it disappeared. When his hand was bare, Novak closed his eyes and tilted his face up to where the sky was losing the last of its brilliance.

A sound – almost a moan – escaped from this throat. It started with pain, became a sigh of release and ended with a shout thrown up to the heavens. Slowly, Novak opened his eyes. He shoved himself away from the rail, found his balance and began the walk back to his car.

Chapter 65

"SO YOU DON'T put too much stock in it then?" asked Ming Wah Choy.

"What?" said Enzo Lee. "Out of the mouths of babes? That kind of thing?"

"Yes."

They had taken Megan Kim to the San Francisco airport in the morning. They said good bye to her just as she was being whisked through the security screening in the custody of an American Airlines ticket agent. The agent would hand her off to the attendant on her flight to New Orleans. Her mother and Police Chief Cliff Davidson would be waiting on the other end.

Megan had hugged them both goodbye. Lee lifted her up and spun her around a couple of times, making her giggle.

"You're making me dizzy," Megan protested.

"I think you can handle it," said Lee.

She promised to return late the next summer to attend the two-week science camp at the San Francisco Exploratorium that Choy had arranged. She was paying for Megan's plane fare and her mother's if she would come as well.

Just before disappearing through the metal detector, Megan turned, flashed her brilliant smile and said, "You make a nice couple."

"Well, she's a perceptive kid, right?" said Lee.

"Yes."

"And you probably had that glow," he said.

"Hmm," said Choy. "*I* had that glow." She reached over and pulled the end of the belt in her white terrycloth bathrobe that Lee had squeezed into. She had on a blue one. They were lying on the plush carpeting of the living room floor in her condo with the gas fireplace turned on low. Glasses of Silver Oak Cabernet were within reach. They faced each other, both resting on an elbow. The loose knot came undone and the white robe fell open.

Choy put her free hand on his neck and let it roam, first around his chest, then his stomach and further down his unclothed body. The whole time she stared into his eyes and maintained a solemn expression until she made him gasp. Then she looked up at the ceiling unable to resist a smile before locking eyes with him again.

"And what do you think she picked up from you?" she asked.

Lee slid his hand into her robe, being careful not to interfere with her hand which still was finding things to do inside the white robe.

"Intense desire," he said.

Lee fondled Choy's breasts and ran his fingers lightly up and down her stomach, going lower each time. Her breathing got heavier and she chewed her lip until she couldn't suppress a small groan.

"Ahhh," said Choy.

Lee rolled her onto her back.

"What? Again?" she said in mock surprise.

"I think we've got some time to make up, don't you?" he said.

"Yes," Choy said with a little yelp and a sharp intake of breath. Then she ran her hands up from his buttocks to his shoulder blades, feeling his muscles as they settled into a comfortable rhythm. "Lots and lots of...um...time."

"Just do me a favor," she added. "No more leaping over tall buildings...or jumping into moving sailboats, okay?"

"Don't know…if I can promise that," Lee said through his panting. "How about…if I promise…to always be…slower than…a speeding bullet?"

Chapter 66

Bayou La Batre, Alabama
April 2007

CHIEF CLIFF DAVIDSON was returning from an early lunch when he saw the two young boys playing on the edge of a large grass field outside the main church in town. He pulled his patrol car over and watched. One was a black kid he didn't recognize. He was pretty sure the other was Billy Kim's boy, a year older than the last time he had seen him at the trailer. He was out of diapers now, wearing cut-off jeans that ended at his ankles, a tattered T-shirt and blue flip flops.

The pair ran in a small circle in the middle of the field. They still had the stiff-legged gait of toddlers. Davidson knew that in a few months they'd have their running legs and there would be no holding them back. Each carried a stick they must have found on the ground and used them to take dead aim at each other as they carried on a running gun battle.

"Pew, pew, pew," said the Kim kid, sighting down his stick.

"Pew, pew," replied his companion, returning fire as he ambled in an arc around the other boy.

Davidson watched for a couple of minutes from his car. When he got out they ignored him until the door of his cruiser shut. Then they turned toward him, two three-year-olds standing side by side in grass that hid their feet, sticks hanging down from their hands. They watched him lumber across the grass toward them. The black kid sucked his thumb.

When he was 10 feet away, Davidson suddenly dropped to one knee and held his right hand out, two fingers pointing at the boys with his thumb upright.

"Pew, pew, pew," he said, giving his arm a slight shake to mimic the recoil.

Their faces exploded into huge grins and they were quickly moving again, dancing around the big man with their stick-guns pouring out a steady stream of noise bullets. They were relentless as they circled him.

Davidson was on both knees now, his arms outstretched toward either side. He twisted his head from one side to the other, alternating shots at each of the boys, tracking them in their gyrations.

"Pew, pew, pew! Pew, pew, pew!"

The gun battle went on for a ridiculously long time until Davidson decided he'd better die before exhaustion set in. He clutched his chest with one hand and his stomach with the other, made a long groaning noise and slowly slid down to the grass. He twisted onto his back with a pitiful gurgling sound that ended when he flung his arms out.

The noise fusillade had peaked when they saw him going down. Once he was prone, they drew closer and tapered off to a few desultory shots. They came nearer still, curiosity mixed with concern. Had they actually killed the big man?

Davidson popped open his left eye halfway, just enough to see the Kim boy. The kid looked down at him. Then up and across at his friend. He smiled and gave Davidson a wave. Then they both took off trotting across the grass away from the police chief.

Davidson rolled on his side to watch them. They headed toward a brick building on the other side of the large field. He knew it was used by the nearby church to store extra furniture and equipment.

For the first time, he noticed the pair standing on the concrete pad next to the windowless end of the building. Grass grew up through the many cracks in the concrete. A pole protruded at the other end of the pad, holding a rusty metal basketball backboard with a slightly bent hoop affixed to it. The police chief couldn't remember it ever having a net attached to it.

Walter Novak wore shorts that exposed his long pale legs and a polo shirt faded to a dull blue. His white hair was in its usual state – swirling uncontrollably. Megan Kim looked half his size. Her hair was a couple of inches longer than the last time Davidson had seen her.

They faced the brick wall. In unison, their left arms swung into the air, releasing yellow-green tennis balls upward toward the sky. Their right arms lifted upward, rackets dipping behind their heads and then rising to meet the balls just past their zenith as they began to fall. The balls flew forward in a downward arc, hitting the concrete at the base of the brick wall and then bouncing up on the wall before settling to a stop a few feet away.

Then they reached into a wire basket on metal legs that stood between them with a pile of balls inside. They looked at each other, making sure each was ready. Then, up into the air again the balls flew, followed by the sweep of the rackets, the serves bounding off the strings, the balls hitting concrete, brick wall and concrete again before finally stopping – coming lazily to rest.

Davidson watched a couple more serves while sitting in the grass. He heard them both laugh at a shared joke. He thought about walking over to them but decided, finally, to head back to his patrol car. He had reports to complete. Maybe he'd track down Novak later and see if he wanted to accompany him to his favorite peach pie spot. He was pretty certain he was seeing something important in progress. And he didn't want to disturb it.

The End

.

Learn more about the world of Megan's Cure and Enzo Lee!
Go to www.robertblowe.com where you can see real-life settings from the book
and get the background on the story.

Other books by

ROBERT B. LOWE:

Divine Fury and *Project Moses*
Enzo Lee Mystery Thrillers

DIVINE FURY

An Enzo Lee Mystery Thriller

Isaiah 59:17

"He puts on righteousness like a coat of armor and a helmet of salvation on his head. He wears clothes of vengeance. He wraps himself with fury as a coat."

Chapter 1

Montana, 2004

THE RAGGED, HIGH-PITCHED strains of the hymn drifted through the hardwood floor of the main church sanctuary above.

"On-ward Christ-ian sol diers, march-ing as to war..."

More than a dozen kids. All fourth graders or younger. He had watched them march in the dusk through the spring snow and up the stairs of the church. They wore snow boots, puffy pint-sized parkas and ski caps in reds, blues and pinks with tassels hanging from the earflaps and bouncing off their shoulders.

Then – silence. The muffled sound of the choir leader saying something unintelligible. Her strong soprano started the next song followed fitfully by the children as they jumped in at different spots in the first stanzas.

"Mine eyes have seen the Glo-ry of the Com-ing of the Lord..."

Walberg focused on the hardware in front of him illuminated by the flashlight lying on the portable table. Five more tables lay stacked against the wall, resting on the faded green linoleum covering the basement floor. Folding chairs were piled nearby. They awaited the next Sunday's pancake breakfast when they would be packed with God-fearing members of Christ Episcopal Church, the largest house of worship in the small town of Bliss, Montana.

It was cold in the basement and he could see wisps of his breath in the limited light of the flashlight. But it was still much warmer than outside and his fingers worked the pliers and wire cutters easily.

He had chosen an alkaline six-volt battery as the power source because he knew it would set off the detonators without any problem even in cold or wet conditions. The wire was 18-gauge, solid copper sheathed in black PVC. Strong enough to tolerate jostling but easy to work using either the pliers or his fingers. The key triggering mechanism was cannibalized from a device that worked similar to a garage door opener but with a longer range of operation. He'd picked it up in Salt Lake City the weekend before.

He stripped the insulation off the end of the wire, exposing an inch which he hooked around the second terminal of the battery using the pliers. He screwed the plastic cap down until it clamped hard on the copper wire. He was finished.

He carefully put the tools back in his jacket pocket, picked up the flashlight and inspected the table surface and the surrounding floor to make sure he'd forgotten nothing. Then, he moved to the outside door. It was sturdy metal with an automatic closing mechanism. He searched in the snow outside the door, spotted a small twig and jammed it against the frame so the door looked closed from a distance but remained unlatched.

Walberg only donned a ski cap when the thermometer dipped into the single digits. Tonight, he wore his usual dark brown cowboy hat. He'd done this since high school to distinguish himself from newcomers to the area. Walberg had been born and raised within 50 miles of Bliss and was happy if everyone knew it. Aside from three years in the U.S. Army, this had been his home his entire life. With the hat and his old, suede-leather jacket, he looked like a thin, down-on-his-luck version of the Marlboro Man

The parking lot had been plowed earlier in the day, but the few inches of fresh snow completely muffled his footsteps. In the quiet, he could hear the children clearly now, nearing the end of their song. He moved toward the far end of the lot and the singing grew faint until he could barely hear it when he reached his 1998 black Chevy Blazer.

He opened the driver's door, reached into the left cup holder in the center console and found the remote switch that he'd left there. It fit easily into the palm of his hand. Still standing outside the Blazer, he closed the car door and found the button on the remote. He stared at the church until he found the center basement window that was just a few inches above ground level. He estimated the distance at 120 yards.

Suddenly, he noticed that the singing had stopped. He heard the children's voices again. But they weren't joining together in a Church hymn. The sound was altogether different. He recognized it as the excited chatter of young kids at the end of something. The end of class. The end of school. In this case, the end of choir practice.

"Dammit," Walberg muttered. He had expected the practice to last at least another 20 minutes. As he watched the church, he saw the main doors thrown open on the far right side of the building and the kids scamper down the stairs – a few in the front, then the main surge, and finally the stragglers who moved slowly and carefully down the steps.

Two of the children ran across the parking lot, heading directly toward him. In the front was a girl, tall for her age with long blond hair bouncing outside of her baby blue ski cap. Behind her ran a younger boy with his jacket hanging open.

They slowed when they got close to him. The girl veered, keeping some distance. She looked at him warily.

"Hi, Uncle Steve," she said.

"Hi," Walberg replied without emotion. "Get in the truck. I've got something to do."

He heard them start to bicker as the rear doors closed and they grabbed their seatbelts. Walberg turned his attention back to the church. It was quiet now with the children out and scattered, mostly on the other side of the building where their parents had parked.

He moved his thumb over the remote until he felt the raised button. Watching the dark basement window, he pressed the button. He saw a faint light go on inside the window. He pressed the button again, and the light went out. He waited five seconds and pressed the button a third time. The light came on again.

Walberg was satisfied. The switch worked as expected. With the right explosives, he was confident that he could plant and detonate a bomb remotely. He pulled a cloth bag out of his jacket pocket and walked back across the parking lot to retrieve the hardware from the darkness of the church basement.

Chapter 2

San Francisco
Sunday, April 18, 2004

THREE CLANGS OF an old cable car bell that someone had rescued from a city garage decades ago signaled last call at the Masonic Pub six blocks from the entrance to Golden Gate Park. It was the signal for most of the two dozen remaining patrons scattered among the old wooden tables and bent cane chairs to settle up and head for home.

For Scott Truman, however, the triple tones meant that the most important part of his night was beginning. It was time for him to return to his blue-walled cubicle in the offices of the University of San Francisco Medical Center a few miles away.

He wasn't particularly dedicated to his job crunching health statistics at the hospital. But he was extremely committed to Sonia, his girlfriend whom he had wooed for more than a year with a single-minded purpose and perseverance that had far surpassed any other endeavor he'd undertaken in his 26 years.

Their first night together had led to a month when they'd spent virtually all of their non-working time with one another. They were so active in bed that they had to prearrange "sleeping" nights so they could catch up. She sat in his lap while they read magazines at the laundromat. They took turns spooning their choices from Mitchell's Ice Cream into each other's mouths. He feigned injuries so he could run slower and stay near her when they jogged in the park.

Then, Sonia was gone. Off to Australia on a one-year internship on some marine biology program. When she didn't call for four days, he started to panic. She had known about the internship for months. Had he been a vacation fling in reverse? A home fling?

Eventually, Sonia called and explained that she'd had trouble getting a new telephone and that her employer forbid long-distance calls for personal reasons. Truman had then made it his mission to explore all the international telephony options.

His first thought was taking advantage of an Internet-based telephone service. But Sonia wasn't exactly a high-tech savant and would be in the arms of some Aussie before that solution was pieced together. How fast were the connections Down Under, anyway? The best idea Truman had was the WATS line at work. Until anyone said anything to him, the five hours he spent on the phone with Sonia each week were free – the best price he would ever find. He had a vague fear of getting caught, but greater faith that the bureaucracy overseeing a $90 million budget had bigger fish to fry. At least he hoped so.

Meanwhile, Truman kept having images in his mind of Sonia in her tiniest bikini snorkeling on the Great Barrier Reef with some guy who was taller, stronger and more tanned than him and with a huge knife dangling from his belt. Calling in the early morning from California had the dual benefit of concealing his heavy use of the WATS line plus tying up Sonia's evening hours that could otherwise be used in ways Truman tried not to consider.

It was 3:30 am when he finally said goodnight to Sonia.

Wearing an orange USC sweatshirt and gray cargo pants, Truman made his long way through the canyon maze formed by the many cubicles at the medical center. Then, he heard the sound of something being moved...furniture, computers, a file cabinet...something. That was strange. He'd seen watchmen outside but never anyone inside the offices at this hour. And, it was the weekend.

He considered just escaping then, hopefully unseen by the person who was also in the office. But he had to walk right past where he had heard the noise. It would seem more strange if he *didn't* acknowledge whoever was there, presumably a co-worker.

He poked his head around the opening of the cubicle where he thought he'd heard the sounds. It was one of the larger ones that belonged to a senior researcher. Truman saw a guy with his head under the desk wearing blue pants and a gray jacket over a white T-shirt.

"Hi," he said. The guy was so surprised that he bashed his head against the desk before spinning around and looking up at Truman from where he sat on the floor. Truman was glad he didn't recognize him. Maybe he could get out without giving his name or having to explain why he was there at this odd hour.

"I just heard you so I thought I'd look in on my way out," said Truman.

"Oh. Yeah. Right," said the guy. He looked around 40, maybe 20 pounds overweight, glasses, slightly disheveled. "I'm...uh...uh...I'm Oscar. Tech support. Just trying to fix some network problems."

"I see," said Truman. The guy looked a bit nerdy. Computer jock certainly fit. "Kind of a weird time, though."

"Emergency," said Oscar. "They needed it fixed now."

"Okay," said Truman. "Well, good luck." He turned away and resumed his walk toward the exit.

"Yeah," he heard behind him.

Truman was relieved. His secret – the clandestine phone calls – seemed safe. It was strange though – some guy fixing a computer at 3:30 am on a Sunday. If he were't so paranoid about his phone calls, he might ask around about it on Monday. But the next question would be why he was in the office at the odd hour. There was no point in calling attention to himself in that way.

"Let sleeping dogs lie," he thought to himself.

He didn't hear Oscar fumbling desperately for the cell phone in his jacket pocket as soon as Truman turned away from him or the short conversation he had with his partner waiting outside the building.

Oscar went back to replacing the Logitech mouse connected to the computer under the desk with one that was virtually identical except for the modification he'd made to it. He had installed an extra small chip inside the plastic casing. The next time someone entered their password, software stored in the modified mouse would have free run of the hospital computer network. Among other functions, it created an invisible tunnel through the network firewall. Data could flow in and out of the system and be totally invisible to the firewall and other security systems in place. Otherwise, the mouse behaved normally and would remain in place for a couple more years until it broke or was finally replaced by a newer model.

Oscar moved the PC back into place and prepared to go downstairs and out through the doors at the medical center's loading dock. Meanwhile, Scott Truman arrived at his Toyota Corolla in the hospital parking garage a block away. When he put his hand on the door handle he heard the scrape of a shoe behind him.

"Hey, Buddy," a voice said.

Truman turned to find a handgun with an abnormally long barrel aimed at his chest. It fired three shots, silenced so they were no louder than a man tapping his finger on a table, and sent bullets tearing through his stomach, heart and liver.

PROJECT MOSES
An Enzo Lee Mystery Thriller

Exodus 11:1

"And the LORD said unto Moses, Yet will I bring one plague more upon Pharaoh, and upon Egypt; afterwards he will let you go hence..."

Chapter 1

San Francisco, California, 1994

TALL AND SLENDER with well-coiffed silver hair that touched her shoulders, Judge Miriam Gilbert was a handsome woman with sparkling blue eyes who still attracted admiring looks from men, even if the looks were somewhat less carnal than in the past.

At the age of 52, after a decade as a San Francisco Municipal Court Judge, Miriam Gilbert had long ago developed the most important quality required for a jurist charged with resolving the petty crimes and minor civil disputes that filled her courtroom – infinite patience.

But, she was struggling today to remain stoic behind the particle board and formica bench at the front of the courtroom. She watched the middle-aged juror twist her fat hands until the knuckles were red and swollen. The woman shifted uncomfortably in her seat as she scanned the people sitting around her in the jury box.

The juror was about Judge Gilbert's age but the resemblance ended there. She wore a blue, vaguely nautical dress at least two sizes and 15 years too young for her. Her face was loose and malleable, shifting back and forth between fear and disdain as she looked at her fellow jurors.

Raising her hand like a child in class, the woman fought her sobs as she spoke through lips painted blood red.

"I am not crazy!" she said. She took two deep breaths. "They kept yelling and yelling at me. And I am *not* going to change my mind."

"He is innocent! *That* one did not prove his case." Her face trembling, the juror jabbed a lethal-looking fingernail at the prosecutor just beyond the jury box.

Orson Adams stared back at his accuser, removed his tortoise shell-rimmed glasses and frowned.

The muscles around Judge Gilbert's left eye twitched slightly. She didn't mind so much that the hung jury was going to waste four days of trial time devoted to a minor case. That was par for the course. What bothered her was a headache that had started about the time the bailiff knocked on the door to Judge Gilbert's chambers and said: "They want to come out. I think they've run out of names to call each other."

The judge cleared her throat, a signal that the histrionics and squabbling that had emanated from the jury box for the past ten minutes were over. She stared at the empty notepad in front of her for a few seconds before looking up.

"It is apparent to me that this jury will not reach a unanimous verdict," she said. "They have deliberated for two days - as much time as it took for the state and the defense to present their cases. Therefore, I declare a mistrial."

"The prosecution will inform the Court within one week whether the state intends to retry this case. I thank the jury for its efforts. I know it has taken much of your time to be here and that the last two days have not been easy." Judge Gilbert made it a point to nod in the jury's direction.

Then, she looked over at the defendant, an almost emaciated young man with dirty blond hair tied in a ponytail. He sat beside his attorney, a corpulent man wearing dark-blue pinstripes, pink tie and a forced smile that looked more like a snarl.

"Mr. Warrington will remain free on bond," she said.

An hour later, the lawyers, jurors and courthouse staff had joined the evening traffic jam. With her black robe now hanging in the closet of her chambers, Judge Gilbert wore a long-sleeved white blouse and a pleated beige skirt as she settled behind her large desk stained yellow to bring out the wood grain through the heavily polished sheen. Behind her were volumes of California cases, bound in blue leather. A cup of Misty Mint tea sat on her right, hot and steaming. Next to it lay two capsules of Darvon painkiller. The headache was worse. It now seemed to fan outward from the center of her brain to her scalp.

Judge Gilbert looked over the assorted papers laying on her desk. She picked up a large envelope that she had opened in the morning. It was teal blue and embossed with a logo in darker blue along the left side that she had never seen before. It was a rising spiral with flowers and bunches of grapes hanging from it.

Judge Gilbert reached into the envelope and pulled out a yellow rose that had been pressed flat. She held it to her nose, inhaled and was rewarded with the aroma of cinnamon. She was reminded of hot apple cider and sweet potato pie.

She set the rose on the desk and grabbed her letter opener, a gift from a former law clerk. She inserted it under the flap of another envelope and tore it open with a satisfying rip. She skimmed the letter inside. Then, Judge Gilbert turned to the next envelope sitting in the tray on the corner of her desk.

The next morning the body of Judge Miriam Gilbert was still at her desk when her law clerk went into her chambers. Her head lay on the desktop, eyes staring at a blank wall. Her silver hair was stained brown where it lay in a puddle of cold tea.

***

ORSON ADAMS WAS more than a little miffed when he was assigned the Warrington case. After three years of prosecuting crime, he had enough seniority to avoid the dog shit cases. Here was a burglary with nothing actually taken, just forced entry with intent to steal. The fact that the case had ended in a hung jury that afternoon was the capper. What a colossal waste of his time.

Adams hadn't handled a case in Municipal Court for a year. Being back there the past four days made him wonder if he was spinning his wheels as a prosecutor. He had progressed rapidly through the District Attorney's office. Being one of a handful of black prosecutors in the office didn't hurt. Still, maybe it was time to get out on his own. Spread his wings and go private. He could defend the scumbags he had been putting behind bars, pocket the big fees and buy a house in Tiburon.

Adams rounded the elevated indoor track at the Run N Racquet Club for the 33rd time. He was in excellent shape at 30 and, with his tailored suits, Adams cut a dashing figure in the DA's office. He frowned again at the memory of the matronly juror who had blown the whole goddamn trial and blamed him...HIM for failing to prove the case.

"Bleeding heart hag," he muttered to himself.

He should have guessed that the middle-aged juror might take a maternal, boys-will-be-boys attitude toward Warrington. The ages were right. During jury selection, Adams hadn't even tried to inquire into whether the juror had any children. Adams had found that older women usually make great jurors for the prosecution. He wasn't accustomed to worrying about them being on the jury unless they wore peace medallions or were former Berkeley radicals.

Adams finished his 44th and final lap and slowed to walk two more, just to warm down and keep the lactic acid from pooling in his legs. He stopped for a moment at the railing overlooking the racquetball courts.

Down below on Court One, surrounded by glass on two sides, a pair of attractive blonds wearing headbands and Spandex tights and tops in purples and pinks were grunting enthusiastically as they pounded a blue ball around the court.

The smaller woman was named Diana. She had a gorgeous body, buxom yet athletic. She was a fixture at the club and invariably attracted a crowd of male spectators as she and her playing partners sweated through their skintight outfits.

Adams made his way downstairs to the men's locker room. He showered and stuffed his running clothes back into a Nike gym bag. He put his tie in his coat pocket and flung the jacket over his shoulder.

Adams walked in the breeze across the four lanes of Folsom Street. It was balmier than usual and the wind carried the faintest smell of the ocean. The scent made him hungry and his mind shifted to restaurants. Last night they had eaten Thai. Maybe Diana would like the new South of Market restaurant, the one that specialized in seafood cooked on a gigantic rotisserie imported from Naples or somewhere. How did they cook fish on that thing, anyway? Wire baskets?

When he heard the engine gunning behind him, Adams barely had time to turn his head before the black pickup slammed into him.

Afterword: Reflections on Big Pharma

The first medical scandal that came to my attention was the Thalidomide disaster.

In the late 1950s and early 1960s some 10,000 babies were born with serious birth defects. The most common defects were arms or legs that had never developed, leaving flipper-like appendages. I still recall the photos of children with tiny, useless arms sitting in a chair while they used their remarkably agile toes to tie knots or perform other daily tasks.

Then, as someone who was news-obsessed even at a young age and would eventually become a newspaper reporter specializing in investigating scandals, I paid close attention to other medical disasters over the years. They were riveting stories.

The Tylenol murders when seven people died after taking Tylenol capsules that someone had spiked with cyanide.

The spread of AIDS through blood transfusions in the early years of the disease before tests to detect the HIV virus were perfected. The father of my close high school friend died that way.

There were recalls every year of a handful of medicines and medical devices right up to the present day. Vioxx. Fen-phen. Breast implants leaking silicon. Artificial hips leaving metal shavings inside patients. The problems ranged from addiction and heart attacks to liver failure and amnesia. Sometimes the medicine just turned out to be ineffective or the device failed too soon.

Yet, all of this happened against the backdrop of astonishing medical success. Breakthroughs in medical science seemed to hit the headlines every day. Organ transplants became everyday events. Diseases that once killed or maimed millions – like smallpox and polio – became nearly extinct. Fatal cancers became curable. Bypass surgery. Artificial joints. Cholesterol-reducing statins. Magic Johnson survived AIDS.

That intrigued me – the duality.

On one hand, there was the world of medicine – including the pharmaceutical industry – acting like God. It promised us extra years of life that would be pain-free, physically active and devoid of depression.

Then there was that darker side.

The one that rushed pills onto the market either neglecting – or hiding – the additional tests that would later show that the medicine promising so much good actually caused harm.

The sales and marketing arms of Big Pharma quietly paid doctors and scientists to tout their wares at medical conferences, bought physicians' loyalty with presents and lavish vacations, and abruptly pulled funding when studies started to find trouble in their products.

Drug companies stopped work on promising cures because the afflicted were too few – or too poor – to bring in big profits.

In just the past few years, the problems have hit an all-time high, at least in terms of penalties levied against the industry. Billion-dollar settlements have been paid by Johnson & Johnson, GlaxoSmithKline, Pfizer, Abbott and Merck. Most often it's been for overreaching with the new wave of psychotropic drugs, but painkillers and faulty artificial joints have had their place as well.

Invariably, it seems, the drug companies wait too long to pull a medicine or device once there is evidence that it's faulty. Instead, they ignore victims, stonewall regulators and hide evidence as long as possible while they wring out the last drops of profit.

I guess that's why I chose to shine the spotlight on Big Pharma in Megan's Cure – the Jekyll-and-Hyde nature of the business. Plus there is so much at stake. Often it truly is a matter of life and death. – *R. Lowe, February 2014*

ROBERT B. LOWE

Acknowledgments:

I am fortunate to have a number of friends and relatives who helped expand my understanding of the medical profession, hospitals, cancer research and the internal workings of laboratories. Between approach shots and 20-foot putts, Dr. Scott Lee told me about his work more than two decades ago searching for genetic keys to unlock the mysteries of cancer. David Egerter, whose long career writing about drugs for the industry requires expert knowledge of the underlying science, listened patiently while I lobbed questions and plot scenarios at him between lattes at the Boot and Shoe (yes…it's a restaurant). My sister Janice Lowe and her husband, Paul Wise, are both pediatricians at Stanford Hospital and helped me pretend I knew something about medicine and hospitals.

On the editing side, my wife Candace Turtle and friend Laura Pepper Wu nudged me back on the rails when I began to slide off. My former college roommate Carl Vonderau, who also writes mystery thrillers, gave me a fantastic critique full of recommendations. I implemented many of them to good effect. Paul Vollmer generously helped me with a detailed line edit, catching a ton of mistakes. My daughter Chenery, whose plans include medical school, both gave me excellent copy editing as well as helped paint the picture of a modern research lab.

I must also thank a large network of family and friends and who are huge supporters of my books. Writing is lonely work. There are moments of elation, warranted or not, but also plenty of despair. You only have to look at your bookshelves to see the many examples of work that you can only dream of equaling. The pats on the back are much appreciated.

I'm also grateful to the many readers who have not only plunked down a few dollars to read about Enzo Lee's latest adventure and the ongoing events in his life, but often take the extra time to write a review or comment on Facebook. I do listen to what people have to say – good and bad. Collectively, those comments have taught me a lot about my own writing and greatly influenced the development of the Enzo Lee series. – *R. Lowe*

About the Author

ROBERT B. LOWE was a newspaper reporter for 12 years for publications in Arizona and Florida. He won a Pulitzer Prize for his investigative reporting. He attended Harvard Law School and practiced law in California's Silicon Valley before turning to the business side of high tech, both managing and founding young software companies. He applies his background in the journalism, business and legal worlds to his fiction. He resides in the Bay Area where his novels are set. **Megan's Cure** is his third novel. The other novels in the Enzo Lee series are **Project Moses** and **Divine Fury**.

Made in the USA
San Bernardino, CA
29 October 2016